FORREST FOR THE TREES

Green Valley Heroes Book #1

KILBY BLADES

www.smartypantsromance.com

Copyright

This book is a work of fiction. Names, characters, places, rants, facts, contrivances, and incidents are either the product of the author's questionable imagination or are used factitiously. Any resemblance to actual persons, living or dead or undead, events, locales is entirely coincidental if not somewhat disturbing/concerning.

Made in the United States of America

Print Edition
ISBN: 978-1-949202-66-3

Dedication

To my village

PART I

Chapter One
SIERRA

"Oh, I have earned the hell out of my cupcake," Sierra said out loud, thinking ahead to the s'mores cupcake she'd had Joy set aside for her at Donner Bakery. She always earned her end-of-day treats. So much exercise that she never had to count calories was one of the many perks of being a national park ranger. As was permission to talk to herself. Because who was listening, except the trees?

But she rarely earned her dessert and the bourbon drink she liked to have at the end of a long day before she crested the hill that overlooked Bluebell Fields, the name she'd made up for the picturesque wildflower meadow she passed near the end of her route. That usually came at around 16,000 steps, according to her pedometer. But it was barely noon on a Tuesday—not even her busiest day of the week—and she'd already passed 12,000.

She had erratic weather to thank for that. Temperatures that rose more than 5° above normal had pretty much defined her summer. Hotter weather meant changes to delicate ecosystems; it meant harsher conditions for hikers; and don't even get her started on what it meant to animal behavior.

Mitigating all of this meant that more duties landed on the Park Service. Already that morning, Sierra had monitored conditions for a congress of red-cheeked salamanders. She'd maintained a watering system that had been built for a rare species of elk. She'd checked in on new calves that had been born to one of the cows a few weeks earlier, in mid-June. And that barely scratched the surface of her official work.

"Dispatch to Betts four-one-five."

Her radio sounded abruptly—quick static followed by Rick's commanding twang. Rick was efficient, precise and a very loud talker both on and off of the ham. She'd never asked what path had brought him to become a radio dispatcher, but he seemed born to do this job.

"Dispatch, go ahead." She plucked her repeater off of her belt and pressed the side button to speak.

"Verify your position, four-one-five. Over."

Following protocol, Sierra pressed the test button on her emergency beacon, which transmitted a signal Rick was meant to receive. A second after, she rattled off the coordinates from her GPS watch. Rick was meant to compare the beacon data with Sierra's spoken coordinates to measure the accuracy of the device.

"35.5628° N, 83.4985° W. You get the beacon? Over."

"Verified," Rick came back. Then, "The fire-warning level has risen from Moderate to High. Over."

"Ten-four," she acknowledged evenly, even as her heart rate spiked.

"We still on for a drink on Friday?" Rick asked. "I need a second opinion on Kevin. Over."

Sierra smirked. "I'm pretty sure your first opinion was correct. Over."

Rick's track record with men was even worse than hers. But he was a good friend and said track record had been the source of much bonding and commiseration.

"I'll buy the drinks. And be careful out there. Over and out."

Her radio gave a final crackle before going silent. As she clipped it back on to her belt, she let loose the words she'd kept at bay.

"Motherfucking shit."

Yeah. She cursed out loud, too. She usually saved bad language for giving the universe a piece of her mind when the 49ers fumbled the ball. She was from Sonoma County. She would resume her weekly TV cursing when the season opened in the fall.

Slowing her walk, she angled her face to bite down on the straw threaded through the shoulder strap of her pack. She'd be no help to anyone if she got heatstroke and collapsed in the woods. It meant she had to set aside her Superwoman complex and practice what she preached to hikers about twenty times a day: she had to pace herself and hydrate.

It might take her until after sunset, but she had to make all of her stops—the unofficial ones, too. Jake Stapleton wasn't supposed to be living on federal land. Jake Stapleton also wasn't bothering anybody. And she had it on good authority he had reason to hide and no better place to go. She hadn't actively hidden him, but she hadn't reported him, either. What he had or hadn't done didn't matter to the fact that he was in this forest. Conditions were dangerous, and he needed to know.

Sierra was still busy hypothesizing on Jake's situation—wondering whether it was true that he'd taken his one way out. In town a while back, it had been the subject of no small speculation. Jake's father, Mortar, was a known felon who'd done time on and off at the Riverbend Maximum Security Penitentiary in Davidson County. He'd been back in Green Valley for just under a year after time inside for trying to kidnap Ashley Winston.

To hear some people tell it, being born male and being born into the Wraiths meant you had no choice but to go in. And that, even if you left for a while, you were right back in the second you returned.

To hear others tell it, there was an out, but only one: to leave Green Valley the day you came of age. No son of any Wraith rumored to have exited in this manner had ever been seen again.

Her musings were halted by the last interruption Sierra wanted: the faintest aroma of fire. It took her a minute to figure out the direction from which it came. On days this hot, she left her Bernese mountain dog, Everest, back at the ranger station. If Everest were with her now, she'd have long-since led Sierra in the direction of the fire.

Picking up to a jog, she hastened along her unmarked path. Most hikers who descended upon her little corner of the Appalachian Trail were well-trained. But there were always a few who ignored all safety and common sense. It didn't take long for a small plume of smoke to come into view.

At least it's at a campsite.

Campsites had clearings, and clearings meant less dry vegetation to carry embers off in the summer wind. A recent series of suspicious blazes had everyone on high alert. There had been three of them—and they'd occurred under such strange circumstances that a fire set anywhere in her territory would warrant an astonishing amount of scrutiny.

Sierra approached the campground with caution. You never knew who you were gonna get. People drank, carried firearms, and did all manner of other prohibited things. It didn't help that she was a woman, let alone a Black woman, let alone one who was barely thirty. People weren't used to authority coming wrapped in a package that looked like her.

"Hey, girls ..." Sierra began in her sorority sister voice. She didn't like to call grown women "girls," but "Hey, ladies" was what men around here opened with when they wanted to talk to you and your friends at the bar. Judging by the expensive camping gear Sierra had spotted from thirty paces, they weren't local.

"Oh, hey!" the first woman bubbled, turning her attention away from the pot over the cooking fire. "Great day, huh?" She motioned to the sky with her spoon.

Sierra pegged them for nineteen or twenty. If their gear hadn't been a dead giveaway, their accents certainly were.

"Wanna join us for lunch?"

"Thank you, no …" Sierra answered quickly. "I'm here to tell you that you can't cook with fire during the day. Do you have a permit?"

Sierra asked the question neutrally, curious to see how they'd play their cards. When people were genuinely clueless, she went easy. But when people knew the rules and didn't follow them … well, that was a different story.

"Oh my gosh—we are so sorry!" The woman extended out the "oh" of her "so" in a way that reminded Sierra of how people talked back home.

"The guy we ran into at the bottom of the hill told us we didn't have to have one." The second one crossed her arms as she chimed in. "He said we could pick one up at the ranger station."

Sierra ran into this every day: hikers leading other hikers astray with misinformation.

"Fires are only permitted on some areas of the trail," Sierra explained. "Part of why you have to get a fire permit is to confirm that you've read the full set of rules."

"That's not how the other ranger made it seem," the second one challenged again.

"What other ranger?" Sierra narrowed her eyes.

"The guy ranger." Her righteously indignant expression was replaced by a dreamy smile. "The hot one," she clarified.

Her friend elbowed her.

"What? He was totally hot."

"What did this ranger look like?" Sierra demanded. The parks

7

were teeming with crews of scientists. Could be, one of them was giving hikers unauthorized advice.

"He had a uniform like yours, except blue ..." The first one dug in her pocket. "Here. He took a selfie with us."

Sierra stepped forward with interest and craned her neck to get a glimpse. She scoffed in disdain when she saw it was Forrest. She scowled when she saw his smug, bearded smirk. He stood between the two women, both hands extended before him in a way that proved he'd held the phone for the selfie. His forearms weren't visible, but his shoulders were. His shirt was snug-fitting—either that, or he just filled it out really nicely. Each of the two women cuffed a bicep so strong it dwarfed their hands.

Forrest Winters was, indeed, *not* a national park ranger. What he was, was a thorn in Sierra's side. The way he swung his big axe, fixed her with his chameleon gray eyes, and always talked about his jurisdiction had a way of breaking her concentration.

"He's a fire marshal," Sierra admitted. He was *the* fire marshal, really—the one responsible for determining the cause of all of those suspicious fires. During any normal season, he'd have come around only once in a blue moon to personally inspect fire conditions. Since the investigation had started, he'd been around all the damn time.

"Either way ..." She pulled out her card. "I'm a park ranger and I'm telling you to put your fire out. If you have any questions, you can call the number on this card or visit Sugarlands, the ranger station in Gatlinburg. For now, I'll have to stay to make sure you properly extinguish this fire."

And Sierra did stay, seething and smoldering much like the embers of the ruined fire, still hot even after the initial spark had died. The two hikers—who weren't at all happy—may not have been the only ones headed to the ranger station to file a grievance. Sierra would have her cupcake—maybe two—before the day was done. But first she'd find Forrest, who really ought to quit charming hikers and get back to doing his own job. Forrest Winters would hear where he could shove his fool claims of sweeping jurisdiction. Before the sun set, Sierra would give him a piece of her mind.

Chapter Two

FORREST

Forrest never minded visiting Greenbrier Ranger Station. Though, it wasn't exactly on his way. It was up past Sugarlands, a third of the way to Mt. Cammerer, just west of Little Pigeon Creek. The sandwiches he carried in the cooler he packed into his truck every morning were nothing to sniff at. He'd finished both of them earlier in his shift. But he sure did like the food at Greenbrier.

Not to hear them tell it, but park rangers were a spoiled brood. There were things they took for granted. Like the luxury of a sit-down toilet, running water, and a table for eating lunch. There were ranger stations aplenty. But Forrest was a fire marshal. He was lucky to see a ramshackle hovel that belonged to the Federal Fire Service every fifty miles.

Something Forrest didn't take for granted was that Greenbrier had bacon bites. If he showed up at the right time of day, there might even be some left. What possessed Sierra Betts to bake these delicious treasures in the wee hours of morning, only to provide them for the snacking pleasure of the hungry parks service masses searched him. But he didn't plan to mention the oddity of the habit, lest Sierra stop.

"Hey there, Forrest," Wendell greeted. Forrest made it a point to know the ranger schedule. Wendell would just be coming on shift. Said shift had already started, but Forrest suspected he came early and lingered longer than needed for the bacon bites, too. Wendell wasn't a punctual man, except when it came to eating anything his wife didn't cook. He might've been the only man in town to show up to a barbecue or a fish fry on time.

"Hey, Wendell. What's doing?"

Forrest had already walked past the visitor lobby, swiped his badge and navigated to the inner office. It was set up with six desks, bullpen-style. Four belonged to rangers who were permanently staffed to that station. The other two were for people like Forrest—floaters from other agencies who happened by.

"The usual." Wendell had on his service belt and his equipment was laid out on his desk. "Not as bad as yesterday, but it's still hot as balls."

All the desks faced a center aisle. There were three on each side of the long, rectangular room. Forrest had walked through the door on one end, dropped his bag onto the floor and placed his axe next to it, blade down and handle propped up against the side of the desk.

"That why you're in here procrastinating?" Forrest joked. He liked to give people a little shit. It broke the monotony of routine and the loneliness of the job. Plus, it wasn't against the law to have a little fun.

"Damn." Wendell looked toward the wall clock, then turned his attention back to retooling his belt. By the time Forrest reached the break room, Wendell was popping a final bacon bite into his mouth, pushing his chair in and fixing to go.

"See you on the other side, brother," Wendell said amicably, before putting his hat on and hastening out the front door. Forrest was A-OK with Wendell's departure. The fewer people who were around when he raided the fridge, the fewer people there were to judge him.

Locating the large, square Tupperware Sierra used to carry her bites, Forrest took the entire container to his desk. After a long day of unannounced tower inspections and revisiting the fire scenes, he was glad for a cool, quiet place to dive into the administrative stuff.

Since Sierra would be coming off shift, Forrest figured anything he wanted was fair game. Chances were, the bites nobody ate by the time she packed up got thrown away. So, really, by eating them, he was doing Sierra a service.

Hello, beautiful ...

Forrest couldn't help the smile that spread across his face as he picked up his first delicious bite. Each scallop-sized bundle was bacon-wrapped perfection. He'd never been able to figure out exactly how she made them, but they held hints of all things wonderful: the tang of scallions; the yeasty goodness of bread; and the decadent goo of melted cheese.

Without anyone there to watch, he wasn't shy about eating it whole, popping it into his mouth like sushi; when he had an audience, he was more discreet. He might have moaned around that first mouthful and he definitely closed his eyes as he chewed. Everything was zen until his ecstasy was shattered by the growl of an angry feminine voice.

"You."

Forrest had just swallowed when the single word was spoken from the door with no small measure of accusation. Still, his smile widened the second he recognized her voice.

"Ranger Betts," he greeted with a short nod, ready as ever to lay it on thick. Sierra Betts had never liked him. She might have, if he hadn't broken her California bear figurine the first day they'd met. It had been an honest mistake of his axe handle, an errant swivel which had knocked over the ceramic statue perched at the corner of her desk.

He'd apologized profusely. He'd offered to replace it. Twice.

She'd refused to accept either gesture and hadn't really warmed to him since. She wasn't cold, just openly disapproving. If her intention had been to ward him off, her standoffishness hadn't swayed him; Sierra Betts was cute when she was mad.

"Always lovely to see you. And, can I mention? Your bacon bites are particularly delicious today."

"Do you know what I just came from doing?" She ignored his flattery.

His smile faded as she came closer, but not from the angry look in her eyes; he detected the aroma of fire.

"Tell me you didn't find another scene."

Some firefighters had lost partial ability to detect the smell of smoke, but Forrest could still smell the slightest hint. Sierra had been around a fire—recently. Even from five feet away, it was coming off her clothes.

"Not another crime scene," she dismissed, though she still seemed mad as hell. "What I did find was almost as bad. A pair of hikers cooking with an illegal campfire who swore up and down they got permission from you."

Forrest felt a wave of relief at the news. He'd take hiker shenanigans over the threat of real trouble any day. Turning on the charm he somehow couldn't help bringing every time he got around Sierra, he answered.

"I'm a fire*fighter*, Ranger Betts," he said with emphasis on the "fighter" part. "You ought to know telling people to set fires isn't what I do."

"Maybe you were distracted, Marshal Winters." Sierra stopped next to his borrowed desk and stood over him in what could only be described as a menacing posture. If she was trying to intimidate him, it wasn't working. What she didn't know, because she hadn't been in Green Valley long enough, was that Forrest liked a take-charge kind of woman. Everything about her sass turned him on.

"Distracted?" he repeated.

Sierra hummed in affirmation. "More focused on taking selfies with park visitors than confirming they have the correct information. I assure you, the two women whose unauthorized fire I extinguished did not."

Forrest sighed, recalling which hikers Sierra was talking about. They'd been nice enough but not the sharpest tools in the shed.

"I can't help it if tourists enjoy meeting park officials. Far be it from me to deny a selfie. It's all part of the experience."

Sierra stepped closer. "What is *not* part of the experience, Marshal Winters, is phrasing park rules in such an ambiguous way as to confuse hikers. I'll thank you next time to state the rules of my park in no uncertain terms."

Forrest pretended to look hurt. "Come on, now. You know I have jurisdiction over this area."

"Fire jurisdiction," she corrected. "Campsites and trail mainte- nance are presided over by rangers. And this territory is presided over by me."

He flashed another charming smile. "Why can't it be our park instead of just yours?"

Since he'd been promoted to Federal Fire Marshal, plenty of people were lined up to kiss Forrest's ass. One of the things he liked about Sierra was the fact that she didn't. He'd seen a few people blink at her irreverence once or twice, not that she ever did anything the more audacious of her male colleagues hadn't done themselves. Only, people reacted differently when bold behavior came from a woman— especially one who looked like her.

"I mean it, Forrest. I should've been off shift forty-five minutes ago. Now I'm not gonna make it to town before stuff closes."

Forrest did feel badly then. He knew better than anyone how exhausting these shifts could be, especially in this kind of heat. He dropped his persona long enough to push his chair back and really take her in—to assess her condition and get a better look at her face.

Her skin was flushed, but it was hard to tell whether the pink at the tops of her cheeks was a sign of heatstroke or seasonal sunburn, or even anger given her frustration with him. Her shirt and skin looked dry. All the other symptoms he could screen for—like clammy skin or a rapid, weak pulse—he'd have to touch her to assess.

"And do you have smoke in your eyes or something?"

Shit. Had he stared too long? He always enjoyed taking Sierra in. Sierra Betts was beautiful. He was fascinated by her smooth, delicate skin and the wild curls that she always wore up in a bun. A wisp or three always escaped its hold by the end of the day. Her slender, heart-shaped face had sharp eyes and kissable, Cupid's bow lips. When his gaze took leave of her lips and flew back to her eyes, her accusing look wasn't pointed toward him—it was pointed toward the Tupperware.

"The lid says *Ranger Snacks*," she pronounced with emphasis. "I can't feed every volunteer, researcher, and firefighter on the trail. They're not for anyone who just happens to drop by."

Forrest forgot about heatstroke for a minute and smirked. "Word has it, Captain Quimby helps herself to as many of these as she wants. She likes when you use the cheddar cheese, but I prefer the pimento."

Sierra's eyes widened, then narrowed, for a brief second before she reached out and swiped up the Tupperware in one motion. Forrest was glad for the extra few he'd already taken from the container and placed on a napkin at its side. Sierra gave him one final, stern glare, then completed the short walk to her desk. That was another thing he liked about his floater space: it was right across from her.

Watching her sit, he caught a glimpse of the 49ers mug on the corner of her desk. If she wasn't already riled, he'd have made a comment. The Seahawks' new kicker was looking good in preseason practice. Too good not to rib her about when the time was right.

"Anything new on the fires?"

He looked back up at the sound of her voice, soft and worried, like her gaze. Their bickering over bacon bites and hikers was over. For some of the rangers, investigating the fires was just procedure. He'd figured out a while ago Sierra cared. She was as tough as any ranger he'd ever met and she wanted everyone to know it. But the fires got to her—just like they got to him.

"I'm waiting for the labs to come back on this last one, to confirm the accelerant used was butane and to see what else the forensic analysis turns up."

"But?"

He'd have to watch his poker face around her.

"But ..." he relented, "I'm close to linking them. And ruling all three as arson."

The decision that was common sense if you looked at the facts of the case would be a big, fat pain to push through. Procedurally, there needed to be evidence and it needed to line up. Officials from three different agencies and five different divisions needed to be involved. And then there was the paperwork—mountains of it—for every aspect and stage.

Sierra threw him a look that said, *it's about time,* though the words that came out of her mouth were, "What cinched your decision?"

She sat down at her desk, then turned to face him by swiveling her chair.

"The time elapse, for one." Forrest started in on the speech he would have to give to Chief Frank Barnett when it came time to plead his case. Forrest could determine the cause of the fires, but it was up to the Park Police to pursue the culprit. "The fires happened over a span of five weeks, which means we're not dealing with tourists. Whoever's setting the fires is local, or living in these woods."

Sierra half-crossed her arms and brought one finger to worry at her bottom lip at the same time as she chewed it. It was a cute habit and it took effort not to stare at her lips. It occurred to him that bringing her around to his way of thinking wouldn't be a bad thing. Frank Barnett was turning out to be lazy as hell when it came to this investigation. It couldn't hurt to have a ranger on his side.

"So, you think it's a local ..." Sierra repeated slowly.

"That's where I'm placing my bets. Setting a timber fire used to get you about five years. The right judge could give him twenty. You ought to know, being from California. With all the big wildfires lately, they're cracking down."

Sierra appeared to think so hard for the next few seconds Forrest didn't think there would be any harm in eating another bite. As far as he was concerned, the ban on sharing with fire marshals started tomorrow.

"All right. But what if it's just some kids?" Her voice softened.

This was the hard part. A good half of the foolhardy things he'd seen in his career were just that. Forrest had been young once, and when he was, he'd done like every other teenage boy: a bunch of stupid, dangerous things.

"Look," Forrest said. "I don't want to lock up a kid for sixty years. And if it is a fifteen-year-old, it'd go through juvenile courts. But if you're eighteen and you're starting fires in Smoky Mountain National Park—a goddamned national treasure by all accounts—I hope they lock you up and throw away the key."

Chapter Three

SIERRA

Jake Stapleton's camp was well-hidden, situated in an odd bend of Little Pigeon Creek, down a steep, rocky hill that wasn't easy to descend. Sierra wouldn't have found him six weeks earlier if she hadn't been with Everest and if they hadn't been tracking a lost gray fox that had escaped from the research center. Everest's nose had led her to Jake.

He was a capable outdoorsman—not uncommon for Tennessee. Plenty of people hunted and fished and made camp for days. But Jake had more than camping skills. He was flawless when it came to covering his tracks.

"Jake!" Sierra hollered as she came up to the perimeter of his camp. Everest was at her side, tags tinkling. It was another hot day and the dog needed some water and a rest.

The first two times Sierra had gone back to check on Jake, he'd retreated into the forest. She'd gradually lured him out of his apprehension. It had taken weeks to convince him she cared more about checking in on him than she did about kicking him out of the park.

Sierra had learned a few things about him. He didn't like when she walked right through to his clearing. It tripped booby traps he had set up around camp. He also didn't like when she disturbed vegetation or did anything else that would make it easy for someone experienced to track him there.

She'd learned to approach the same way he did—from behind on the banks of the creek. Making him nervous was the last thing she wanted to do. He'd never brandished a weapon, but she'd seen knives and this was the South. It wasn't outside the realm of possibility that he had a gun.

"Hey …"

It was a good sign that he relaxed when she stepped into his clearing. But he was still a teenager. Even on a good day, she didn't get much from him. He sat on a thick-cut log that had been upturned next to a pile of charcoal ash. It served as his cooking pit—another smart choice that kept him hidden. It was harder to smell fish cooking on coals underground than it was to smell it cooking over an open fire.

"I brought your favorite." She set down her pack and sat on the second log. The fact that there were always two made her curious to know who visited him.

His camp was in full camouflage mode. The beige, eight-person tent he lived in was well-shaded, as was the hammock he'd strung up between two trees closer to the creek. A camouflage tarp concealed miscellaneous equipment, including a medium-sized Yeti cooler that must have been a bitch to hike in.

He watched with interest as she unlaced her bag—much bigger than her standard day pack. It was the one she only carried when she'd planned a visit to him. Since he was never much for words, she'd do most of the talking.

"Bacon bites." She announced what he already knew, passing him the thawed baggie-full she'd thought for him to eat now. Another dozen meant for him to keep in his cooler were frozen solid.

"Thanks." This was always the point at which he threw her a genuine smile—one that showed her what he must have looked like as a younger kid. He was hardened in some odd, unfortunate way. Moments like this reminded her he was still just a sullen teenager hiding in the woods.

Jake made quick work of relieving her of the frozen stash and took the proffered ice packs along with it. After he'd settled them in his cooler, he returned the ones she'd brought earlier that week. Their temperature was barely even cool. By then, Sierra had pulled out and filled a water bowl for Everest. She'd placed it a few feet back from the log under a spot of shade.

"You must be a good fisherman"—she jutted her chin to his smoldering pit as he sat down and opened the smaller container of bites—"to catch anything this late in the summer, with the creek being so low."

Jake struck Sierra as a shy kid—and kind of a serious one. He shrugged before taking his first bite. "I've got a lot of time."

His jet-black hair was scruffy in the back and flopped long and low in the front—enough to nearly conceal Jake's bright blue eyes. He was taller than average, with a lean, capable build. She'd never seen an actual fishing rod, but it didn't mean he didn't have one hiding back there somewhere.

"How many can you catch in a day?" She wanted to get him talking.

"Evening time's best. Maybe around two or three."

"And that's enough to live on?" Now she was the one who was fishing.

Humor lit his features. "There's a reason why they call it Pigeon Creek."

Sierra rolled her eyes, which her glasses may have prevented him from seeing. He might also not have noticed her gaze shift to survey the scene, looking at the campsite to assess its condition.

"For real—you good for food?"

She'd seen evidence of an emergency stash—a cache of Top Ramen and bags of dried beans. But she didn't like how relieved he seemed every time she brought him food. He may have been surviving, but his situation wasn't good. She would feel a lot better if he had a dog.

"I'm doing all right," he said around a mouthful of bacon and bread and cheese. His answer was always the same. But since there was only a snowball's chance in hell of him ever volunteering the information if he really was in trouble, Sierra would continue to ask.

"The fire risk was elevated yesterday," she started in, "from Moderate to High. They put out a few brush fires already this week."

"Good thing I'm right next to the water," he returned. "Fire comes this way, I'll just submerge myself in the creek."

She threw him a reproachful look. "Come on—you know that's not how it works."

Both fell silent and Jake watched as Everest had her fill of water, then pat his leg and threw out a "C'mere, girl," to coax her to him for a good pet.

"Look. I know you're in a bad situation, even if you won't tell me what it is. Guessing you don't have anywhere better to go is why I haven't kicked you out. But looking the other way while you're squatting on federal land is different from letting you stay in the path of danger. I need you to figure something out."

She quieted then, not wanting to lecture—not needing to beat a dead horse, and not expecting him to be ready with an instant solution. She was glad for a rest and a shady place to catch her breath. She also figured a little companionship wouldn't hurt Jake, both human and canine. The few times she'd ever seen him smile had been to greet her dog.

On her own time, Sierra had asked around surreptitiously about his situation. As far as she knew, he still hadn't been seen in town.

She didn't know when or how he got his supplies, though she had long suspected he had help.

After enough time had passed that Sierra would be missed if she didn't start heading back, she had a final drink of water and began to pack up her bag, but not before taking out the final item she brought.

She'd noticed early on that each time she happened upon his camp, books had been scattered around—through the door of his tent; with a bookmark in the hammock; or open and facedown on the stump. Jake Stapleton was a bibliophile.

The last time she'd been to his camp, the resurfacing of one of the earlier books she'd seen seemed like a sign that he was running out of new things to read. She was sure she didn't have the same tastes as an eighteen-year-old boy, but a good book was a good book. She had no idea whether he'd like *The Amazing Adventures of Kavalier and Clay*, but she set her own copy down on his stump. It was the thought that counted, right?

After strapping on her pack and organizing her hydration straw, she turned back to Jake one final time. She'd have to work out a better plan to get him to break camp and leave. In the meantime, she could at least threaten what would happen if he wasn't vigilant.

"The closest access road is a mile and three-quarters that way. You won't find it on a regular map. Travel south half a mile and you'll come right up to a section of the trail. You'll see a sign on the inter-section that posts the fire hazard status for the day."

She reached into her pocket for the final item she'd thought to bring him: one of the detailed area maps that only rangers and other park agency officials carried. It had more information than most park visitors cared about or needed to know. They showed the locations of hazards and infrastructure and resources that could be abused or exploited if they were public, but she wasn't worried about that. Allowing him to study it was the least she could do.

"That sign gets updated every day at six o'clock in the morning and again at four in the afternoon. Check every day as soon as you wake up, then again at four o'clock sharp. If you ever smell smoke or that sign *ever* says the fire risk is extreme, you get out."

* * *

"Is Joe coming in soon?" Sierra's Green Valley best friend and fellow California transplant, Jaya, craned her neck to look past Willa Hill, scanning faces in assessment of who was behind the bar.

"I don't think he's working tonight." Willa sounded apologetic. The pretty blonde had served them at least ten times before. When the food came, Jaya would switch to something simpler: she liked a rum and Coke when she had the fried chicken and a sweet tea when she had the ribs. But the martini she liked before her food was always particular.

"He makes me the fresh blue cheese olives," Jaya said a bit wistfully under her breath, picking the menu up off of the table and searching for something else. Jaya was a woman who believed a properly made dirty martini was nothing to trifle with. She'd once waxed poetic about shaking rhythm and olive juice.

"Can I get you something different?" Willa knew better than to convince Jaya to let a different bartender try. They'd all been down that road before. When food or drink didn't suit her discerning tastes, she let you know. Jaya was Indian American with a fiery personality that made her seem much bigger than her five foot four. Originally from New York, she had come to Tennessee by way of Los Angeles. Sierra was a softer touch—pure Northern California. Jaya liked to rib her about it. California nice and Tennessee nice didn't mix.

If Jaya didn't like something, she sent it right back. If Sierra didn't like something, she didn't complain; but she also wouldn't eat it, which would cause any Southern server to ask her what was wrong.

California protocol insisted she deny that she wanted anything different, which kicked off a real stalemate.

Sierra plucked the menu out of Jaya's hand. "We'll both take a plate of the fried chicken. She'll take a mojito. I'll take a sidecar."

Jaya had once said the bartender currently on duty made a decent mojito. Sierra didn't know his name, but she recognized the guy. Familiar faces were one of the things Sierra liked best about Genie's. They made Sierra feel like she was at least somewhat part of the town. Genie's Country Western Bar had live music sometimes and a good jukebox when it didn't—both of which Sierra liked. It was the easiest place to get a drink and relax in Green Valley.

"You know twice as much about this town as I do," Sierra said, after their drinks had been delivered. They had lived in Green Valley for about the same amount of time. Jaya was a writer and borrowed much of her inspiration from real life. For her, people-watching was research. She made it a point to observe the goings-on.

"Who would I go see if I wanted more information about the Iron Wraiths?" Sierra got to the point.

Jaya swept dramatic black bangs from where they half-covered her eyes and looked at Sierra like she was crazy. The rest of her long, magnificent hair was swept up into a perfectly messy top bun. Whereas Sierra's hair was stubborn—insistent in its spiral curls and difficult to wrangle—Jaya's hair was versatile. Sierra had never seen her wear the same stylet twice.

"No one. The only thing you need to know about them is leave them alone."

"The fires in the park—they think they're being started by someone local. Call in the usual suspects, right?"

Guilt by association wasn't how Sierra liked to think. Just because the Wraiths were known for troublemaking didn't mean they were behind the trouble in the park. But learning about the Wraiths could kill two birds with one stone.

Jaya lowered her voice and whispered. "Why would a motorcycle club set fires in a national park?"

"That's what I'm trying to find out. All people ever say about them is that they're bad—that they cause trouble and they shake people down. But I need names and criminal profiles."

Sierra didn't mention that she wouldn't mind doing a little digging on Jake. The more she knew about his situation, the better she could help.

Jaya seemed suspicious. "Why isn't the sheriff's office doing this?"

"It's out of Green Valley Sheriff's jurisdiction. The case is under the Parks Police. There's a lot of procedural red tape that could take weeks. And I don't have time to wait. While I'm here, busy investigating, Parks Police hasn't even ruled it as a crime."

Jaya cringed. "When's your performance review again?"

Sierra thought of her pregnant boss, who was currently on bedrest but working from home.

"It should be about five weeks, but it depends how long Olivia lasts. The baby isn't due for another eight, but you never know. Did I even tell you? Clint Grissom is my interim supervisor and you know he doesn't like me. All the fires have been in my territory. I just … I really don't want something like this hanging over my head."

Jaya gave Sierra a half-pitying look—one that fell short of full commiseration, a sure sign Jaya was about to say something Sierra wouldn't like.

"You could always ask Forrest Winters."

Her innocent voice didn't fool Sierra at all.

"Uh … no."

"Why? Because he broke your California bear?"

"Not just any bear—my good luck charm."

"Sierra. That bear is in every gift shop in the state."

"He's a Seahawks fan," Sierra said as if her mouth had suddenly filled with vinegar.

Jaya rolled her eyes. "Has bad luck befallen you since he broke your bear?"

No, Sierra didn't admit.

"What kind of person always has an axe in his hand? A crazed serial killer, that's who."

"You're the one who sounds crazy," Jaya informed her, with a shake of her head.

Sierra took a self-righteous sip of her drink, then gave her real reason—the one she hadn't wanted to say.

"Forrest Winters is not my friend. He and his old boys are half the reason why people like me get shut out. In no other world would I have to prove myself against Dennis Peck."

Sierra couldn't help the sour look that came over her face the second she thought about him. Not a day went by that he let her forget that he was gunning for her promotion. Never mind that the quality of his work didn't hold a candle to hers. Who needed actual chops when you spent your days hunting and fishing with the brass?

"Look. I know it hasn't been easy for you—not being from here and being one of the only women. But cutting off someone who can get you what you want won't help. The best way to smash the patriarchy is to succeed."

Jaya wasn't wrong, but Sierra wasn't ready to relent.

"Forrest isn't the only man in town who knows about the Wraiths."

"Maybe not," Jaya admitted. "But he would understand why you were asking, and the man is extraordinarily well-connected. Everyone in town likes Forrest Winters—even me."

"What's to stop him from going straight to the chief of the Parks Police and telling him I'm jumping the gun on a criminal investigation?"

Jaya shrugged. "Threaten not to let him eat your cooking anymore."

Chapter Four

FORREST

"Fine day for fishing."

Park Superintendent Ed Ellis settled into his seat in Forrest's boat, plain clothes on and ice-cold beer in hand. Forrest had seen the man out of uniform, but something about the loud Hawaiian shirts he wore everywhere when he wasn't on duty always took Forrest by surprise.

Being the highest-ranking park official meant no one gave him too much shit about his quirks. If he weren't the boss, he would have been heckled. Today's shirt was patterned with leaves and flowers from tropical trees and plants and, inexplicably, billiard balls. Forrest's standard fishing attire consisted of cargo shorts and a button-up—the fast-wicking kind that had SPF engineered into the fabric.

The seats on the bow-end of the deck faced one another, but Ed angled his body forward, speed wind from the boat's motion beginning to tousle his graying-blond hair. In Forrest's own hand was coffee, which he could safely resume drinking now that he'd maneuvered his boat away from the dock. His house disappeared behind them as he made quick work of propelling them to the middle of Bandit Lake.

"Plenty of bass right now," Forrest remarked, thinking of the dozen he'd caught and filleted the week before, now Ziploc-bagged and newspaper-packed into his freezer. If bass for dinner was the goal, Forrest could have easily supplied the whole office. But sustenance wasn't why Forrest was up at five in the morning with Ed Ellis and Frank Barnett on his boat.

"You like these outboards?" came the voice of the latter.

Forrest turned to regard Park Police Chief Frank Barnett, who stood behind the cockpit, bent over the stern to look down at the motors. The man stood well under six feet tall and sported a dark handlebar mustache that Forrest had always thought to be a bold grooming choice.

Frank had a thing for vehicles. It mattered not to him whether it traveled by air, land, or sea. He always wanted a peek under the hood. Forrest wasn't surprised he'd picked up on the presence of new outboard motors. There were two, non-gas—owing to an official regulation prohibiting gasoline motors on Bandit Lake. Forrest was lucky to live there. Another regulation stated that houses on Bandit Lake could not be bought or sold—only passed down, as Forrest's house had been passed down through his mother. Owning a house inside a national park had afforded him a mountaintop treasure that sat on one of the most pristine lakes in the U.S.

"Newer model. Got a lot more horses than my first electric set. It's nowhere as powerful as Ed's. If it needs to, it can sustain ninety minutes at twenty-five MPH."

"Well, I prefer the sound of a motor," Frank informed him, steadying himself on one of the center console supports as he walked up toward the bow. "These electric ones are getting too quiet. It's like those Prius cars. The way they sneak up on you—it just isn't right."

Forrest drove a hybrid himself, a fact he wasn't sure whether

Frank knew. Forrest's personal car spent the majority of its time in his garage.

"You seen that Tesla Cybertruck?" Frank went on. "Looks like a goddamned spaceship, but they've got the nerve to call it a pickup."

"I wanna see the electric version of the F-150," Ed chimed in.

"I'd ride in one, but you won't ever catch me buying an electric car. What's next? Electric motorcycles?" Frank groused.

"You'll be driving one soon enough," Ed informed Frank with an amused smile. "Washington's already talking about turning over the whole fleet—a five-year plan to go zero emissions on vehicles in all national parks."

Frank waved the idea away with his hand, sporting a put-out look before, during, and after the next long gulp of his beer. For a guy who couldn't have been fifty, Frank was a bit of a curmudgeon. Forrest thought of it as law enforcement syndrome. The strange mix of real tragedy and stupid shenanigans you saw on jobs like his could do something to a man. Forrest wasn't nearly as jaded. His father hadn't been either, and Hardy Winters had been a fire chief in the USDA Forest Service for twenty-five years.

"I don't know about electric trucks ..." Forrest cut in. "But I'm all for innovation. There's a few things on my wish list that would change the game. In-helmet thermal imaging displays ... *drones* ..."

The way he said it got a chuckle out of both men, which had been Forrest's intention. His were small maneuvers, each one vital to his game of chess. Men like these didn't get behind your ideas because you presented them well in a PowerPoint or wrote pretty emails. They got behind you if they knew you and had seen you were competent—bonus points if they liked you and double bonus points if they knew you'd get behind them when they needed you to.

"You sound like my son." Ed gave a little roll of his eyes. "Always playing with his gadgets and his toys. He needs to get himself a woman. And, *you* ..." He threw Forrest a pointed look. "We need to find *you* something to do."

"I know they sound expensive, but I'll tell you what—these fires springing up in the park? We'd know who was setting them already if we had better tech."

"A whole lot of things would be easier with more budget." Frank didn't miss a chance to jump in. Mentioning the B-word was another strategic maneuver on Forrest's part. "What the hell do we have to do to get the director to loosen up the purse strings?"

The director he spoke of was the National Park Service director. National parks were under the U.S. Department of the Interior. The secretary of the Interior was a cabinet member who reported directly to the president.

"That's Washington's purse strings," Ed came back easily, clearly skilled at telling his own direct reports they couldn't have more money. "Trust me when I tell you, we ain't getting one more dime this year. Right now, they're tighter than a nun's asshole."

Forrest laughed along, which wasn't as easy as it seemed. The talk was salty and the jokes were crass. The other two had started drinking before they'd even gotten on the boat. Since starting his new position, Forrest had a new appreciation for his father. He also saw more clearly why the man had dragged him on so many fishing trips earlier in his career. He'd been grooming Forrest for the politicking that he had known would come.

Only, since Forrest had started as Fire Marshal, it had been *too much* politicking. It had spared him the trauma of running into fires again, but it hadn't always felt like a step up. His title got him more respect than when he'd been a USDA fire chief, but he didn't feel closer to doing what he needed to do.

Once upon a time, his goal had been to innovate how wildfires were fought, nationwide. He'd worked hard to earn advanced degrees in fire science and had risen quickly through the ranks. His obsession with wildfires had once been rooted in pure intellectual interest. Then, two years prior, in a burning forest in Southern California, his best friend had died fighting such a blaze.

Todd's death had changed everything. It had made Forrest impatient for change. It had made him expand his focus from merely fighting wildfires to preventing them. He wanted to change early warning systems, and rethink the way they ran incident command, and improve relief crew resource allocation.

"Suppose I found a way to bring in a drone program that came in at net zero, and that I could find a way to run it that didn't lay off any staff?"

Frank elbowed Ed. "Don't believe a word he says," he advised with a mischievous glint in his eye. "That budget cut line is the oldest trick in the book."

But Forrest stood his ground, making his point with just the right balance of confidence and humility. "If I could pull it off, budget-wise, a successful drone program sure would make the park look good. People look up to Great Smoky for a reason."

Forrest quieted long enough to let the notion percolate in Ed's head. Attending to the controls, he slowed the boat the closer they got to the spot. He cut the engine, resolved to say no more. Pushing too hard, too fast, was always the wrong play. And if Ed didn't bite today, Forrest would keep slow and steady in his persuasion. Patience was one of Forrest's greatest strengths.

"There's a special commission ..." Ed finally said after Forrest was sure that he wouldn't respond. "They're taking proposals for product ideas they'd develop in partnership with Silicon Valley. Come up with a drone design that's specialized to wildfires and you might have a shot."

My own design?

Forrest had never dared to dream of anything so ideal. Current drone technology had limitations when it came to wind and temperatures they could withstand. He'd researched which ones would do the best in the heat. But he had a lot of ideas about how to alter product specs to do even better with fires.

"How soon would they need my proposal?" Even if the deadline was tomorrow, Forrest would stay up all night writing an application that would earn him his way in.

"Not so fast." Ed threw him a sober look. "It's not whether they pick you, it's whether I can spare your time. And I can't justify putting you on a side project right now. I won't greenlight anything until you get your caseload down. Prove to me you've got all major risks under control. Figure out who's setting those fires. Close that case within a month and then we'll talk."

Chapter Five

SIERRA

"Y̲ou've got one month," Sierra uttered to herself but out loud, once again alone on the trail. "You've got 'til at least August fifteenth." It was the same unhelpful reminder that had dominated her thoughts all morning. Today—the fifteenth—marked the official halfway point of July. Olivia had said Sierra's performance review would happen by the middle of August.

That gave her one more month to solve the case. Only, she couldn't solve a case she didn't have time to work. As the daughter of a retired detective, she'd learned at least that. It didn't help that this was tourist season or that she trekked a mile out of her way twice a week to look in on Jake. Time was the one luxury she didn't have.

On the trails was where Sierra got most of her thinking done, though she couldn't think her way out of this. At least walking helped with her stress. So did having her dog at her side. The only thing Everest loved more than holding court at the ranger station was a long morning walk. She drank from the creek and pawed at butterflies and chased small animals off-trail. Seeming to sense that Sierra was worried, Everest coaxed her into a game of fetch.

But niggling thoughts about solving the case continued to steal her fun. If she could somehow get Olivia to lighten up her other duties, she'd have a better shot. She had a staff meeting later, but that wasn't the place to bring it up. Just as Sierra was thinking about how to broach the issue in their one-on-one, she spotted "the old biddies."

The nickname Sierra spoke in her mind in the most affectionate of ways referred to five of her favorite regulars—mature ladies from Green Valley who hiked in three times a week. They were mycophiles, the technical term for people who liked to forage for wild mushrooms. They wore mushroom-themed t-shirts, carried mushroom-themed accessories, and they called themselves "Morel Support."

"Any luck this morning, ladies?" Sierra asked jovially once she was upon them. Everest had stepped a few feet ahead and made her rounds, sniffing suspiciously at the fanny packs most of them wore. Sierra was fairly sure the old biddies left the park with heavier packs than they came in with. She was also sure they were the only regular foragers who no one ever reprimanded. It wasn't illegal to pick them, but it was a crime to take them out of the park.

"This month's been shit." Jolene was a septuagenarian spitfire and the queen bee of the group. Sierra also speculated that she was quite wealthy. She always wore enough precious gems for a red-carpet walk. Today's sapphires matched a blue t-shirt she wore that said, *Shiitake Happens*.

"A lot of what we've been seeing is picked through or trampled over," another one—Iris—chimed in.

"You call open season on amateurs who don't know what they're doing?" Jolene rejoined.

"You ought to need a permit to do what we do," Iris piped back in. "They ought to have required reading about proper mycological practices. They ought to read our blog."

"I enjoyed your last posting," Sierra remarked.

Their genuine appreciation for fungi was the other reason why Sierra didn't bust them for picking. That, plus she wasn't going to accuse or frisk a group of women their age. Being part of Morel Support gave them purpose. They photographed and cataloged and discussed their finds with palpable love on a blog of the same name. Jolene's college-aged grandson managed the website and helped with the technical aspects of getting it online.

"Kevin does a good job with it," Jolene said with no small measure of pride. "He's even got a couple of his fraternity brothers reading the thing."

Jolene talking about her grandson kicked off a solid ten minutes of the other women gushing and showing pictures of their own grand-children. It was another twenty before Sierra was on her way. But the biddies were entertaining, and Sierra didn't mind. Meeting colorful people was a lot of the fun of being a ranger.

Alone again, she was five minutes into resuming her deep thinking when Everest sped up her happy trot, breaking into a run to get to whatever was around the corner. Sierra didn't step up her own pace, but when she rounded the bend, she craned her neck to see whatever Everest had found. That's when she saw him: Forrest.

"Traitor," she mumbled under her breath at the sight of Everest loving every minute of Forrest lavishing pats and behind-the-ear scratches. When Sierra finally reached them, Everest beamed up at her with a blissful smile.

"Do you walk around with bacon in your pocket or something?" Sierra asked.

Forrest gave Everest a final rub and rose to his feet. "I reckon it's just good, old-fashioned Southern charm."

Reaching toward his face, he pushed up the temple of his sunglasses until they sat on top of his head. Forrest looked down at her, smirk on his face, as usual, having his fun. Only, for Sierra, there was nothing fun about the heat that rose to her ears every time his gaze set on her, clouding her thinking with his smoky eyes.

Forrest's eyes weren't just gray, and they weren't "just eyes." His gaze was penetrating and clear, with dark lashes that matched his dark hair. His irises were never the same, though whatever their hue at any given moment, a dark charcoal ring that looked like drawn pencil outlined the lighter color, adding intensity. Today they shone brightly —the color of wet shale—a stark difference from the last time she'd seen him. They'd turned dark, like slate, when he'd talked about the fires. There was something wondrous, and magical, and devastating about watching the way they changed.

"What are you doing in my neck of the woods?"

Forrest chuckled and crossed his arms. "Your woods again, huh?"

Sierra mirrored his posture. "'Neck of the woods' is a Southernism. I know how *y'all* like your sayings."

He laughed again, his voice rich and deep—another thing about him she had the bad habit of replaying in her mind.

"Better than a pig likes slop." Forrest's eyes twinkled.

It made Sierra grateful for her own sunglasses—windows to her soul, and all. She didn't want to think what Forrest might notice if he really saw her then. He would never stop gloating if he knew of her susceptibility to his allure.

"You never said what you were doing here," she pointed out.

"Following up on some potential fire hazards. Just being vigilant. You know how it is …"

Sierra nodded. "I do."

"I was just down at the ranger station …" he began haltingly. "I wanted to thank you for what you left me—you know, my *fire marshal snacks.*"

Sierra bit her lip against her own smile. "You liked that, huh?"

"Not just me. The guys thought it was pretty funny."

"You told me you could read, so I figured …" She trailed off innocently, and shrugged.

After their last conversation and his repeated, willful ignorance of her Tupperware marked specifically as being "Ranger Snacks," she'd brought in a smaller Tupperware labeled "Fire Marshal Snacks."

"Sad thing is, a different fire marshal must've beat me to it," he continued. "Imagine my disappointment when I opened the container and it was empty."

"Oh, no!" She feigned shock. "What did you do?"

"Picked up the phone and called Ed Ellis. Asked him to put out an APB to track down whoever had my bites."

"Then you helped yourself to the ranger bites, I'm guessing."

He made a production out of looking distraught. "They're not as good as fire marshal bites, but I had no choice."

He didn't take his gaze off of her. When heat rose again in her ears, she knew she had to go. Plus, if she didn't get moving, she really would be late.

"Nice to see you, Marshal Winters."

His smirk melted into a half-smile. "Always a pleasure, Ranger Betts."

He stepped aside, clearing the path for her to go.

* * *

"Hey!" Sierra's face broke out into a smile when Olivia came into view on the conference room screen. Sierra had connected her laptop and logged on. Wendell and Dennis would join her in the conference room, and, owing to doctor's orders about staying off her feet, Olivia would join virtually.

As yet, Wendell and Dennis had not arrived. Wendell was perpetually late and Dennis was coming off of front desk duty. Last Sierra had seen him, he was issuing a long-winded answer to a rather simple question from a pair of hikers.

"Your girl treating her mama right?"

Olivia's belly looked even more swollen than it had two weeks before. That was the last time any of them had seen her in person.

"The baby's doing better, now that I'm taking it easy," she beamed. "It's bed rest that isn't all it's cracked up to be."

"Let me guess. Jimmy?" Sierra asked.

Olivia leaned in and lowered her voice, as if her husband were lurking. "Nervous Nellie out there is working my last nerve. He won't even let me in the kitchen to fix something to eat."

Sierra made a mental note to take over a meal or three. Her own sister-in-law had been on bed rest before her nephew was born. Her brother had gone a little nutty in that situation, too.

"Olivia!" Dennis's too-loud voice boomed from the conference room door. He breezed in at a fast clip, his mere presence evaporating Sierra's short-lived ease. Having a boss like Olivia made the less rosy aspects of her job more tolerable—things like putting up with the Dennises of the world. Not having her around every day was a loss.

Three things were true about Dennis: he always had a drink in his hand, a superior look on his smug face, and he never missed an opportunity to suck up. Sierra could have made sport of anticipating what creative, new angles he would come up with to ingratiate himself to their boss. No doubt whatever he said next would plant his lips firmly on Olivia's ass.

"You miss us yet?" He came farther into Sierra's space than she wanted him to, sitting right next to her and setting down his mug. It was black with a white handle and white writing that said, *My pen is bigger than yours*. There was an illustration of a fountain pen alongside the phrase; only, there wasn't much space between the word "pen" and the word "is." Reaching across her rudely, Dennis angled Sierra's laptop toward himself.

"I don't miss the heat," Olivia replied. "Y'all are really getting it."

"Nothing I can't handle," Dennis volleyed back. "And don't you worry. I'm holdin' the place down."

Sierra caught herself just in time not to roll her eyes. Taking a sip of her own drink kept rude words from spilling. Today, her tea was in a simple white mug with the park service arrowhead emblazoned on front. Her 49ers mug had mysteriously disappeared.

"Sounds like *all* of you are holding the place together," Olivia said with emphasis. "I got another nice note from the head researcher at the institute down in Tremont about all the good work Sierra is doing to support the lab. It's good to know you're representing the department well."

"I've taken the liberty of giving Clint daily briefings on the goings-on in this area." Dennis glossed over Sierra's praise. "He's been appreciative to have an inside track."

Olivia frowned. "Let's not get ahead of ourselves, Dennis. I'm still working. Just working from home."

"I hope I didn't step out of line, Olivia. I didn't want to have to bother you on your maternity leave with things I could handle on my own. Not given the condition you're in. It's God's work you're doing right now."

Olivia was a GS-11, two ranks above Sierra's GS-7 designation. She supervised all the rangers in the near eastern region of the park. Her counterpart, Clint Grissom, supervised the rangers in the far eastern and southern regions. Gaia Abbott—who ranked higher than both Olivia and Clint—was responsible for the northwest area, the region with the majority of the visitor traffic, near Cade's Cove.

Theirs was among the top ten most visited parks in the national system. There was prestige to being in leadership here. Olivia wasn't the highest-ranking woman in the park, but she was known nationally within the ranger service. Sierra had jumped at the chance to work for her.

"Where's Wendell?" Olivia wanted to know.

"Still not here," Dennis reported. "Sierra, why don't you send him a text? See if you can find out where he is?"

Because I'm not your secretary and you're not my boss? Being in the same room as Dennis was an exercise in holding in harsh thoughts she couldn't say out loud.

"She on yet?" came a voice from the door—the voice of Wendell, who came barreling in a solid six minutes after the start of the meeting.

"Yes. *She's* on." Olivia announced herself. Had Wendell taken a moment to look, he would have seen. "Punctuality, Wendell," Olivia chided in her all-business voice that was forgiving and impatient all at once. "Let's dive right in."

"Mind if I drive?" Dennis still hadn't relinquished Sierra's computer. "I put together a summary update for today's meeting."

Lacking any graceful way to get her laptop back, Sierra watched as Dennis navigated to the shared drive and opened to a slide—a table showing each of their names. Dennis had color-coded indicators to show which territories were doing well. Green showed strong performance, yellow was at-risk, and red was off-track.

Why is my territory mostly yellow and red?

Not only did Dennis's dashboard show Sierra as patently failing, Wendell was mostly green with a bit of yellow and Dennis was green across the board.

"Beginning with Area Four, things are holding steady." Dennis started with Wendell's territory. By then, Wendell had opened his computer and begun to follow along.

"As for Area Five, it's been hard work and extra hours, but I've managed to bring my numbers up," Dennis humble-bragged.

"But we ought to talk about Area Six," Dennis continued gravely. "I'm worried about a few things. The number of incidents in Sierra's area has gone up."

You asshole.

Dennis was up for the same promotion she was. There was a vacancy in their area of the park for a GS-9. If Sierra got it, Olivia would still be her supervisor but Sierra would become the supervisor of the other rangers at Greenbrier Cosby.

Wendell wasn't in the running—he was a GS-5. Dennis was the only other GS-7 in Olivia's service. He wasn't above playing dirty to get what he thought he deserved. But he had to know he didn't deserve it. If he did, he wouldn't be so bent on undermining Sierra.

"These numbers are wrong," Sierra cut in, still racing to process how he'd arrived at this skewed version of the data. "This isn't the methodology that was used in previous reports."

"Thanks for noticing, Ranger Betts." Dennis kept his eye on Olivia, even as he addressed Sierra. "If you'd let me, I can tell you why this methodology is better."

"Ranger Peck," Olivia finally said in a voice that held warning. "We have to measure consistently with other parks. Plus, changing the method midstream gets us comparing apples to oranges."

"My apologies, Olivia." Dennis pulled off some masculine version of simpering that kept its dignity while telegraphing regret. "Sometimes I get a bit too eager when I'm trying to take the initiative."

More like sabotage.

"Why don't you let me do the worrying?"

Olivia always seemed to have his number. What worried Sierra was, not everybody saw past his tricks; Clint sure didn't, and he was her on-the-ground supervision while Olivia was out. With Grissom in charge, Dennis might actually be winning.

Chapter Six

FORREST

"Tell me who this Jeffrey James is again?"

Buck had met the man in the parking lot of Sugarlands. The question came seconds after he'd climbed into Forrest's truck. The walk-through of the latest incident site would soon be underway. After a debrief at the station, they'd split into pairs and were set to caravan to the scene.

"Jeffrey James is the sheriff. His station is down in Green Valley but he's got jurisdiction over the whole county, with the exception of the park."

"Why would Green Valley be involved in something like this?"

The question reminded Forrest of how green Buck was. The junior firefighter was no longer a rookie, but just. He was young, unmarried, one year new to the neighboring firehouse in Crosby. Like the Green Valley Fire Department, the one in Crosby primarily served the town. But firefighters from all of the local community houses backed up park patrols during fire season. Spotting the plume of smoke during one of those patrols was how Buck had discovered the third fire. He didn't work for the parks service, but he was on the case.

"Plenty of the troublemakers who come into the park come in from Green Valley. Usually bored kids looking to have a little too much fun. Could be, the sheriff has some ideas."

"Chief Barnett didn't look too happy about him tagging along."

Forrest took his eyes off of the road long enough to throw Buck a matter-of-fact look.

"Frank Barnett never looks too happy about anything."

Forrest thought back to the previous Saturday, to fishing with Ed and Frank on his boat. Get Frank talking about something he liked—like bourbon or football—and he was good company. Mention something he was pissed about—like how much pressure his department was under over the summer—and, man, did he like to complain. His body language at the debrief had said it all: he didn't have time for this shit.

But Frank needed to make time. Never mind that he was severely overworked; he was the big decision maker—the one who all park law enforcement reported to. He was in a better mood during quieter times of year, but the summer heat really brought out the crazies. Frank delegated plenty to his lieutenants, especially in high season.

That's why it wasn't surprising that Clint Grissom had been brought into the mix. He was at the supervisor level on the ranger side. He was too senior to work a patrol beat, but he did manage a large handful of other rangers. Grissom being there explained why Dennis Peck had tagged along—he always seemed to be up that guy's ass. The final member of the investigation team was Sierra, the one ranger who actually needed to be there since the fires were in her territory.

"We should partner with the rangers, you know," Buck commented too casually. "What do you know about Sierra?"

Forrest took his eyes off the road long enough to throw Buck a sidelong glance.

"I know she's too much woman for you. Sierra Betts is fierce. I've seen her get close to a mama black bear to help an injured cub. Saw her one day at the range, too. I've never met a ranger on the preservation side who was better than a halfway-decent shot. But Sierra ... she's a dead-eye."

"There's somethin' sweet about her," Buck kept on, ignoring Forrest's discouragement. "I think that tough-girl thing is an act. I sure wouldn't mind seeing her softer side. All of her softer sides, matter of fact ..."

Forrest couldn't gratify it with a response. The less appropriate the locker room talk, the farther away he needed to be. And the comment hit him in ways he didn't enjoy. If anyone in this town was going to get to see the softer side of Sierra, Forrest thought it ought to be him.

"Well, rein it in, cowboy," Forrest warned. "We're almost at the spot and today is important. You flirt on your own time."

* * *

"Is my presence strictly necessary?" Sheriff Jeffrey James asked with irritation.

It was a bit too late for that. They had caravanned to the point on the access road closest to the scene of the fire. Now three-quarters of the way to the site, their rather slow party hiked through thick forest without trails or paths.

"Five more minutes," Forrest called by way of placation, seeing the man's limits were being tested. The sheriff was unaccustomed to long walks and extreme heat. He was in good shape for his age— likely pushing sixty—but spent less time at crime scenes than he did seated at his desk or behind the wheel of a cruiser.

Clint Grissom also sweat profusely, though it was hard to tell how much of his resting dick face was a result of the heat. All summer, the usually even-keeled ranger supervisor had been in a snit.

Forrest had been too busy buttering Frank up to dig about what might be going on. He'd made it a point not to miss poker night that week and he'd even shown up to crash the party on the night Frank always had a cold one at Genie's with his boys. Forrest had been working overtime to meet Ed's requirements to submit to the special commission. Now, all he needed was for Frank to get Grissom to do his part in getting to the bottom of these fires.

"You been getting along okay up here with all this heat?" Buck asked Sierra.

Buck had made it a point to fall in behind her.

"It's the humidity I'm not used to," Sierra replied.

It was easy to tell that Dennis and Sierra were most acclimated to the punishing heat. The sloshing of liquid and knocking-together of ice cubes was audible from within Sierra's hydration pack.

"You're from California, right?" Buck continued to dig. "Whereabouts?"

"Sonoma County, which is north of Marin, which is north of San Francisco."

"Sounds nice. What's it like out there?"

Marching single file gave Forrest a chance to roll his eyes at Buck's weak game. Buck was a good-looking guy and every bit a red-blooded American boy, but still … how the hell did he get laid with that?

"We're here," Forrest announced before Sierra could answer. The colorful flags marking the ground gave it away. Walking onto a fire scene, even a days-old one, still dredged up emotion—some cross between anxiety and sadness and rage. Forrest did his best to suppress it as he ushered everyone in. Each member of the small party ducked under a section of the yellow-taped, tree-strung perimeter and stood around the border of an inner circle.

"All right." Forrest made brief eye contact with each person. "Thank y'all for being here. You can see the scene has more flags than the initial photos. I'll get to that. In the meantime, I'll turn it over to Firefighter Buck Rogers to describe what he saw when he came on the scene."

Buck looked a bit nervous. He had never presented to people so high up. Most of what he saw in Crosby were medical emergencies and rescuing cats from trees.

"Okay." Buck cleared his throat. "We've named this fire the Little Pigeon Fire given its proximity to Little Pigeon Creek. At approximately four in the afternoon on the date of the incident, I was at the Mt. Cammerer lookout when I spotted the plume as part of my rounds. I called it in and the Crosby Fire Department met me on the scene, where we found this area smoldering. The crew opted not to use an extinguishing agent. The scene remained manned until it fully cooled."

"Could the fire have started spontaneously?" Frank asked.

Forrest shook his head. "This area is completely shaded. Without direct sunlight, a spontaneous fire is unlikely."

"You raised the fire risk to High," Dennis pointed out importantly. "Doesn't that mean the likelihood of spontaneous fires is increased?"

"Overall, yes." Forrest kept his voice calm. "But the fire risk was Moderate on the day of the incident."

Jeffrey James mopped his brow. Frank peered down at the newly flagged scene with interest. Dennis looked at Clint Grissom and Grissom looked at Frank. Sierra raised her eyebrow and looked at Forrest.

"Wouldn't you know whether it was man-made versus nature-made based on the presence of accelerants?" She was waiting for him to mention what they'd already discussed.

"Thank you, Ranger Betts. If you'll all take a look at the flags, please." Forrest pointed toward the area in the middle of the circle. "The orange ones represent areas I tested as part of an expanded forensic investigation. They're spaced one foot apart in the configuration of a grid. As Ranger Betts suggests, the presence of accelerants would further confirm a fire that was not spontaneous—one in which humans were involved."

"I take it you found accelerant?" Frank asked.

"We did," Forrest confirmed.

"Campers carry lighter fluid," Clint Grissom cut in irritably. "I don't know what we're doing out here in all this heat."

"A two- to four-foot radius of concentrated carbon deposits is consistent with your typical campfire." Forrest hid his frustration. "But we found no single ignition point for the fire and no accelerant concentrated to one spot. The accelerant was spread all over."

"What do you mean, all over?" Sheriff James was still sweaty, but he looked intrigued.

"If you'll take a look at the pattern delineated by the new flags— the purple ones—it was confined to a perfect circle."

Forrest paused and looked around as brows furrowed and eyes swept, and as all present took in new information—information that any idiot could see changed the game.

"Why would someone spread accelerant over such a wide area only to put out the fire?" Sierra's gaze flipped up to Forrest.

"That's what we wanted to know," Buck stepped a foot closer to Sierra. "So we ordered a compound spectrum to test the perimeter."

"What the hell is that?" Dennis asked.

"It's to determine what chemical compounds are present when you don't know what you're looking for," Sierra murmured, then set her gaze back on the flags. "It's different from the test that would have been used to detect accelerants."

As usual, Sierra was spot on. Forrest was about to tell her so when Grissom cut in.

"How 'bout you let Forrest answer the questions?" His voice

wasn't sharp, but it wasn't kind either. His arms were crossed and he looked down at the ground.

"Actually, she's right …" Buck chimed in, looking back and forth between Sierra and Grissom in confusion. It wasn't the first time Forrest had seen Grissom take a jab at her. They were usually like this one—microaggressions. Forrest had seen it in the way Grissom treated Olivia, too.

"But you already got a positive test on the accelerant. What does the other test tell you that you don't already know?" Dennis questioned Buck.

Sierra kept her mouth shut but looked at Dennis like he was an idiot.

"It would give a clue as to what stopped the fire." Forrest said what Sierra wouldn't. "Fires don't burn in clean circles. They don't even burn in clean lines unless there's a very strong wind."

"A deliberate, controlled fire," the sheriff concluded, his handkerchief out again. He mopped his brow before swiping at the back of his neck. "Seems like the same person's setting all these fires."

It was what Forrest had been waiting for—someone other than him to draw that conclusion.

"The evidence backs it up," Buck said. "We found compounds like ammonium, diammonium sulfate, ammonium phosphate …" he rattled off.

"Fertilizers," the sheriff replied.

"And the exact same compounds you'd find in a fire retardant," Buck concluded.

Silence fell over the scene. Forrest took another look around. Frank was the only person who hadn't spoken and also the person whose opinion mattered the most. He stood, arms crossed, continuing to inspect the ground as if staring for longer would reveal the answers.

"You look at anything else?" Frank finally asked. "Find any evidence about who they might've been or how they got in or out?"

Forrest shook his head. "No trash, no tracks, and nothing between here and the trail."

"They probably came in and out by the creek," Sierra supplied. "It's low enough this time of year. They could navigate by it and get in and out, undetected."

"What's your *official* determination?" Dennis asked, placing emphasis on the word official and scowling briefly at Sierra. "Isn't that why we're all here?"

Forrest said what he said next with some ceremony.

"Based on the facts of the case—that this fire was deliberately set and subsequently extinguished—I'm officially ruling it arson. Based on new forensic testing done on the two initial fires, I'm ruling those as arson, too. And based on similarities between this fire and the two prior fires, I'm ruling these cases as linked."

"Looks like we got us a serial arsonist on our hands." Buck voiced aloud their conclusion.

"Which is why I invited Sheriff James. While this officially falls under the jurisdiction of Chief Barnett and the Parks Police, my opinion is that these fires are being set by someone who is local to town."

"But you still need to make an official ruling," the sheriff said to Chief Frank Barnett.

The chief nodded. "I'll work with my people on it and call the group back together in a few days."

"I'd like to help," Sierra chimed in quickly. "This is my territory. I may be able to provide guidance about the area that no one else would know. If I understand the profile of our arsonist, I could be a first line of defense in catching him."

"I think Chief Barnett and I can take it from here," Grissom said, once again calmly, but it was dismissive all the same. "You need to focus on your daily responsibilities—not take on more. I'll confer with the chief. I can always call in Dennis if I need help."

Ouch.

When he looked to see her reaction, her face was drawn in a consternation so bitter, Forrest knew instinctively that things between Sierra and Grissom were strained.

"This is real good investigative work," Frank said finally. "Even if the crime itself is strange. Thanks to you, Forrest, and your team for getting us to this point."

The sheriff had his hat off again and was wiping at the back of his neck.

"I'm real interested in where you come out on this one," he began. "But when you decide what you're gonna do, just call. I could do without another walk in the woods."

Chapter Seven

SIERRA

"I 'll take an Uncle Nearest sidecar."

Sierra settled into the barstool at the same moment Joe set down a napkin for her drink.

"Oh, don't worry. I asked him to get one started the second you came in."

For the second time in a week, Sierra was at Genie's—this time with her dispatcher, Rick, sans his latest boy-toy, with whom he had already broken up. Truth be told, Rick was a bit of a heartbreaker. He was five foot eight, just like Sierra, and in shape though average in his build. But he was sharp. Witty. Whip-smart and cutting when he needed to be. He could bend anyone with his sapient, golden eyes.

Sure enough, it was mere seconds before Joe set down the drink that consisted of simple syrup, fresh lemon juice, and bourbon. The glass—frosty with condensation—held liquid of a hue that proved the drink had been mixed just right. Two wide shavings of orange peel were immersed in the liquid itself, and a long toothpick-skewer with Bing cherries on it lay across the top of the glass.

"Thank you," she said in a desperate way that came out more like a gush. One brief toast later and she was taking a long, satisfying gulp. With the kind of day she'd had, Sierra had a feeling she'd need at least three.

"I've gotta get this promotion."

Rick had heard this proclamation before. Fortunately for Sierra, his greatest friend-strength was commiseration. As the only openly gay man who worked on their side of the park, some of their struggles were the same. In his early years, Rick had gotten it worse.

"Just four more weeks," Rick said in a singsong voice. "You can make it that long."

Sierra cocked her head. "But can I make it without killing Dennis?"

She didn't mention that Grissom was in the mix and more hostile than ever. Better to stick to the enemy everybody knew.

"Dennis is all hat and no cattle," Rick said in an indignant voice before taking a sip of his gin and tonic. "Besides, they can't *not* give it to you this time—not after all that you've done."

Rick liked to remind Sierra of her accomplishments—of her high incident resolution rate and the perfect record of zero safety violations occurring on her watch. Getting the supervisory role meant she would spend less time on the ground and more time behind a desk. It meant nine to five from Monday to Friday instead of odd hours and inconsistent shifts. It meant the lifestyle of someone who actually had a life.

"It's not whether I earned it that worries me," Sierra said grimly. "It's what I can't do to protect it. The politics of the parks service are bigger than me. I don't want this to turn into another Shasta."

Even mentioning the name of the park where she'd been on her previous rotation filled Sierra with betrayal. Being passed over for the same promotion at Shasta still hurt. The bullshit reason why added insult to injury. Despite her spotless record, the opening had gone to a notorious hack: the brother of the chief of the Park Police.

"Fortunately for you, Dennis isn't related to anyone important."

"But he *is* a pompous jackass and he *does* have a penis," Sierra pointed out. That was the part that ate at her—her own life lessons made it hard to believe in progress. It was impossible to ignore that, century after century, the same kinds of people, owing to the same kinds of circumstances, tended to emerge the victors.

"At least tell me things are going better on the dating front." Rick waggled his eyebrows. He always knew how to bring it back to lighter topics when Sierra got too maudlin, though Sierra's love life had become a source of depression, too.

She'd received her fair share of attention since arriving in Tennessee—mostly, men she met in Knoxville when she hit the town with Jaya or Rick. Among the few she'd dated, she couldn't complain about their physical appeal. She hadn't minded the Southern gentleman routine, either, but the attraction from her end never lasted. Coming up with three younger brothers, she knew the difference between an overgrown boy and a man.

"It's drier than the Sahara," Sierra admitted.

"Still?" Rick seemed outraged. "I thought it was gonna happen between you and that ranger over in Cade's Cove. Over the radio, he's got a really nice voice …"

"If the 'it' you're referring to is a sloppy kiss and a clumsy side-boob fondle, that's a no."

Rick chuckled around his straw. "You and your stupid kissing rule …"

Sierra was unapologetic. "There is nothing stupid about wanting a man who knows how to kiss. Kissing is glorious, and underrated, and a leading indicator of other important talents. And by 'other important talents,' I mean—"

"Be careful." Rick looked around with put-on paranoia. "I saw Buck buzzing around. You don't want to tell him the way into your heart. He's already hell-bent on breaking that dry spell of yours. Say it too loud and he might just materialize."

Sierra smirked at the notion. Buck Rogers was, indeed, hell-bent on dating her. He was also barely legal. She had happened upon his twenty-first birthday party at this very bar.

"I have enough problems without guilt over robbing the cradle. And, like I told you. I don't want to have to train the man. I want someone who knows what he's doing. Someone like—"

Sierra cut herself off and her smile disappeared seconds after she joined Rick in scanning for signs of Buck. Her enjoyment dampened the second she laid her eyes on *him*.

Sitting at the best booth in the middle of the floor was none other than Forrest Winters, looking every bit as smug and gorgeous as he always did. He was holding court with other law enforcement who worked in the park. It explained why Buck was there. She recognized one guy she didn't know as from the fire service. The one other person she did know sat at Forrest's left hand: Chief Frank Barnett.

Sierra must have been looking too long, or too hard. Forrest looked up from talking. When he did, his eyes affixed directly on her. He didn't pause his speech but he gave a little wink. Sierra scoffed in displeasure, thoroughly resenting the traitorous flush that came over her at his gesture.

It's a flash of anger, she reassured herself.

It had been five days since she'd caught him red-handed eating out of her Tupperware—*marked* Tupperware, she thought. Tupperware that clearly announced itself as containing ranger treats. It had been three days since she'd run into him on the trail and eight hours since he'd walked the investigation team out into the woods. It had been the same amount of time since he'd done nothing to advocate for her place on Barnett's team. It had been three hours since she'd swung by the ranger station at the end of her shift only to find—yet again—that he had pilfered her bites.

Remnants of Forrest's visits were always obvious. He was some sort of maniac about writing in pencil. He sat over the trash can and sharpened their tips with his axe. A telltale mess of shavings in the wastebasket was always left in his wake. Then, there was the *other* evidence of his presence. In the cool confines of the room, Forrest's scent lingered. It was unmistakable—a mixture of some masculine soap, warm pine needles, and fire. There was something else to it she couldn't identify but smelled delicious.

Hastening to look away, Sierra fixed her eyes back on Rick, hoping he hadn't noticed Forrest's wink or Sierra's answering scowl. Rick was under the influence of the same spiked Kool-Aid everyone else in Green Valley had drunk. It loosened them to Forrest's charm; it tricked them into thinking he was a swell guy. Sierra knew the truth in a way no one saw and that no one likely would. He may have had a pretty face, but Forrest Winters was just like every other good ol' boy Sierra didn't care to know. And she knew just where he could stick that Southern charm.

* * *

Sierra had learned early on that she could never be inconspicuous in Green Valley—a dubious fact of being one of few Black women in town. She'd been recognized by strangers within a week of her arrival. Everyone from supermarket cashiers to hardware store clerks and even the teller at the bank had asked how she was getting along after noting that she must be "that new park ranger in town."

Another dubious fact was being continually confused or associated with other Black women in Green Valley. Bobby Jo MacIntyre owned Big Bob's Bait and Tackle, was old enough to be Sierra's mother, and the two women looked absolutely nothing alike. Still, Sierra had fielded a dozen questions from the other half of the town who didn't know she was the new park ranger about whether she was Bobby Jo's daughter.

"Anything I can help you find?"

Sierra was doing her best to dodge the librarian. It was also by habit that she pulled tiny maneuvers that let her peruse in peace. Beyond cases of mistaken identity, being followed in places where people browsed was the other thing that happened to you when you were Black. Sometimes it was innocent—sometimes not. Sierra was so used to being targeted with that very question, she tended to answer by rote, insisting that she didn't need help and would find whatever she was looking for herself.

Only this time, she did need help. A pep talk from her father, retired detective Cedric Betts, had pulled her out of her frustration over Grissom. Her father had been a rule-breaker himself. He was unconventional and a loner, but he'd tackled some tough cases. When she'd gone to him, he'd given her only one piece of advice: know your beat.

The problem was, Sierra didn't know this beat. She knew the park, but not Green Valley. And if she believed that the person setting the fires was local, she needed to get up to speed. She might not have access to police reports, but there was plenty she could research in the Green Valley Ledger about arson cases and suspects mentioned in relation to local crime.

"Oh! Hello."

Sierra finally answered the librarian, whose bright red lipstick and cat-eyeglasses flattered her pretty face—one made even lovelier by hazel eyes and freckles on her nose. She was heavily pregnant, though not quite as far along as Olivia. There was something shy about her, even though she had been the one in pursuit of Sierra—even though helping people had to be something she did dozens of times a day for her job.

"I was hoping to brush up on local history—anything that could help me get to know the town, especially over the past few years."

The librarian blinked. "You are?"

It wasn't the reaction she'd expected. It seemed like a fairly standard request. Most towns with their own libraries also had their own archives.

"Yes ..." Sierra said slowly.

"Oh! It's just I wouldn't have pinned you for a non-fiction type of woman. From looking at you, you strike me as more of the literary fiction or cozy mystery type."

Who *was* this person?

"It's not for pleasure." Sierra smiled, reminding herself that when you didn't act suspicious as hell, people were disarmed. "I'm a park ranger. It makes me half historian, half law enforcement, half environmental expert. Hikers ask a lot of questions, you know. I'm also looking for anything you have on local bird species. Do you have anything like that?"

The librarian gave a shy smile. "That's three halves, by my count. Either way, we have an archive. And I know who you are, Sierra Betts. Word has it you bake the tastiest bacon bites in the tri-county."

"Has Wendell been talking?" He'd been known to sing the praises of her bites outside of Greenbrier Ranger Station. No fewer than five rangers from other stations had asked for them specifically when they'd dropped by, all on Wendell's account.

"Not the way you're thinking." The librarian gave a little wave of her hand. "He came in looking for a recipe book that had something like the ones you make. Sounded like he was going to try to spring it on his wife."

"He could have just asked for the recipe."

The librarian motioned for Sierra to follow her someplace.

"I know why he didn't." The two women began walking and the librarian lowered her voice to a whisper. "His wife is the jealous type. He can't bring home a recipe from another woman, but I'm guessing he figured a cookbook was safe. More marriages than you think hang in the balance of the right book. I've gotten personal thank-you notes for stocking ten copies of *Fifty Shades of Grey*."

It looked to be a short walk across the main floor to a system of hallways and rooms on the far side. Something on a display table caught Sierra's eye as she passed. The covers of two books she'd spotted in Jake's camp reminded her that she'd taken him *The Adventures of Kavalier & Clay*, which reminded her she didn't own a single other book she suspected he might like.

"Hey." Sierra stopped walking. "I'm also looking for a book recommendation ... for my nephew," she lied. "He's already got these two books."

The librarian stopped as well, picking up the first book Sierra had motioned to—the one with a red cover.

"Then he'd probably like anything on this table. Though, I could show you the Young Adult table as well."

Sierra looked closer at some of the books, many of which seemed to have young people on the cover. "I thought this *was* the Young Adult table."

The librarian smiled. "No, that one is." She pointed back toward the display they'd just passed. "This one is LGBTQ literature."

"Uh ... thank you," Sierra managed, her mind scrambling to reconcile what she thought she knew about Jake. "Sorry. I didn't mean to stop us from getting to the archives."

"Now what is it you're looking for, exactly?" the librarian wanted to know. "The East Tennessee Room is on this level. It's a special collection housing local and regional history, though a bunch of it goes a ways back. Some of what's in there'll take you back a hundred years."

Sierra stopped walking when the woman did. They had stopped in front of a door with a plaque bearing that name. Craning her neck to see down an intersecting hallway, Sierra noticed a sign with a downward-pointing arrow next to a staircase. It read: "TO THE ARCHIVES."

"What's the archives room?" Sierra wondered aloud, not answering the librarian's question directly.

"The downstairs archives are full of the kinds of records they don't maintain at the County Recorder's. You know—local periodicals and every annual report ever put out by City Hall. Literature about local schools and local business and crime rates and such. But the East Tennessee Room has more historical artifacts and curated history. I'm guessing that's what you're looking for. It'll give you better fodder for the kinds of stories tourists might like to hear."

Sierra's heart sank as the woman produced a plastic card from some hidden pocket in her skirt and swiped it in front of the panel to unlock the room. What Sierra really wanted was downstairs. Only, she'd already made up a story for what she needed and why.

"Have you ever used an archives space?" the librarian asked, swiping the card and letting them into the East Tennessee Room.

"Being a historian is part of the job ..." Sierra trailed off.

The space was larger than expected. A large, rectangular table sat in the middle. The bookshelves on the longest wall had sections that were labeled. Green Valley history was labeled distinctly from county history. There was even a section on Great Smoky Mountains National Park. A computer in the corner sat in a single bay.

"Is that where I can access the digital archives?" Sierra asked hopefully, motioning to the terminal.

The librarian glanced at the computer before waving her hand. "Oh, no. You can look up books we have here in the library but that's about it. It's the same as all the other computers in the building—a digital card catalog." The librarian's brow knitted and her wide, friendly eyes blinked from behind her glasses. "Is there any specific topic you're looking for? I might know where to look and could save you some time ..."

The woman seemed so helpful and genuine it made Sierra want to tell the truth.

"Well ... apart from digging deeper into Green Valley history, it would be good to hear news about the kinds of things that happen in town. I live inside the park, and sometimes we get kids from Green Valley—kids doing things they aren't supposed to do. I wouldn't object to brushing up on local incidents ... and crime."

The librarian nodded in understanding and threw Sierra a knowing smile. "My husband calls it 'knowing his territory.' You might have run into him. Wyatt Monroe? He's a county sheriff. My name's Sabrina."

Sierra didn't answer for a beat—the same beat her heart skipped at the realization she'd just revealed to a cop's wife that she was poking around.

"There are a few things I can pull for you. And you know who else we can ask?" Sabrina was off to the races now that Sierra had given her more to go on. "Naomi Winters? The head librarian? She helped organize the archives downstairs. She might know the best way to do it."

Naomi *Winters?*

As in, Forrest Winters? Sierra had to kill the idea before things got out of hand. Saying as much as she had had been a mistake. It had seemed a safe-enough bet to say she was interested in crime records when she'd seen Sabrina only as a librarian. But she couldn't forget just how small this town was.

"Oh, no," Sierra backpedaled. "That sounds like a lot of work. I don't need anything that involved. I'm mostly here for the older stuff. I figured I'd have a casual look at back issues of *The Ledger*. You know, if it was easy."

"Oh, okay." Sabrina nodded quickly and adjusted her glasses in a way that told Sierra maybe Sabrina had a habit of getting ahead of herself. "Well, look around here as long as you need."

Chapter Eight

FORREST

I've been waitin' for you, girl ...

Forrest said it telepathically to his Cuban sandwich as he unwrapped the foil and plastic in which it was sealed, taking a deep inhale of the crusty bread and piled-on fixings inside. One of the highlights of any shift was eating his handcrafted sandwich, which he liked to wash down with a bottle of home-brewed sweet tea. No matter the heat outside, his cooler kept both items fresh.

Though his sandwich may have varied each day, he liked to eat whatever kind he brought with a bag of kettle chips and take a load off his feet while he listened to music in the cool, air-conditioned confines of his truck. Today had been another hot day—one not made easier by the fact he'd been out late the night before, drinking down at the firehouse for poker night and shooting the shit. Even the smallest of hangovers felt amplified when you spent your days in the punishing heat. His lunch felt well-earned. More than usual, his sand-wich would taste good.

Forrest had just pulled the two pre-cut halves apart, put the first down on his passenger seat and made to take his first bite of the other when his cell phone rang.

"Shit," he said. *So close.*

But any firefighter on duty at the height of fire season would be an idiot not to answer his calls.

He pressed the call pickup button on the steering wheel of his truck. "'Lo? This is Forrest Winters."

"Forrest, it's Frank. Glad I caught you. Good to see you the other night at Genie's."

Forrest straightened a bit at the sound of Barnett's voice. "Oh, hey, Frank. What's doing? Missed you last night at poker …" He trailed off.

Frank chuckled. "I'm still hurting from three weeks ago and all that money I lost to Grizz. I'll go back when he stops cheating. But listen …"

Here it was—the reason why Frank had really called.

"I'm calling as a courtesy. To let you know where we came out on the Little Pigeon Creek fires."

The way he phrased it told Forrest everything he needed to know.

"What'd y'all decide?" Forrest asked.

"Now, we'll be on watch," Frank was quick to reply. "But I don't have the resources to fully investigate it, which means I can't put it on the books as a crime. If I rule it as a crime, I'm on the hook to solve it. And, especially if I call it arson, if I can't prove I've done enough to prevent another incident, it's my ass on the line."

Forrest fought to control a rush of anger. "It's all our asses on the line if there's another fire and it gets out of hand. My guys are at risk more than yours. And when there's a wildfire, it's not just acreage that burns. Do you know how many living things are tied into this ecosystem? How many paychecks inside and outside of the park rely on tourism? How many animal species would go extinct if we let them burn?"

"Look, man," Frank cut in. "I know all those things. And, believe me—I'd catch the guy if I thought we had a snowball's chance in hell. But I don't have men to spare for a wild goose chase."

"Wild goose chase?" Forrest sputtered.

"That's exactly what it would be. We've got three crimes and zero witnesses. That means I don't even have a description of a suspect to give to my guys. And my men aren't trained detectives—they're first responders. They don't even patrol any of the areas where the fires have occurred. We're just not set up for this."

Forrest quieted, still seething. Frank's points weren't wrong. But the consequences of not responding could be dire. Something else about this bothered him—something he hadn't identified yet.

"Look. I know you're mad about it, and you have a right to be. None of this is any disrespect to your opinion. But I can't put resources on a manhunt in high tourist season if we don't know the man we're hunting for or have any idea of where he'll strike again."

Forrest caught his sandwich out of the corner of his eye, his appetite now gone. "I guess were all up against bureaucracy and budget cuts these days," he conceded. Livid as he was, he couldn't afford to alienate Frank.

"If I was you, I'd make friendly with every beat officer in every agency. Folks who are already on the ground are your best chance at eyes and ears now. Who's that new ranger? The one who's supposed to be good?" Frank asked.

"Sierra Betts?" Forrest guessed.

"No. Not her. The one Grissom brought to the scene. What's that kid's name? Peck?"

Forrest ran into Dennis Peck from time to time, just like he ran into Sierra. Only, he usually saw Dennis at Sugarlands, chatting up Grissom and shooting the shit. Forrest had no clue when Dennis actually made his rounds.

"I'm telling you, man," Frank continued. "The boots on the

ground are your best shot at seeing something. Get the rangers, researchers, and game wardens on your side."

* * *

Six hours and one uneaten sandwich later, Forrest had cooled somewhat, gone for a long drive and begun to regroup around a plan. He might not have agreed with all of the chief's logic but Frank was right about one thing: if his department wasn't going to take it, Forrest would need eyes and ears. And he also needed allies—true allies who would do more than just say something if they saw anything suspicious. He needed someone who would go in pursuit.

What Forrest needed was a partner. Only one person came to mind. And she came to Donner Bakery every Tuesday. It was why Forrest had knocked off early—why he lounged at one of the bakery's inside tables, at the tail end of a slice of banana cake and halfway through a glass of milk. Barnett's *other* reason for not wanting to take the case—to keep it on the ranger books as an incident instead of putting it on the police books as a crime—gave Forrest even more reason to want to talk to her in private.

"Sierra ..." He feigned surprise. "Fancy meeting you here."

She hadn't seen him when she'd walked in, breezing right past him to get to the counter. Forrest had waited a few seconds, taking her in before he announced himself. She was showered and lovely, her hair in a looser bun than usual. Stray wisps kissed smooth skin the hue of sequoia trees. Her cornflower and navy-blue-striped sundress hugged her breasts and opened to a flowing skirt that stopped at her knees. Dainty sandals revealed toenails painted purple. He didn't see her out of uniform nearly enough.

"Forrest ..." she said with the slight frown of a person unaccustomed to seeing him out of context.

He closed the pocket notebook he'd been writing in—an outline of the proposal he would submit to the special commission. Never mind that he hadn't yet gotten the green light. He rose to his feet, and strode to where Sierra stood at the counter. At the same moment he arrived, Joy set an open cupcake box in front of Sierra, showing her the confection before making to close and sticker the pink box. It was topped with white buttercream and sprinkled with dark chocolate crumbs, and had an Oreo stuck upright in the frosting.

"I didn't know you like cupcakes," he lied.

"Everybody likes cupcakes."

"Well, if everybody doesn't, everybody should. Why don't you let me buy you that? I've been wanting to talk to you."

"I can buy my own cupcakes." Already, she seemed suspicious. "And I wasn't planning to eat this here. Can't you just corner me at my ranger station one day and steal my bites like you always do?"

Buoyed by her snark, he smiled. Something in the way she said it made him think she welcomed his little drop-ins.

"Invitation accepted," he responded smoothly. "But what I want to talk to you about can't wait. It's urgent, and sensitive."

He said that last part quietly, looking around to be sure he hadn't been heard.

She blinked. "You want to buy me a cupcake and have a secret conversation with me?"

"I prefer the term *confidential*."

She blinked again.

"I know this sounds weird. I promise you, it isn't. I thought of something that could be good for us both. But we should go some-place to discuss it. Small town, word travels, and all. Will you at least trust me enough to hear me out?"

When Sierra sighed and shook her head, as if preemptively disappointed in herself, it was clear she'd made her decision.

"What are you suggesting exactly?"

"I'm suggesting we go for a walk."

Still looking put out, she picked up her cupcake box by its string.

"Hey, Joy," he hollered, loudly enough to be heard in the kitchens. "Put Sierra's cupcake on my tab."

* * *

The weather was cooler now in town than it tended to be in the park, not just owing to the time of day. Some valleys languished in still, settled air but Green Valley caught a breeze. Walks down Main Street could be pleasant in the summer. Dinner smells from restaurants and the aroma of burnt honeysuckle filled the air. The thought crossed his mind that it would have been nice to wander into one of said restaurants with Sierra, to have a real conversation—not just about work—over a real dinner.

"I can take that for you."

Her hands were full. One hand clutched some sort of wallet strapped to her wrist. The other held the top of her pastry box by its strings. When he held out his own hand, she gave him the box and muttered a quiet thanks. They walked in silence until he turned them off onto a side street.

"Barnett gave me a call about the fires. Told me his determination."

His sidelong glance showed him her furrowed brow.

"Those aren't supposed to be announced until the debrief tomorrow afternoon."

"He gave me a heads-up—you know, as a professional courtesy."

And 'cause he knows it's bullshit and wanted to give me time to cool down.

"He won't call them arson. Won't link the fires. He won't pursue further investigation and they won't be ruled as crimes, all on account of a lack of evidence."

In the seconds it took Forrest to break the news, Sierra's expression transformed. The look of mild annoyance that he always seemed to elicit in her was replaced by something half-angry, half-grim.

"How the hell do the presence of accelerants and retardants at all three fires constitute a lack of evidence?"

This reaction was why Sierra was the right person for the job.

"Barnett knows just as well as everyone else I made the right call."

"Then what is he doing?" she half-shouted with utter consternation.

He stopped walking and looked at her squarely.

"Same thing a lot of these guys do. Covering his own ass."

Forrest broke down what he'd figured out—an extension of what Barnett had all but admitted privately.

"He doesn't think he can catch the guy. He's got nothing to go on to make an arrest. But if he admits the fires are linked, and that it's arson, he's on the hook. He'll be in a world of hurt if there's a bigger fire that sounds like it's in relation to a case he couldn't solve."

Sierra's responding voice was terse. "How will they go on the books, then?"

This was the part that impacted her. "They'll all go in as Level 5 Incidents. In *your* territory."

He gave it a minute to sink in. By not making it his own problem, Barnett had just made it hers.

"This is bullshit."

The vision of her so lovely in her dress was in discord with the fact that she was spitting mad. She smelled sweeter than honeysuckle, but softer somehow—the crispness of hyacinth and the warmth of vanilla all at once.

"Hell yeah, it's bull," Forrest said bluntly. "That's why I wanted to talk to you. If Barnett won't do shit, we've got to take matters into our own hands."

"We?" She put her hands on her hips and narrowed her eyes, leaning in as if she hadn't heard correctly.

"That's right." Forrest stood a bit straighter. "I think you and I ought to work our own investigation. As a team."

Sierra crossed her arms. She was getting that sexy, mad-hot look that only seemed to come out when she was specifically mad at him. It was different from how she looked when she'd only been mad at Barnett a moment before.

"And why would I agree to something like that? Like you said, Barnett made his decision. I can't go over his head. Case closed."

Forrest couldn't help his answering smile.

"Unlike most of the other yahoos assigned to this case, you actually care about catching the culprit, and you have real skin in the game."

She narrowed her eyes and leaned forward, getting into his face a little. Damn, if it wasn't hot. For the first time since cooking up his scheme, Forrest began to think about what it would really be to partner with her. Investigating would lead to theorizing. Theorizing would lead to validating or invalidating working ideas, which, with Sierra would definitely lead to arguing. Arguing would lead to extreme attraction and tight pants and a whole lot of other things that sounded like perks and problems all at once.

"If I care so much about my skin, why would I risk anything that seems like insubordination, let alone with someone who could blow the whistle on both of us if he got caught?"

Forrest raised an eyebrow. "Who says I'd be the one to get caught?"

She shook her head in a pitying way. "You haven't thought this through."

He crossed his arms and leaned back on his heels, flashing his best self-congratulatory smile. "See? That's where you've got things wrong. I've thought it *all* the way through and it's bulletproof. My plan is resplendent in its sheer perfection."

"Right ..." she said slowly. "Well, I can see you're really excited. And thanks for thinking of me, but you're gonna have to find another partner in crime."

"I prefer the term *partner in justice*."

The fervor of her continued refusals gave him pause.

"Well, partner in *whatever-you-want-to-call-it*, this isn't really my kind of thing."

He leaned closer, his voice quiet and low as he stared into her eyes. "You may have everyone else tricked into thinking you're some squeaky-clean, golden-girl rule-follower, but I've got your number, Ranger Betts."

She leaned in even closer. "And I've got *your* number, Marshal Winters. You're just a food-stealing hotshot who likes to win."

Then, she held out her hand, looking up at him expectantly, and said in a way that told him the conversation was over, "I'll take my cupcake now."

Chapter Nine

SIERRA

"You ought to bring your friends more often."

Rick didn't spare Sierra a glance as he peered down at the parking lot of Sugarlands Ranger Station from the second-floor window of the dispatch office. He'd flipped up the microphone on his headset and swiveled his chair around to get a better view. Sierra had rolled in a second chair next to him. The office was all naked wood and beams, just like every other room in every other ranger station in the park. This office had desks for three dispatchers, but Sierra had never seen more than two on shift at once. The other one was on break.

At the moment, said parking lot was filling with various trucks and cars belonging to the members of the fire investigation team. The meeting to officially share what she'd heard from Forrest the night before would start in ten minutes. Sierra had already poured out her sob story to Rick, who had pledged his help. Four of the other six members had parked but none had entered the building. They stood in two groups, laughing and talking in the lot.

"Trust me. They're not my friends."

Sierra's voice was grim. She needed to get that in check before the meeting began. She also needed to wipe her bitch face off and turn her game face on. Easier said than done, considering her run-in with Forrest had caused her to lose half a night's sleep and taken every ounce of joy out of eating her cupcake. When she'd finally given up on a good night's rest, she'd shuffled to the kitchen and started in on a batch of Rick's favorites: no-bake peanut-butter balls.

"You said Buck was in your corner …" Rick did look over at her then, his caramel eyes just as saucy as his voice. Rick stuck a perfect ten every time for his pointed looks. He had a way of pinning you with eyes that knew and saw all and commanded you to admit it.

"For all the wrong reasons, unfortunately." Sierra pulled the Tupperware from Rick's hand and helped herself to a peanut-butter ball. "The way things are going, he might win by default. If I don't get this promotion, I'm stuck living in the park for at least another year. Which means I'll probably never have sex again."

She didn't need to remind Rick again of how online dating had gone over like a lead balloon, or how her whole social life hinged on living closer to civilization. She could never start flirtations with cute, bookish men she spied at the library or thoughtful ones she found at cafes without access to casual, everyday routines that happened when you lived in an actual town. As it stood, she only showed up in Green Valley for short periods on days when she had a specific task or plan. Sometimes the drive wasn't even worth the trip.

"Please, girl. Don't nobody 'round here feel sorry for you. You turn on your porch light and you'd have company lined up out your door. And you're mighty particular for someone who's always complaining you need a man."

Sierra threw him a look of her own, because was he serious?

"I don't *need a man*," she corrected. "What I would like is some company. And I prefer my gentlemen callers to be a certain maturity level and age."

Back at Shasta, Sierra had enjoyed the company of wildlife researcher Chris Chisholm just fine. They'd been friends with benefits —nothing else. Back then, she'd been content with no strings and a snug embrace to keep her warm on cold winter nights. Now, she wanted more.

"And maybe *some people* ought to be a little pickier," she went on, rising from her chair and handing him back the container. It was almost time for the meeting.

Rick's radio chose that very moment to crackle to life. She could see the change in his demeanor the moment he heard the call. In any calm moment, Rick was a master shit-talker. On the radio, when it was his job to protect park inhabitants, he was all safety and business.

"Call me later," he mouthed.

Sierra nodded and whispered, "Remember what I said. I can't compete with what they've got. If I'm gonna find this guy, I need your ear to the ground."

* * *

Sierra nodded her hellos as she made her way into the conference room, keeping up her pleasantries as she shuffled in and shuffled past, scanning her eyes over the screen at the front of the room. Olivia hadn't been able to accompany them to the crime scene, but she could be present for this meeting. It was always possible that she had a conflict or a doctor appointment. Barring that, she would want to be on the call.

Forrest had been right about one thing: Barnett was passing the buck—making his problem somebody else's problem. Olivia calling him out on his bullshit was Sierra's best hope. By the time they were all seated and it was clear that Frank was about to begin, Sierra pulled out her phone. She wanted to see whether Olivia had accepted the meeting invitation. At the very instant Sierra discovered that Olivia's name had never even been included on the invite, Frank's voice broke through her thoughts.

"First things first. I want to commend Fire Marshal Winters and Firefighter Rogers for the high caliber of their investigative work, for their team's quick response and dedication to the case. And I want to say personally that I don't doubt their findings. I do believe someone set these fires deliberately and had a plan for extinguishing them. I do believe the fires are suspicious. And I hope that whoever set them is caught."

Sierra's gaze shifted to Forrest, who smiled graciously—convincingly—through his acceptance of the praise. It was something that had never come easily to Sierra: hiding her displeasure, especially if the bitterness of injustice was at play.

"The problem comes with doing the catching," Barnett continued. "And, the fact of the matter is, no matter how much we want to catch him, we don't even have a profile on this guy."

Barnett paused once again as heads nodded all around—all except for Sierra's, Buck's, and Forrest's. Buck looked as pissed off as Sierra felt.

"I can't put men out there unless I can tell 'em what they're looking for and where to look. I'm short-staffed as it is. But this is a serious issue. And the last thing we ought to do is drop the ball.

"That's why I've decided to assign a special investigator to take on that challenge." He made eye contact with the people around the room. "Rangers are the boots on the ground and the eyes and ears around the park. I'm pleased to assign Ranger Dennis Peck as the leader of an ongoing grassroots effort to catch the culprit."

Sierra felt as if the air had been sucked out of her lungs, though she was too busy processing the scene in front of her to remember to breathe. Her gaze swung to Dennis, who was busy nodding acknowledgment of his new role. He held a white coffee cup that said *Rise and Grind* and his face was just as smug as ever.

* * *

The hours that it had taken Sierra to fall into a restless sleep were no match for the rude, rhythmic percussion of she-didn't-know-what that woke her up. It infiltrated her consciousness, drilling its insistent way into her exhausted mind. Worse yet, the sound persisted. Some corner of her brain remembered garbage trucks making their noisy rounds up and down her old street in the early morning and the occasional construction project that produced odd spurts of noise. Then another part of her brain—the part that was waking up and gaining steam— remembered. Man-made ruckus wasn't a thing when you lived alone in the woods.

Holy shit.

Sierra pried one eye open but shot straight up in bed as if her body knew instantaneously that it had to come all the way awake, but her eyes were still deciding. It was barely daybreak, but just enough sun had begun to make its way through and chase away the remainder of the night.

On instinct, Sierra crawled silently from bed, slipped on a short, striped robe and a pair of galoshes, and grabbed the walkie that always sat next to her bed. On her way out of her bedroom, she grabbed the shotgun by the door. The rhythmic drumming kept up from outside, though the cadence was slow. Whatever animal was out there, it had to be big and lumbering. Only, none of the bigger animals she could think of liked to come around at dawn.

"Everest," she whisper-called as she made her way from the bedroom to the front. Her dog stood curious but silent, pacing by the door. Whatever this beast outside was, it had gotten her dog's attention, but not enough to worry her. Everest knew enough about the strange sounds and disturbances of the forest that she didn't bark Sierra awake at just any odd turn.

Everest trotted up to Sierra, circling her once and heading back to the entrance, as if to herd her closer to the door. But Sierra diverted toward the window, where, from inside the darkened house, she could take a glimpse with minimal detection.

Nine times out of ten, even if an animal was causing property damage, the play was to leave it alone. Straining her eyes to see by the early light, she looked out the window and to the right, toward the heavy-lidded trash cans fifty feet away. At the same time as her eyes saw nothing by the trash cans, her brain put together that the sound wasn't coming from the right—it was coming from the left. What she saw next nearly gave her a heart attack.

A hulk of an axe-wielding man stood by her wood pile, wound back in a wide motion, then drove the axe down with practiced precision. Her astonished eyes followed the motion as she watched the log split perfectly in two. Her jaw slacked as the muscular figure leaned to the side and picked up another log, set it upon her block and wound back again, jacked arms driving the axe down heavily once more.

"Damn you, Forrest Winters," Sierra whispered out loud, but made no move toward the door. In the privacy of her own living room, she would let herself look—would let herself surrender to the sublime hypnosis of watching that man chop wood. No longer perplexed by the origin of the sound, she leaned in to appreciate the beauty of the simple task, and relished every tiny illumination of the rising sun.

He wasn't in uniform, which likely meant he wasn't on duty today. He wore simple brown leather work boots, jeans, and a blue plaid shirt. Said shirt was loose enough to allow for the twist of his midsection as he moved his body but snug enough to accentuate his form. The sleeves of his shirt were rolled up to his elbows, and on his hands he wore gloves that cut off just above his wrist. Those strong forearms she had tried desperately not to notice were corded and flexed and strong. Her nipples puckered like they would have if she had been hit with a cool breeze at the very same time a wave of heat flushed over her.

And then it happened—the same thing that happened every time she was confronted with Forrest—the one thing she didn't want it to. His gaze flipped up to her in the middle of her flush—not a confused gaze that searched out something based on some sixth sense that he was being watched. A knowing gaze that fixed right upon her.

That single, infuriating motion was all it took for Sierra to remember herself. To remember how Forrest incensed her. To remember that he had shown up at her cabin, uninvited, at the crack of flipping dawn. Uncaring that the only things covering her were a sleep shirt and a short robe, she put down the walkie and threw open the door, gun still over her shoulder as she stalked out into the morning. She had half a mind to rack the slide, just to see him squirm.

"You're trespassing," she informed him. "And you woke me out of a dead sleep. What in the hell are you doing up here, Forrest?"

"Mornin' to you, too, Sierra." Forrest didn't stop his motions—he just continued in perfect rhythm, which only made every single little thing about him more annoying.

"Can you stop chopping my wood already? I asked you a question."

He gave a final swing of the axe that came down so hard, the log he split flew out wide in opposite directions, and the axe stayed lodged and upright on the chopping block.

"I figured you'd be up early. Isn't morning when you make your bites? They taste like you make 'em fresh."

He pulled his gloves off as he spoke, sticking them in his back pocket and brushing off his hands. Unintimidated by her shotgun, he crossed the distance that would bring him to her door. Mount Everest, guard dog extraordinaire, hurried to Forrest's side and he bent to one knee, indulging her with pats and rubs.

"I think we got off on the wrong foot," he continued after rising back to his full height. "I know it's been some time, but the fact that you don't like me much is clear. Which is a real shame, because you and me could be good together."

"What did you just say to me?"

"Working together," he clarified, putting his hands up in the universal sign of peace as he continued to walk toward her. "I think you and me could be good working together, for all the reasons I told you before and for all the new reasons given how things are shaping up. You and me could be a great team."

"You've got your team." It took effort for Sierra to keep the venom out of her voice. "You and Dennis won't need any help from me."

All afternoon, Sierra hadn't known where to direct her anger. Should it have been toward Forrest for giving her some big speech about wanting her to be his partner in justice, then dropping her like a hot potato to get what he wanted from Dennis Peck? Or was she mad at herself for passing up an alliance with the one person who had the clout to place her front and center to the investigation, just as he'd done for Dennis?

"Peck? Why would I be working with him?"

"You said you needed a ranger to help with the investigation, didn't you? That a ranger would be the ideal person—eyes on the trail, boots on the ground."

"I didn't say all that. Well, I said some of it. But I didn't mean I wanted Dennis. I meant I wanted you."

Without the sun to lighten them, his gray eyes were as dark as nickels, shining with something she'd never seen. He'd drawn close and Everest sniffed and licked at his hand. Sierra couldn't bring herself to chide her dog for her manners. She was too busy trying to work all of this out in her mind.

"Me?" She still didn't understand.

"Yes, you. Why the hell would I want Dennis on my team? He

doesn't give a rat's ass about the fires. All he wants is somebody to do all the work so he can get all the glory. Why would I want to work with a person like him?"

Because you're exactly alike, Sierra thought but didn't say out loud. It all made perfect sense in her head. Everything she disliked about Dennis and suspected that Dennis disliked about her applied to Forrest. Forrest took people out on his boat, and went to poker night and came from a family that had lived in this valley for years. In Sierra's mind, that practically made them twins.

"Well, if you didn't want to work with him, why would you tell Barnett that he ought to head up the investigation?"

"That wasn't me. That was Grissom, all the way."

Could he be telling the truth? Sierra disassembled and reassembled puzzle pieces in her mind. If she was wrong about that, she was wrong about every unfavorable accusation she'd mentally hurled at him since the day before.

"Look, Sierra ... I came to you because you're smart. You know your job and you know your territory and if anyone has what it takes to catch this guy, it's you. And—excuse me for being so forward about it—but you could use a win, and a friend. Dennis knows how good you are. Give him a chance and that boy'll throw you under the bus in a second."

Forrest's words were true. And they hurt. And it bothered her he knew that much—that she was so transparent to a man she'd placed at arm's length. And she didn't know how to flip a switch in her mind to suddenly befriend the man she loved to hate. Did this mean she had to start letting him eat her bites?

"You broke my bear," she complained weakly, her last holdout to what was clearly a promising idea. She would acquiesce in a minute, but she couldn't have him thinking he could just waltz in there and tell her what to do.

He sighed and pinned her with his dark gray eyes. "I don't know how many ways to apologize for that. And I know you don't approve of the way I eat your bites. But I wouldn't eat 'em if they weren't so good. And if there were some way to repay you, I'd repay you, only you don't seem to appreciate it when I do things I think you'll like."

"Things you think I'll like?" she repeated.

He jutted his chin back toward the block. "You know … chopping your wood. Your pile was looking a little low."

The smug smile had dropped from his face and the look about him was almost kind.

"Look, Sierra. It's up to you, whether you ever let me on your good side. But I can at least make it equal. You know, so you don't dislike working with me so much."

Sierra sighed, feeling like an asshole.

"So is that it, then? I bake you bacon bites and you chop my wood? We solve this thing together and call it a day?"

"There is one more thing …" He trailed off.

Of course there is.

"And just what would that be?"

"I want us to keep our partnership a secret."

PART II

Chapter Ten

FORREST

"What? No gun this time?"

Forrest asked it in lieu of a proper greeting after Sierra swung open her cabin door. She was fresh-faced and fresh-smelling and—unfortunately—fully clothed. He'd had a good chuckle about the spitting-mad, shotgun-toting, bathrobe-and-galoshes-wearing version of her on his way down the mountain the previous morning. The curve of her smooth, chiseled calves stretching up from her boot all the way to the hem of her night shirt had followed him all day.

"No need." She leaned against the doorjamb, crossed her arms and raised an eyebrow. "This time, I knew it was just a deranged fire marshal at my wood pile. Not some hardened serial killer."

She still hadn't invited him in. He really didn't mind. It gave him a reason to stand there and look. On the job, she never showed nearly as much skin. The ranger uniform was designed to protect—long pants and long sleeves kept off bugs and warded off scratches from branches on the trail. Forrest liked her immensely in khaki shorts and a simple, gray V-neck that exposed her smooth, tawny arms.

"I brought doughnuts." He remembered himself long enough to

hold up the pink pastry box that dangled from his finger. Apple cider doughnut from Daisy's Nut House were a simple enough offering. He wanted to start this day off better than the day before.

"I made breakfast." She confirmed what his nose had told him and what he had only dared to hope might be for him. "I hope you like bacon bites." She smirked as she waved him in.

Forrest was more than a little curious to get a glimpse of where she lived. He'd been disappointed when she hadn't asked him in the day before. Hers was one of the nicer ones—one of only a half-dozen historical cabins that hadn't been opened as an attraction or closed up altogether, but turned into an official home.

"Nice place." His eyes washed over the room with appreciation, taking in the way she'd designed the open space. A well-loved sofa in a deep teal blue sat atop a patterned area rug. The lines of chartreuse in the zigzag design alternated with gray and white and added a burst of color to the room. The sofa and rug faced a fireplace and took up the leftmost third of the space. An open kitchen formed a sideways "L," with countertops, a range, and other appliances lining the right side and back wall.

"Let's sit." She motioned to the area farthest to the right. Her table sat beneath a window that faced the back part of her wraparound patio and overlooked the creek. It could serve as a dining table just as well as it would a desk. With a file of papers sitting on one half and a place setting sitting on the other, it was some of both.

Forrest sat and Sierra puttered around between the table and the kitchen, not waiting for him to ask whether he wanted it before pouring coffee in his ceramic mug—a 49ers mug—and bringing over a carton of organic half-and-half.

"So tell me about people who set fires." Sierra set a plate of bacon bites between them and settled into the seat across. The first part of their protocol was meeting off-hours. They couldn't count on having enough privacy if they were to meet at Greenbrier. Plus, Forrest had less of a reason to be there nowadays, with Dennis in charge of the investigation.

"You've got four kinds of arsonists—four very different criminal profiles. The first is motivated by financial gain. Most convicted arsonists burned down buildings, usually to commit insurance fraud."

"Probably not our guy, then." Sierra wrote something in her notebook.

"Not unless you can think of someone who stands to profit from burning protected land."

"What's the second kind of arson?" Sierra worried the end of her pen lightly with her teeth.

"Covering up a criminal act. It's an extension of evidence tampering. The idea is to obscure what happened or to make it more difficult to prosecute a crime. About half of those kinds of fires involve a body. Our forensics found no human or animal remains, so that part doesn't fit. But it's common to find accelerant where it doesn't belong."

"Kind of like our fires."

"Kind of like our fires." Forrest nodded. "These kinds of arsonists don't set fires willy-nilly. They need to destroy something specific and they always go for a controlled burn. That aligns with the three fires we've seen."

"So we're stuck on motive," she murmured.

"Either that," Forrest thought aloud. "Or we're stuck on opportunity. Maybe the crimes happened someplace else and someone is using this land to destroy evidence because they have no other place to dispose of what they did."

Sierra still looked troubled. "I'm stuck on the perfect circle. How much evidence could you hike in on foot? A backpack's worth? Maybe two? That theory doesn't explain why it's such a wide radius."

"I'll agree with you there," Forrest concurred. "My hunch is the crime is being committed in the park. The only question is … what?"

All manner of possibility had crossed Forrest's mind: cock fighting and burying bodies and all the other things people went far out of the way to do. Only, none of those made sense.

"What's the third kind of arson?" Sierra finally asked.

"Revenge. Crimes of passion. Think betrayed spouses, spurned lovers, sibling rivalry … That kind of arson is usually about property damage. Its motive is to hurt an actual person by asserting control over something they love or own."

"So we're thinking it's not financial gain and we're thinking it's not revenge because all of this is federal property. And we're thinking it could be to cover up a crime."

"Either that or we're dealing with the fourth type of arson. Pyromania."

He liked the way her hair fell down in front of her face—and the way she habitually tucked it back behind her ear—as she continued to jot down notes.

"Say more."

Forrest took a sip of his coffee. "Pyromania is an impulsive behavior. Pyros can be all ages, but most studies of pyromania have been done on kids. Some start as young as five or six."

Sierra frowned more deeply than she had frowned at anything yet. "What about means and opportunity? How does a six-year-old get hold of lighter fluid and fire retardant?"

"Fire retardant, I agree with you. Lighter fluid, you'd be surprised."

"But how would a kid even get into the park?"

"A young kid wouldn't but a teenager could. It would have to be a teenager, too, to navigate off the trails. Whoever did this has some level of training when it comes to the backwoods."

Sierra looked even more distressed. She'd taken methodical notes throughout the conversation, but—rather suddenly—she stopped writing.

"Doesn't coming deep into the woods to set a fire seem, I don't know … just a little too ambitious for your average teenager?"

"Your typical teenager, yes," Forrest agreed. "But don't think of pyros as typical teenagers. Your average pyro lives in a troubled home. He doesn't have a positive father figure, may be a self-isolator or a social outcast, may have seen fire used inappropriately by other people and may be industrious and intelligent enough to find ways to habitually set fires."

"All right …" Sierra trailed off. "Tell me about the motive. Why do pyros set fires?"

"Theories range from control fantasies to pyrophilia. Kids in bad situations may want something they can control. Problems at home can lead to a desire for destruction."

"What's the difference between pyromania and pyrophilia?" She was writing again.

"Pyrophilia is an excitement or arousal that comes from setting them and watching them burn."

"I guess they teach you a whole lot in fire school." The way she said it made him chuckle.

"College, too." He liked that she looked impressed. "I majored in psych."

"Not what I would have guessed …" But the signs of interest that washed over her face for a moment disappeared just as quickly. She got back down to business. "Let's make a list. What are we looking for, both inside and outside of the park?"

"It's still too early for a decent profile." This point was exactly where Frank had known the case would get stuck. "I'll go through some back channels, talk to my buddy, Grizz, down in Green Valley."

"We should also follow the supply chain," Sierra chimed in. "Find out who's been buying fire retardant and what brands. Not all fire retardants have the same ingredients. We also ought to run plates on cars that entered the park on the incident dates."

"That last one's a long shot. There aren't cameras at every gate. Avoiding the camera would be their best shot at never getting caught."

Sierra threw down her pen and leaned back in her seat. "Still, we ought to check. If there's one thing my dad taught me, it's that a hell of a lot of criminals are dumb."

Chapter Eleven

SIERRA

Sierra was so relieved for a day of respite from the punishing summer heat that she didn't mind the afternoon shower, which —when you took the tree canopy into account—came down more like a trickle. The air was warmer than usual and the rain fell on tree branches and soil, giving the thick of the forest a tropical sort of feel.

It made for slippery rocks and careful footing down slopes and the precaution of walking sticks, all three of which added up to slower going. But with a summer as dry as this one and the fire risk what it was, Sierra was thankful for every precious drop.

This time, she'd driven her truck to the closest point in the road and walked into Jake's camp from the other side. She also wanted to time the alternate route. With the fire investigation, the degree of contingency planning she had to think through with Jake in mind was frightening. Letting him stay in the park was one thing when she'd thought of him as just an off-trail camper. But this was turning out to be different.

Sierra wasn't surprised to find his camp closed up—hammock

empty, tent door closed and tarp over his things. It was overcast, but as she approached, she saw no glow coming from his tent.

"Jake?" She did as well as one could, knocking on the door of something soft. It made a little tapping sound and the section of tent move with the weight of her hand.

Immediate zipping from inside the tent told her he was home. Only, this wasn't home. This was an unauthorized campsite in Great Smoky Mountains National Park. And for the first time since she'd discovered him, she really did want him out.

"Oh, hey …" He unzipped the door all the way, crouching only a little as he did. The tent roof rose pretty high. "It's raining. You want to come in?"

"Thanks." Sierra wiped her boots on a makeshift doormat he had outside the tent—in this case, a thick towel.

"Ho-Ho?" he offered. Sierra hadn't eaten one of the convenience store delicacies in a long time. It said something about where he was getting his food. She was slow to fully arrive inside, having left her pack outside and underneath the rain flap near the door before grabbing her standard peace offering—a container of bites. Each one accepted the other's offer.

A good ranger knew how to hold up a conversation that ascertained plenty about a camper's status, all while making it sound casual. As usual, she was assessing—judging his physical and mental state. Despite living in the woods, he seemed clean—maybe not shower-clean, but hygienic. Junk food diet aside, he seemed healthy and well.

"How's your Plan B coming?" She devoured the last of her twin chocolate cakes at the tail end of a debate about which gas station snack was best.

"It's coming. I've got a buddy I can stay with, but he can't take me in just yet."

"Do you have another friend who could take you in until you get into that situation? The fire risks are changing and I really need to get you out of this park."

His eyes widened in a way that showed her she had his attention.

"I've been checking the sign every morning, just like you said. I've been on the walkie, too. Figured I'd hear if there was something going on."

"You might ..." It wasn't a half-bad idea. "Though, there are frequencies that only law enforcement uses. Most of what you'll hear, you'd be hearing from other visitors in the park."

He blinked. "Huh."

"That's one thing that worries me about you being out here," she dug in. "The fire risk is only getting worse and there are times I won't be able to get to you."

"But the fire risk should be lower for the next several days, right? I mean, it's raining ...'"

"True, but it's not an end-all solution. The longer I let you stay here, the more irresponsible it is of me, and the less fair it is to you."

What Sierra didn't say—what she couldn't say—was how much she felt for his situation. Digging around for information had left her with the sense that things with the Wraiths were much worse than she'd thought.

According to Rick, the motorcycle club was in a state of disarray. A few key players had wound up dead or sent to prison. Lately, they'd been linked to more violent crimes. Their numbers were dwindling and they were actively recruiting members.

"You don't have to keep coming out here. I'm fine taking care of myself."

Only, something in Jake's voice told her he wasn't.

* * *

Eager Beaver's Hardware and Lumber took up half a block and faced Main Street proudly. Its windows were wide and full of elaborate, themed displays. On the left side of the double-front doors was a Labor Day motif. A banner that read, *Relax. You deserve it.* was hung up from end to end. A casually dressed dummy sitting in a patio chair wore a smile on his face and appeared to gaze down at a glass with an umbrella drink.

The store's mascot—predictably—was a beaver. Half a dozen rather realistic likenesses had been integrated into the display. One hung comically from the back of the patio chair. One stood on a pedestal with a large palm leaf, as if fanning cool air upon the dummy. Another carried the tray that held the dummy's drink.

Sierra had practically lived at Eager Beaver's when she'd first arrived in Green Valley after the rude discovery that her cabin was mostly bare. Apart from the kitchen table and her log-style bedroom set, the space had been devoid of furniture or decoration. That was how Sierra had come to know old Mr. Stokes.

She had bought everything from a paper towel holder to privacy shades, to decent light fixtures for the bathroom, to a trash can for under the kitchen sink. Any item on her wish list that he hadn't carried in the store, he'd special ordered. The man had to be in his seventies, but—no matter the time of day or day of the week—it was always him who was minding the store.

"Welcome to Eager Beaver's, where the prices are *dam* good!" he hollered from the back. His back was to her and he seemed engrossed in something. She smiled at the familiarity of his standard greeting. Stokes did like a good pun. He brought them into nearly every conversation and liked to brag about how he'd thought of the tagline himself.

"Afternoon, Mr. Stokes," she hollered back, making her way to the rear counter, where the register was.

He finally looked up. "Haven't seen you in a while." He wasn't a full-on curmudgeon, but half of one, a right she supposed he'd earned from managing to keep himself alive for so long.

She smiled warmly. "What can I say? You were too good at helping me get my place in shape."

"How'd that wood splitter work out?" He was engaging in a gruff grandpa kind of way.

At the mention of the wood splitter, Sierra's thoughts turned to Forrest and how he'd looked both times he'd stood in front of her house with his axe, her wood splitter discarded on the ground as he chopped without an assist.

"You know? It worked out all right."

"Anything I can help you find? You've been down these aisles so many times, I don't know what guidance you'd need from me."

"Good memory," she praised.

This might just work out as she hoped. His sharp recall had shown itself before. Even months after she'd bought this or that, he remembered her home projects with precision. If there was something to be known about fire retardant that had been purchased at his store, Mr. Stokes would remember who had bought it and maybe even why.

Sierra gave him a little salute and made her way down one aisle after another. Fire retardant could as easily be in the home safety section as mixed with the industrial supplies. It took her a good few minutes, but the two-gallon jug of something called "Fire Away" was a solid find. She picked up the heavy bottle and read the front label, cross-referencing what she saw with research she'd done before she arrived.

From what she could tell, it was something you sprayed on the outside of a building exterior. It created some sort of barrier that made it so your house wouldn't burn. A neat row of Fire Away bottles sat on the shelf closest to the floor. The space next to them was conspicuously empty. Sierra looked more closely. A stock-out of any fire protection product would be a clue.

She half-expected it to be the same product—maybe in a different size. But the label stuck to the shelf below announced a different product: "Fire Stopper."

When she made her way back to Mr. Stokes and hefted the bottle onto the counter, it landed with a thud.

"I'm looking for some fire protection for my cabin," she lied. "Is this the stuff you just throw on your roof?"

"It is," Stokes answered with a bit of humor. "You worried about that cabin of yours catching fire?"

"Maybe," she returned with a coyness that met his humor. "The warning level in the park keeps going up."

"I'd sooner sell you a good pole saw for fifty dollars than see you waste your money on that. There wouldn't be so much wildfire damage if people just cut back their damned kindling."

Sierra had to agree. She also had to agree that the price for two gallons of Fire Away—seventy-five dollars—seemed hefty.

"You might be right about that," she conceded. "I don't know if I'd wet down my house, but I'm thinking about wetting down the perimeter. Do you think I should use Fire Away or the other one—I think it's called Fire Stopper—that's stocked out?"

"That's the difference between the two of them." Mr. Stokes leaned a hand on the counter and began to explain. "Fire *Away* is meant for roofs and textiles and things. Fire *Stopper* is meant for that there you just mentioned. Only, right now, I'm stocked out."

Sierra's heart rate sped. She was getting closer. "Must be a popular product."

"Usually, it's not," he corrected. "I see a surge in demand every time someone comes out with one of those doomsday apocalypse shows. Those preppers buy all kinds of crazy things—night-vision goggles and bunker-building supplies. I wouldn't have pegged you for one of those types. I guess you got time for reality TV."

Sierra chuckled. "So you're telling me there's a type?"

"They get younger every year. The ones who bought me out of that Fire Stopper are just kids."

"Anyone from Green Valley?" Sierra wanted to know. "You ought to tell them to invite me to their prepper secret meeting."

Sierra knew from her father how to run a down-low interrogation. Conducted properly, one didn't need to feel like it at all.

"To each his own." His half-pitying look confirmed his view that her interest in Fire Stopper was a waste. "And the boys who bought it all up aren't from here. 'Course that's no surprise. I've got three times the selection they've got at the place up in Cedar Gap. Lots of folks I sell to aren't from 'round here."

Sierra smiled at his pride. "Then I guess I'll take the Fire Away now and the Fire Stopper when your next shipment comes in. When do you think that might be?"

"Friday. I'll be sure to set you one aside."

Sierra took out her credit card and slid it across the counter.

"Thanks, Mr. Stokes. And if those prepper boys come back in here again, be sure to catch their names."

Chapter Twelve

FORREST

The Green Valley Fire Department was located on its own little back street off of Walnut, on the edge of downtown behind the field. The brick building was simple but stately, with architecture reminiscent of the simple stations built in the sixties and seventies.

From the street, the building was a hulking rectangle, wider than it was tall. Above the second-floor windows and on top of the doors, molded concrete added flourishes that complemented the brick.

The garages that held the truck bays aligned left and took up most of the space. A gleaming ladder truck could be seen through the first door; the second revealed a smaller engine; and a third bay had a fire ambulance parked inside. A patch of lawn with three flags— Tennessee Fire, State of Tennessee, and the United States of America —separated the oversized driveway from a pedestrian walkway. Impatiens in reds and pinks and whites had been planted in rows on either side of the path leading up to the lobby door.

"Sonofabitch," Grizz Grady said by way of greeting as Forrest walked into the station, foregoing the lobby entrance to come right in through the middle garage. Following Grizz's voice, Forrest snapped his gaze to the open part of the upper floor, where Grizz peered down from the edge of the lounge.

"I was hoping I'd find you here." Forrest walked toward the familiar steel stairs and climbed up to reach his friend. They'd never worked for the same agency, but they'd been on relief crews together. Grizz was a solid firefighter—well-trained and a real team player who helped the younger guys on their squads. Like Forrest, he'd grown up in Green Valley, but they'd just missed each other in school.

"Come to cry about that two-fifty you lost?"

Grizz didn't talk a lot of smack in general, but he had some pride when it came to his poker. He was known in town as a bit of a shark.

"I never gamble with more than I can afford to lose," Forrest came back with an easy smile.

The poker game was an institution. There were always full-timers and volunteers from the surrounding stations, but it was held at the Green Valley firehouse. The other regulars were also in law enforcement—Clint Grissom and Jeffrey James and a few more who liked to gamble. Forrest made it a point to show up every few weeks, to keep current on all that was happening in town.

When Forrest finally reached the platform, he extended his hand and they did the bro-shake thing. He caught a glimpse of Todd's tribute plaque from of the corner of his eye. It happened sooner or later, every time he was in the building. His best friend had worked for Green Valley Fire. Just last week, Forrest had been down in Knoxville, looking in on his widow, Violet. It seemed like she was still having a hard time.

"Trouble in the park." Forrest distracted himself by getting down to business. "Some suspicious Class Bs. Consumer-grade accelerants."

"You got any leads?" Grizz walked both of them into the lounge space. Green Valley Fire had things pretty tricked out: a sixty-two-inch flatscreen for watching sports and two stocked fridges, one with the soft stuff for duty hours and another with the hard stuff for after.

Forrest didn't know who had the hookup, but they always had good food to eat on the table commonly known as "the buffet." Scanning the selection, he noted that today was tacos. The logo on the accompanying napkins told him they were from Los Panchos, the best place in town. He didn't know how they did it, but Los Panchos somehow squeezed the shell shut after the taco was filled so that when you ate it, nothing came careening out.

"That's why I came to see you." Forrest refocused, remembering his task. "Parks PD more or less closed the investigation. Said they didn't have the men to put on the case. You know how the cops are. They always want a suspect. Don't know how to investigate shit without a witness to tell 'em who did it and do half their job."

Grizz nodded in agreement. It wasn't uncommon for there to be friction between police and fire. Firefighters were trained to think in terms of prevention. Cops were more reactive than anything. The way you fought fire in a community was a lot different from the way you fought crime.

"Word has it, there were three," Grizz reported.

Forrest wasn't surprised he'd heard. Some of the guys in law enforcement were just as bad as his gossiping cousin, Scotia. People finding out about fires this strange was only a matter of time.

"That's right." Forrest leveled with him. "And there's gonna be a fourth if someone doesn't take it seriously. They've got some young buck on it—a ranger named Peck who doesn't know that territory well. I'm doing a little sniffing around. Making sure we're turning over every stone."

"Yeah, I know Peck. He's come to the game with Grissom a few times. Seems like a bit of a lap dog. Real ambitious."

"That's one way to put it." Forrest gave Grizz a look. "When was the last time you saw him?"

"Ran into him fishing on Saturday up at the lake."

"He ask you about the case at all?"

Grizz shook his head. "Not a word."

It confirmed what Forrest suspected: Peck wasn't too invested in the case. Asking whether there was anyone in town who liked to set fires was Investigation 101.

"So I'll ask the question he should've," Forrest said. "Do y'all know of anyone who sets fires who might've taken their little habit to the park?"

Grizz took a minute to think. They had stopped behind the long, leather sofa where Forrest had sat countless times to catch games.

"Some kids started a dumpster fire last month when they were running from the cops and tried to burn up a bag of weed."

Forrest chuckled. "It must've been a big bag."

Grizz crossed his arms. "You know? It was. The officer saw 'em with about half a pound. Turns out they were college kids from over the border."

"Sounds like the cops on the Carolina side are getting kind of loose."

"Oh, they've always been loose," Grizz rejoined. "But it's getting worse. They've had to double up bouncers at the Pony for all the underage ones who want to get in."

"NCU has always been a whole lot of party and not a whole lot of school. I just wish they'd keep shit in their own backyard."

"Sorry I can't be of more help," Grizz apologized. "But I really can't think of any fires we've ruled as suspicious. Most of our calls nowadays are EMT. Either that, or purely accidental."

"No need to apologize." Forrest held out his hand to shake again. "No known arsonists in town is probably a good thing."

"You leaving already? Stay a while. Have a taco. Drink a beer. You look like you're off duty."

Forrest eyed the taco table again, thinking of the other stops he had to make only briefly before reasoning that a guy had to eat.

"Thanks. Don't mind if I do."

* * *

Half an hour, three tacos and one visit to Donner Bakery later, Forrest strode into the sheriff's office, hoping he'd timed it correctly to miss Flo McClure. Unmarried, in her fifties, and a bit of a hard woman, the town had assumed the sheriff's receptionist would die a spinster. Then, she'd gotten drunk one night at a family dinner and come out of the closet. This development at least partially explained why Flo had always been impervious to Forrest's charm.

Loretta Boggs, on the other hand, was far from impervious to Forrest. She covered Flo for an hour at lunch each day. Unlike Flo, who was all front desk, Loretta was usually behind the curtain. She processed crime scenes, filed evidence, and managed records. In Forrest's experience, having as many allies as possible across agencies was always worth the trouble. Forrest could make sure it was Loretta at the front desk if he timed it just right.

Her story was a tragic one, though you wouldn't know it to look at her. She'd been a widow for going on four years. She'd been called out to process a crime scene—to photograph a man who had died *in flagrante delicto*. Only, the apartment had belonged to a nineteen-year-old college student and the dead guy had been her husband.

"I brought your favorite." Forrest announced himself at the reception desk seconds after he breezed in. Loretta had been too engrossed in her magazine to look up. By the time she did, he had already set down a clear-topped box containing one full-sized blueberry pie. Forrest made it his business to know the guilty pleasure of everyone on his butter-up list.

"Oh my stars!" Her expression lit up in delight when she broke out of her reading and took in the pie box, then Forrest's charming smile. She let her hands—and her magazine—fall to the counter. She sat at a desk, but the counter was high enough that Forrest could lean his elbows on it from where he stood. Loretta liked it when he stopped and talked, mostly because she was an all-out flirt.

Forrest had met plenty of amateur flirters. He'd seen the batting eyelashes and the playful winks and the subtle slips of phone numbers. Most lady-flirting had a "come and get it" kind of feel. Loretta's flirting was different. It was looking for something. Forrest could only imagine what being cheated on with a woman more than ten years her junior could do to a woman's self-esteem. He didn't think there was anything wrong with being part of puffing it back up.

"How you been, Loretta? You're lookin' good, girl."

It wasn't even a lie. In her mid-thirties, Loretta was a beautiful woman.

She smiled slyly. "I could say the same about you."

Flirtation aside, she was great at her job. She was someone to keep in your good graces if you ever needed to call in a quick favor that related to knowing about who was committing crime.

If the sheriff wasn't in, Forrest could default to asking Loretta, who could get him at least half of what he wanted to know. On a fire case, she might even have been the one who had processed the scene. For the time being, he would start by asking for Jeffrey.

"Is the sheriff around? I could use ten minutes of his time."

She barely looked at the phone as she picked up the receiver, dialed an extension, and kept taking in her eyeful of Forrest. "Hey, Jeff. You busy? All right, well, Forrest's here. Imma send him back."

"Always good to see you, Loretta." Forrest knocked once on the counter and made his way around the desk, using his hip to nudge open the barrier gate she had to buzz in. As he pushed through, he gave her a little wink. He could tell—it tickled her to bits.

"When are you gonna ask me out, Forrest Winters?" She leaned forward in her seat and folded her arms in a way that left little to the imagination.

"I guess whenever I muster up the courage, darlin' ..."

As Forrest made his way down the hall toward Jeffrey's office, he thought of Buck. If he liked older women so much, maybe he ought to leave Sierra alone and get to know Loretta.

Five minutes after sitting down at the sheriff's desk—after pleasantries had been exchanged—Forrest raised the issue with Jeffrey. This time, he kept the "lazy cop" commentary to himself. Truth be told, Jeffrey was a different kind of law man than Frank—a better law man, if you asked Forrest. But he couldn't come out and say it.

"You heard from Grissom or that kid, Dennis Peck, at all?"

Jeffrey shook his head. "I half-expected to. Figured they found their own leads."

"Not as far as I can tell," Forrest replied. Then, he made every excuse in the book for Grissom. For a good minute, he toed Frank Barnett's line about how all of them were short-staffed at this time of year and how difficult it was to pursue a case with no witnesses.

"Now you know I don't want to step on Frank's toes ... but he's not resourced to run this investigation. Grissom's in charge, but he's tied up in other things."

"But you're the fire marshal and you care about stopping who's starting fires."

Forrest didn't deny it. "I don't want to go over anyone's head. I just want to solve the case."

Jeffrey nodded in understanding. "So tell me how I can help."

"I'm not asking you to get involved," Forrest assured him. "But if I could rule out a few things, it would go far to ease my mind. Thought it wouldn't hurt to ask whether you could think of anyone who was ... troubled."

"There's a lot of troubled people in this town," Jeffrey replied with an eyebrow raise. "I've gotten three calls about Patsy Swine this week. Had to go out to Odin's place to check things out. Now, you tell me what kind of world we live in when I'm spending half my gas budget checking out calls about a domesticated pig."

"What the hell did Patsy do?" Forrest wanted to know.

"Not a damned thing." Jeffrey sighed. "Odin's not the one causing trouble. It's some of his kin making the calls. Playing tricks on him over some family vendetta. You ever had to write up a report on whether a pig had an alibi? Trust me—Green Valley's got plenty of crazy to go around."

Forrest blinked. "Well, I'm not talking about that kind of crazy. The profile I'm looking for is someone who's disturbed. Someone with destructive tendencies—maybe a vandal. A person who's caused harm for no apparent reason, not for revenge or personal gain."

"Not while I was on duty ..." Jeffrey reached toward his computer and keyed something in. "Most of our property damage is your typical stuff," Jeffrey murmured as he scrolled. "Eggs and toilet paper on mischief night ... retaliation against cheating husbands. Nothin' I see here looks worse than teenagers having too much fun, or good, old-fashioned revenge."

Jeffrey's comment about teenagers reminded Forrest of his profile.

"Any kids without a lot of supervision who you might classify as troubled youth? Someone with an abusive or absentee father?"

Jeffrey crossed his arms and sat back in his chair.

"Yeah ..." Jeffrey nodded somberly. "We've had some of that over the years. More than I care to admit. The abuse situations we've handled as best we could. But being an absentee father isn't against the law. We've got kids in all kinds of situations—folks in the military, mom or dad's in jail ... We've got a few kids whose dads are off working on a rig."

"Anyone on a bad path with access to a car?" Forrest still asked, even though it was already clear to him that no one was coming to Jeffrey's mind.

The sheriff just shook his head. "I already looked into arson cases and dispatches involving fire. I looked at it myself—to satisfy my own curiosity the same day we toured the scene. If I'd have turned anything up, I would've called you right away."

Forrest sighed and sat back in his chair, letting silence fall. "What do you think is going on? You been doing this job for how long? You must have some idea."

"I don't," Jeffrey said plainly. "But I'll tell you what. I can spot the oddball cases a mile away. Whatever's going on here, it's just plain weird."

Chapter Thirteen

SIERRA

You busy tonight?

Forrest's text came in just as Sierra was setting down the final items she needed: a spray-mister, a bottle of anti-frizz curl elongator, and a new detangling brush. Her hair was sopping wet and she wore a cotton robe with a thick towel draped around her shoulders. The flatscreen was on and the newest episode of *Insecure* was queued up.

The truth was, Sierra *was* busy. Taming her tight curls in the Tennessee humidity was serious business. Tonight, she had a much-needed date with her do. Since moving to a new climate, it was like her own hair was a stranger to her. The tried-and-true regimen that worked in California's dry heat did her no good in the Great Smoky Mountains. Her goal was to figure things out well enough to wear her hair down from time to time. She was sick of her everyday bun.

Why? What's up?

Sierra shot off her text, then sat on the floor in front of the sofa.

Her laptop was off to the side and she had queued up the hair tutorial she would multitask-watch. This particular video had a lot of upvotes, but, in Sierra's experience, 100% of hair-tubers made their styles seem twice as easy to achieve than they actually were. But figuring it out on her own was her only option. There wasn't a Black hairdresser for a hundred miles.

New information. Dinner at your place?

Sierra's stomach flipped and her brain worked to process the three things she felt at once: panic at the thought of pulling her house together, excitement at the prospect of seeing him, and—lurking shamefully—self-loathing at said excitement. What she didn't feel was as much regret as she should have about postponing her date with her hair. The naked truth was, he'd been on her mind. She wanted to see Forrest.

I'm a little busy. What time were you thinking?

She didn't want to seem too available.

I could be there with takeout in about an hour.

It might take half that for Sierra to do an abbreviated version of her routine. Her coffee table looked like she'd robbed a beauty store. The curl elongator was only the last step in a long process of wetting and parting and sectioning and conditioning and brushing—a process that one had to do right and that would take at least an hour and a half. Now, she would have to improvise. But what were her other options? Not making progress on the case? Not getting her fix of Forrest?

All right, come on over.

* * *

Fifty-five minutes later, Sierra swung her door open to find Forrest on her porch, two heavy bags dangling from his fingers. His charming smile widened unabashedly the second he took her in. That had been happening more lately—him looking upon her with an appreciative gaze rather than just playful, heckling eyes. And he wasn't shy about it, either.

In place of a greeting, Forrest took his time, letting his gaze wash over her as he stood at her door. From the wide, slow circling of his eyes around her face, it was clear what he was taking in. Sierra readied herself for whatever snark he might have coming. It wasn't like she'd never gotten comments about her hair.

It was impossible to *not* notice when she wore it down. Untied, her buoyant curls could not be contained. They hung heavy—past her shoulders—when they held the weight of water but tightened and lifted until their ends barely kissed her shoulders when it dried. It was just hair, but Forrest had a way of finding her buttons and making it his business to push. He was taking so long, she was seconds short of snarking him first.

"Your hair is beautiful."

Sierra opened her mouth, then closed it, falling short of a witty response. It was the one thing she hadn't expected. The way he'd said it had felt awestruck and utterly sincere. She had never been good with compliments and it felt too vulnerable to take one from him. So she answered the only way she knew how: with a proud lift of her chin and a witty retort.

"Of course it is."

She waved him inside and he followed her to the table, informing her that he'd picked up Chinese. There was no Chinese restaurant in Green Valley which meant that he'd been in Knoxville when he'd texted. The chili she would have thawed out didn't hold a candle to the deliciousness she could already smell: the vinegar of General Tso's chicken and the char of shrimp fried rice.

Her second surprise came when Forrest fell in next to her at her kitchen counter, opening cabinets and drawers, finding plates and spoons for the containers and setting up a mini buffet from them to serve. It was hard to believe the same man who she had bickered with just last week was in her home again, moving in lockstep with her.

"So what'd you find out?" Sierra asked after they'd settled at her table and she'd opened each of them a beer.

Forrest didn't respond until after he'd had a big bite and a good chew of orange chicken. He looked the kind of hungry she felt at the end of a long day and she imagined he had to eat a fair bit to maintain his bulk. No amount of trying not to stare made her not notice how good he looked filling out the dusty blue of his Henley, which only brought out the brightness of his eyes.

Sierra distracted herself with a bite of egg roll. Unlike the thin, flattened wraps of the egg rolls back home, these were thick and pockmarked with tiny bubbles. They were greasy and absolutely delicious.

"There are no known fire starters in town—no reported incidents from Green Valley Fire and none from the sheriff. Jeffrey James looked in the county database for me. I think we can rule out a pyro or a troubled youth."

Sierra felt a pang of relief for Jake. If their profile indicated a troubled youth, with him being born to the Wraiths, Forrest or anyone else who found it out could pin it on him.

"So we've narrowed down to the last type of arsonist," Sierra concluded. "The kind who's covering up a crime. That's consistent with my findings."

Forrest raised an eyebrow.

"I went down to Eager Beaver's. Turns out fire retardant is expensive. Our culprit is someone with cash. A product Stokes confirmed could function as a perimeter blocker was sold out. It costs seventy-five dollars a bottle."

"A business expense, then ..." Forrest set down his chopsticks. "Serious criminals committing a serious crime. Sounds like we ought to look at the Wraiths."

All the relief she had so recently felt drained from Sierra's body, filling her once again with a sense of dread. Profiling the suspect as a Wraith would keep Jake in the path of danger.

"It still doesn't answer the question of what or why," she pointed out.

"Maybe not. But we gotta dig. Last time the Wraiths were linked to crimes in the park, there were bodies."

"So we dig," Sierra said simply.

"Uh-uh. *I* dig," Forrest said. "The Wraiths are some dangerous boys. Any looking into of them is something we've got to do carefully. There are people I can visit."

"Great. I'll come with you."

"No, you won't."

The familiar, hostile feelings returned, reminding Sierra everything she didn't like about this man. Forrest Winters was pushy—entitled—and if he thought she was just some chess piece who he could put anywhere he wanted, well, he had another thing coming.

"You know, your sales pitch was pretty good, but you suck at execution."

"Execution? Execution of what?"

"That whole speech you gave me about forming a partnership? About how well we'd work together and how we needed to be a team? Sure seems like you're not feeling too collaborative right now."

"Sierra, please. You do not want me to take you anywhere near the Wraiths." That half-cocky, half-charming smile fell from his face. His eyes darkened to granite and his voice became grave.

Sierra broke eye contact long enough to choose her words.

"Look. I don't know what you see when you look at me, but you can let go of the misguided notion that I'm some delicate flower. You don't know all I have to add to this or who I really am. If you're not gonna bring me in, you can do it yourself."

Forrest shook his head. "You don't know what you're asking for."

"And you don't know what you're passing up. There's a reason why I have an unresolved incident record of zero. Did you know my dad's a detective? Boy, I grew up squeezing information out of my teddy bears."

Sierra hadn't meant to be funny, but a glint of humor quirked up the corner of his lip.

"I don't think anyone would describe you as a delicate flower, Sierra."

That soft, patient voice of his was back again. His eyes took another slow perusal of her face, just as they had when he had first shown up at her door.

She bit her tongue against any of the at least five things she wanted him to know in that moment, all too raw for her to say out loud.

She picked up another morsel of chicken, certain this one wouldn't be as tasty as the last. But the sooner she finished her food and sent him the not-so-subtle clue of clearing her plate, the sooner he would leave.

Forrest hadn't taken a single bite since his comment. Instead, he continued to stare—not in a creepy way, just a scrutinizing one that made her feel even more ridiculous for shoving food into her mouth.

"I thought about what you said."

She dipped her last bit of egg roll in what was left of the duck sauce, her final bite to freedom. "Thought about what I said about what?"

His voice was deep and low. "About it being a club—a bunch of good ol' boys doing things the way they've always been done."

Sierra swallowed thickly, certain now that he saw her as some bitter shrew. "Did I really say it like that?"

"You were too polite. But I'll admit, there's something to it."

Sierra didn't know what to say to that. Forrest Winters was the last person she'd have thought to be talking to about social networks and how they keep some people on the margins.

"What made you think about it?" she finally asked.

He threw her a half-amused look she couldn't decipher. "Other than I listen when you talk? You said something important. Did you think I'd just dismiss it?"

She grasped for an elegant response. Him caring enough about it to bring it up again was the last thing she had expected.

"Not that you would dismiss it … I didn't think you'd give it thought. I mean, it doesn't really impact you."

"There's one thing I've learned as a firefighter: a team doesn't work unless everyone's in it. You thinking you're not part of the team is a problem."

However true it might have been, it wasn't easy for her to hear it said out loud.

"I'm a member of the daytime team. It's the after-work team that's harder. That's what happens when you look like me and you're not from around here."

"And that's what you think me not wanting to take you to see the Wraiths is about."

"You tell me. Would you take Wendell?"

"No, I wouldn't take Wendell. There's things I can ask—and things they'll tell me—because they know me. Things they won't tell me any other way but out of sight and one-on-one."

Sierra didn't concede the point, but she understood that logic. It made her think again about Jake—this time, about how she could never take Forrest along for one of her visits. Jake would clam up and Sierra wouldn't blame him. Forrest Winters was law enforcement. In town, you only ever saw him out with the park brass, firefighters, or cops.

She didn't know what made her more uneasy: hoarding information about Jake—information she knew Forrest would deem relevant to the investigation—or teaming up with a man who was a bit too tied into the way things had always been done. Sierra had no doubt that Jake Stapleton would be regarded as trustworthy and help-worthy by her alone. Forrest would treat him like a suspect.

"Can I ask you a question about that?" Forrest had taken another bite of chicken and chewed thoughtfully before swallowing and wiping his mouth. He had also jutted his foot out and sat back in his seat. "I don't want to sound contrary, but there's something I'm curious to know." He wiped his fingers and took a pull from his bottle. "Why haven't I ever seen you be the one to make a move?"

She shook her head, not knowing what he was getting at.

"There are circles, then there are *circles*." He said the second one with emphasis. "Not getting invited on the hunting trip is one thing. But why not join in when you have a chance? For some of the situations you're talking about, you don't need an engraved invitation. Poker night, for one. Even just grabbing a beer at the bar … those are things you don't need anyone to invite you to."

Forrest wasn't wrong. And he also wasn't joking. If he could be so thoughtful about it, so could she.

"I guess I just don't feel comfortable." It cost her something to admit. "I don't know what you talk about, or how clean it is, or how much I would relate to it. For all I know, you spend all your time talking about Duck Dynasty and complaining about your wives."

Forrest frowned. "What's wrong with Duck Dynasty?"

Sierra rolled her eyes. "Duck Dynasty isn't the point. The point is, what if trying to be part of the club only highlights everything we don't have in common?"

He put his beer bottle down and leaned forward.

"All right. But what if it highlights everything you do?"

Sierra sighed, knowing how petulant it would make her seem to shoot his argument down, and knowing at a deeper level that she really ought to be more open. She picked at the label of her beer bottle.

"It's just hard to imagine. Let's face it—I'm an avocado-eating, Prius-driving, California liberal. I have almost nothing in common with people around here."

"You and me have lots in common."

She sent him a disbelieving look. "We do?"

"We both come from law enforcement families. We both think the wildflower fields are just about the damned prettiest place in this whole park. We both know God didn't invent cupcakes so someone could make a dill pickle version. And we both care a whole lot about who set those fires."

"I didn't know you hated those cupcakes." Sierra gave a little smile.

"It's not natural." Forrest looked perturbed. "Neither are the sour cream and onion ones Jenn makes. And don't think I haven't told her so."

Even as she smiled, she thought about the rest. When he put it in those terms, it did feel like they shared a lot.

"You do realize most folks like those things ..."

"Maybe," he hedged. "But you'd know a hell of a lot more about people if you took the time. Everything I know about you, I know because we've been together outside of work."

"Half the things you know about me, you know because you show up to bug me everywhere you don't belong."

"See?" He smiled. "You're proving my point. Persistence pays off."

She shook her head and reached for another egg roll. He made it sound so easy.

"Maybe it'd be less intimidating if you let me take you a few places." His voice was calm and even and warm. It held something earnest, even though, moments before it had held something light and joking.

He didn't wait for her to answer before he asked. "You know how to play poker?"

Chapter Fourteen

FORREST

"Just the man I was hoping to see."

Forrest plastered a smile on his face as he strode through the door of the inner office in Greenbrier Ranger Station, tamping down disappointment at the sight of the wrong ranger. Running as late as he was meant he would only have half a chance at catching Sierra. Unless she was running much later than him, she'd have already gone for the day.

It was a triple disappointment. Had he gotten there two hours earlier as planned, he would have beaten her back before the end of her shift, been in time to help himself to a few bites, and to drop what he'd gotten for her in her drawer for her to find the same day. Now, every element of his plan would have to wait. She wouldn't get her gift until tomorrow. And her being gone meant that so was the Tupperware for her bites.

"Forrest fuckin' Winters," Dennis said in an overly familiar way that Forrest was sure he didn't like. Forrest didn't mind when people were casual with him, but Dennis didn't know him like that. Still, snubbing Dennis would achieve nothing and could possibly even set the investigation back. For that simple reason, Forrest would let him keep on thinking they were buds.

"What's doin'?" Forrest was all practiced congeniality. He dropped his bag on the floater desk. Dennis put down his coffee long enough to come up and shake his hand. "You comin' or goin'?"

"I'm not even supposed to be on now." The way he said it was laced with pride, like working overtime should've earned him a cookie.

"Fire investigation?" Forrest probed, thinking again about all the questions Dennis hadn't bothered to ask Grizz or Jeffrey.

"Not today." Dennis doubled down on self-satisfaction. "Clint's got me working on something else."

As Dennis walked back to his desk, Forrest pulled his steel water bottle out of the side pocket of his bag and made his way to the water cooler by the front. Sensing that Dennis wanted him to probe for what he was working on, Forrest was deliberately slow to ask. Dennis stood waiting, one hand on his hip and a coffee cup in the other. Today's mug had a picture of the grim reaper and said *Death Before Decaf.*

"Anything good?" Forrest asked after he'd filled his bottle and taken a long sip of his drink.

Dennis perked up. "Clint's got me on poaching. Not just in my territory, either. He wants me to work with the Carolina side—head up anti-poaching efforts for the whole park."

"I thought Fish and Wildlife was in charge of that." Forrest knew good and well that Dennis wasn't talking about animal poaching. People willing to break federal laws for a trophy kill were rarely the smartest, sanest, or soberest people you'd ever meet. You had to be a lot better than Dennis to do that job.

"Not game poaching," he clarified. "*Ginseng* poaching," he said as if Forrest had never heard about the problem. Never mind that he'd grown up in the park.

"Folks are still doing that?"

"Not just any people. The worst kind." Dennis crossed his arms and let a sour expression come over his face.

"What kind would those be?"

"The people who sell 'em to the black market. I'm not just talkin' hippies and stoners and the ones who buy into all that new-wave, California bullshit. I'm talkin' 'bout the scumbags who sell the stuff for top dollar, to China."

It was a view Forrest had heard before.

"My dad used to take me through the forest looking for it when I was a kid," Forrest replied. "The education programs have worked pretty well."

Dennis just scoffed. "Come on, now. Criminals don't want to be educated. They just want to make a buck."

"You might be right," Forrest hedged. "But the more people who know the right way to pick them, the better the species' chances."

"I guess ..." Dennis relented. "But I'm gonna catch a bunch of those poachers, all the same. Anyone who steals from a goddamned national park deserves to be charged with a federal crime. It belongs to the United States government. Selling it to Asia is goddamned un-American."

Not wanting to go down that road with Dennis, Forrest mentioned the other thing on his mind.

"How's the fire investigation coming? Anything I can help with?" He hoped Dennis would take the bait. The more Dennis invited him to keep investigating, the more reason Forrest would have to do exactly that. It could also get him and Sierra access to a few more resources.

"Slightly stalled." Dennis wove his head from side to side in the universal gesture for ambivalence. "Clint's got me busy with other things. He's been doing two jobs lately, you know, with Olivia out on leave. Since I'm his right-hand man, I'm working overtime myself."

"Just let me know if you need anything," Forrest offered again. "Me and my guys know a few things about fire."

"Thanks for the offer. Clint made the priority on this pretty clear. He wants me to personally oversee things, but I'll punt the busy work —probably supervise Sierra."

The comment got Forrest's hackles up. He didn't like the way Dennis talked about Sierra—like they weren't peers. Add in how low a priority this investigation seemed to be and how cavalierly Dennis talked about an arson case in front of a federal fire marshal, and Forrest was getting mad.

It told Forrest three things: Dennis had to be one of the people who irritated Sierra. Forrest had only been talking to the man for five minutes and Dennis already irritated the hell out of him. Secondly, the way Dennis threw Grissom's name around with such authority meant he thought Grissom was in charge and would protect him from all manner of things. It was a rookie mistake—cocky and overconfident —not taking into account the hierarchy and who from which agencies had clout.

But the third fact was the most telling: Dennis sure seemed dumb enough to think a sham investigation could keep the fire situation in hand. Dennis, of all people, ought to be shaking in his boots. If there were another fire—let alone a worse one that burned real acreage and created real losses—Grissom would distance himself and all blame would fall upon Dennis.

"Sierra knows her shit," Forrest said by way of response. "And it's her territory. If your hands are so full with poaching, why not just give it to her?"

"I could ..." Dennis trailed off. "But I figured it'd be good to get used to things. Before long, I'm gonna be her boss."

A full hour later, long after Dennis had gone, Forrest continued to stew, working out with precision exactly what it was he didn't like about the man.

Even when it came to little things, Dennis was out for himself. It went against everything firemen were taught. When it was life and death, there was not a single inch of room for ego. All personal whims and interests had to be disposed of and put aside. Forrest had seen men work together who hated one another personally, and not just work together—truly come together in hours of need, to become greater than the sum of their parts.

But something else was bothering Forrest. At first, it had seemed like Dennis was acting alone—an equal-opportunity kiss-ass. More and more, it seemed like he and Grissom were in cahoots. Only, Grissom wasn't known for taking younger guys under his wing. Forrest rarely saw him with his own direct reports who worked in his area of the park. Why did he and Dennis seem like some sort of team?

Tomorrow AM?

Forrest was broken out of his thoughts when a text came through from Sierra. Receiving anything from her made him smile.

Smiles for her were something he only allowed himself in private. Not because *he* was afraid of what it meant—because she wasn't ready and now wasn't quite the time.

Can't tomorrow. Gotta work. Anything urgent? he texted back.

Nothing that can't wait. Thanks for confirming you're not coming.

An unbidden thought that should have occurred to him long before infiltrated his mind.

Why? Expecting company?

It was none of his business. He held his breath as the dancing dots on his chat screen told him she was actually going to respond.

No. But if I hear someone chopping wood in the middle of the night and I know it's not you, I'll get my shotgun ready again.

Her text was followed by an emoji, and not one of the cute ones either—one of the red ones with devil horns. Enjoying that little touch was secondary to his sense of relief. She wasn't expecting company. It didn't prove she was single or that she wasn't seeing anybody, but another day when no such evidence surfaced felt like victory.

He pressed the reaction button that said "Ha, Ha" then pocketed his phone and made to leave. With no one else in the office, it was safe for him to place the small, white box into the top drawer of her desk.

Taking a final stride into the break room, Forrest took a long shot by opening the fridge. He was feeling peckish. Even if he left right then, he still had a good half hour before he could make it home. If he was lucky, there might be leftover catering from a meeting. If push came to shove, he could default to Cup of Soup, but he was hoping it wouldn't come to that.

Forrest resigned himself to disappointment as he swung open the door. The absence of her Tupperware was bound to deflate him. He had come to enjoy any sign that she was near. What he saw when his eyes adjusted made him blink hard, twice. The little container he hadn't seen in a while—the one that said *Fire Marshal Snacks*—sat front and center on the top shelf. This time, it was full of bites.

Chapter Fifteen

SIERRA

Anything good come in last night?

Sierra flipped open her laptop and messaged Rick the second she came into the office, an hour earlier than usual. Patrolling her territory more thoroughly meant leaving time to cover more ground. Today, she had her weekly check-in with Olivia. She also had counter duty, which would further reduce the amount of time she could canvass her territory within the park.

She wanted to catch Rick before he went off shift. True to his word, he'd been checking in to report anything out of the ordinary. Apart from whatever he heard when he was on duty, he had access to activity logs from when he was off shift. He scanned those daily and told Sierra about anything with even a hint of a connection.

Just folks having a little more fun than is good for them. You know how this place gets at night.

"A little too much fun" could mean anything, from drinking, to drugs, to shooting guns, to teenagers going parking. The park was closed after sunset, but plenty of folks—mostly kids—came to party.

What you saw depended on what shift you worked. Daytime was a lot of helping through-hikers and monitoring conditions. The calls that came in at night ranged from trivial to completely wild.

Anything ongoing? Sierra wanted to know next.

That one was a standard question she would have asked any dispatcher as she came on to her shift. Some days, you walked into a situation-in-progress.

We've got a streaker by Ramsay Cascades. White female. Late teens to early twenties. Park Police is on the scene, trying to talk her back into her clothes.

Sierra gave pause. It wasn't every day that a streaker was a woman. Stripping down naked and showing what no one wanted to see was a distinction Sierra had observed almost exclusively with men. Having witnessed multiple incidents, Sierra was convinced that men were obsessed on all conscious and subconscious levels with their penises. She'd never met a streaker who had been able to conceal some modicum of showmanship and pride.

5150? Sierra shot back.

It was one of their incident codes. An official calling a *5150* meant there was knowledge or suspicion of a mental health issue. When people acted strangely, it was hard to tell, but making an early call according to your best judgment was part of the job.

It's a clear 236. She told them what she took—now she's just paranoid and won't let them get close. I

A 236 was an intoxication code pertaining to hallucinogenic drugs.

LSD? Sierra guessed.

It was making a comeback on the recreational scene. People on LSD weren't easy to deal with if they were having a bad trip.

Not LSD. Shrooms, Rick clarified.

Anything else? Sierra hoped their streaker was the universe's idea of enough excitement.

That's it. For now.

He added a smile emoji at the end. The belief that more crazy would come from the simple act of alluding to the fact that it might was common law enforcement superstition. Incidents like this sometimes gave way to streaks of crazy—crazy that could last for days.

After signing off, Sierra pulled out her Tupperware and walked with anticipation to the kitchen, eager to see whether Forrest had been by. The idea to leave him bacon bites had come to her on a whim. It was a simple enough gesture, to leave him what he would have taken himself. If he'd shown up the night before and seen them, he'd have appreciated the joke.

When she came into the break room, she was pleased to find the smaller Tupperware, washed and empty, sitting on a corner of the counter. Well, almost empty. A piece of paper appeared to be inside. Smiling widely even before she peeled the lid off, Sierra hastened to open the container to read the note.

Thanks. They hit the spot.

Next to written words, he had doodled a piece of bacon.

Sierra was glad no one else was in the office to witness the goofy grin she couldn't wipe off her face. Trying her best to not overthink things, she resolved to get to work. Upon returning to her seat, she woke up her laptop and made to retrieve her notepad from the top drawer of her desk.

If she'd been relieved a moment before that no one was around to see her grin, she was doubly relieved that no one was around to see her find the white box, and triply relieved that no one was around to see her snort-laugh when she opened it. Forrest had gotten her a Seahawks mug. Inside was another note:

Ask and ye shall receive. You said you needed another cup.

* * *

Sierra might have had Forrest and his persnickety coffee cup to thank for her jovial air at the front desk, even though the guests she was helping could kindly be described as deluded. The woman who had spent fifteen minutes grilling Sierra about how to "get up close to the animals" was living in a fantasy land.

At the moment, said woman was spouting off about having just wasted the entire morning at Cade's Cove hoping to see elk, but she—as she had so colorfully explained—"didn't see shit." As the woman spouted off, Sierra was hyper-aware of the buzzing of her cell phone in her pocket.

She was guessing it had something to do with the photo she'd texted Forrest of the Seahawks cup. She'd tacked on a Post-it with the words "Glasses for Kickers" written in black Sharpie and had thrown in a few dollar bills and some change from the bottom of her purse. She'd sent over the photo with a short note of explanation: *So Jason Myers can see the goal post.*

"Well, where can we see some bears, then?" the woman demanded after she was finished complaining about the shortage of elk. Never mind that she'd gone looking in the northwestern part of the park, when most elk were in the Cataloochee area in the southeast. The woman was sunburnt and skinny and heavily jeweled—middle-aged, though she didn't look old enough to be retired. In a bright pink sundress, she looked more ready for a backyard barbecue than she did for the park. From the twin wedding band worn by the man standing next to her—who hadn't gotten a word in edgewise—Sierra could only guess they were married.

"Bears are most active around dawn and dusk." Sierra motioned to the map she had spread out in front of them. "Your best bet is to take this loop trail and stop along the way. In the back of this book, there's a quick guide to vegetation. Look for them around blackberry, blueberry, and huckleberry bushes."

The man seemed to be tracking Sierra's instructions, but the woman didn't spare the map a glance.

"Isn't there any way to see them up close without havin' to go hiking up a trail?" she went on.

They'd spent the better part of fifteen minutes talking in circles about what other wildlife they might see. They'd already established that bobcats were nocturnal, foxes were rarely seen during this season, and wolves didn't even live in Great Smoky Mountains National Park.

"Well, you don't want to get *too* close. They're beautiful creatures, but they're still wild animals. We recommend a safe distance of at least one hundred feet."

Conscious of the line forming, Sierra closed the book. The woman plucked her glasses off of her face and pinned Sierra with sharp blue eyes.

"Well, can't y'all train the bears to come up to the road?"

Sierra blinked. "No, ma'am. Our role is to protect their habitats and monitor their well-being within the park. We don't train the wildlife here."

She turned to her husband with a plaintive look. "Well, how are you supposed to get a picture with 'em if you can't even get close to any?"

"Ma'am. Please do not attempt to take pictures with the bears."

Sierra looked at her watch. It was just past 11:50. Dennis was meant to have been there to relieve her twenty minutes before. He was definitely in the office. His bag was next to his desk. If he didn't show up soon, she would be late for her meeting with Olivia. And regardless of when he showed up, she would still have to finish up with whatever guest she was helping. She could only hope the next ones didn't take long.

Come on, Dennis, she muttered under her mental breath. In futile hope, she took a final look around. Still seeing no sign of him, she gestured for the next pair to step forward. It was another couple who looked sweeter than the last, but she knew instinctively, they wouldn't be quick. Someone needed to do something about Dennis.

* * *

"I am so. Sorry. I'm late," Sierra said in a rush, still walking down the hall as she connected onto her meeting. Her laptop teetered precariously on the underside of her right forearm, and she moused awkwardly with her right. Dennis had been thirty-five minutes late relieving her. Now, hustling toward the conference room, it was going on a quarter past noon.

"No problem," Olivia came back good-naturedly, then frowned. "Are you walking down the hall?"

"I just got off the desk," Sierra explained.

"Busy morning?"

Sierra wouldn't go out of her way to rat out Dennis, but she wouldn't lie for him either.

"I was waiting to be relieved from the desk."

"Ah, okay." Olivia nodded. "Well, I've got a hard stop at twelve thirty, so let's jump in. I got two more glowing letters about you from visitors. I forwarded you copies this morning."

"People still write letters?" Sierra quipped, wanting to buy herself a few more seconds to get situated. Closing the door behind her, she settled into her seat.

"One of them was an email. It came through the general feedback inbox. The other one was a letter. Maybe you ought to take a look." Olivia said it with a bit of intrigue.

Sierra hastened to do just that. When she located the email and clicked on the attachment, she blinked upon discovering an official-looking letter on USDA letterhead. Her eyes flew down to the signature line before she even read the letter, too wild with curiosity to not look and see who it was from.

"I helped Elaine Lee and didn't recognize her?" Sierra blurted inelegantly. Elaine Lee was the forest service chief. She was one of the top-ranking officials at the Department of Agriculture.

Olivia somehow beamed and smirked at the same time. "No. But her daughter visited the park last month, and she sure raved about you."

"Wow." Sierra blinked.

Olivia chuckled. "Wow is right. And congratulations. A letter like this'll be a feather in your cap. I've already asked headquarters to send you the original. That one's a keeper."

Sierra was eager to read the content of the letter, but refocused on Olivia, who crossed off something in her planner. Olivia always had a list of agenda items to discuss and their time was short.

"So how are things going with the fire investigation?"

This was the part Sierra had rehearsed. She didn't want to sound petty, but Olivia was Dennis's boss, too. Sierra didn't want his side to be the only one Olivia heard.

"I've changed my patrol pattern," Sierra began. "I paid a visit to my friends on the research side and asked them to keep eyes out. There are other avenues we could pursue, but I'm staying in my lane."

Olivia had been taking notes in her planner.

"Staying in your lane?" She stopped writing and looked up.

"You know, now that Frank Barnett put Dennis in charge of the investigation."

Olivia's eyebrows rose to her hairline. "When did that happen?"

"Last week. Frank says he can't investigate without suspects or a profile. The ball's still in our court."

"Right." Olivia shook her head. "So it won't show up as a crime on his books, but it'll be an incident on ours. That's lazy policing if I ever saw it."

Sierra kept quiet, hanging on to see what else Olivia might have to say on the matter, and what she planned to do about it.

"What else is happening?" Olivia wanted to know.

"Just dealing with the heat," Sierra reported. "Coming up with new ways to support animal hydration. There's a system I'm trying out with that new gang of elks—the one with all the calves. I'm keeping good track of how it works. I was hoping when things calm down a little, you'd authorize some time for me to write a research paper about it."

"You've been tracking it that closely?" Olivia's eyes were on her notebook as she wrote. Her subtle smile foreshadowed approval.

"My early findings show enough promise that I think we could use them to apply for grants that would allow us to scale up."

Olivia finally stopped writing and looked up. "That sounds amazing."

When Olivia looked down at her watch, Sierra also checked the time. Thanks to Dennis, they only had four minutes left.

"I just have one more question," Sierra put forth. "What happens when you have the baby? How do I officially launch my new work plan for the fall?"

It was a delicate way of asking bigger questions: when would she find out about her promotion? Who would sign off on her goals for next year? Olivia had alluded to the fact that it would happen early, in around three weeks. Olivia was meant to drive the process—not Sierra—but nothing was on the schedule.

"How about you list out your accomplishments from this year and start thinking more about next year's project goals?" Olivia replied. "Is two weeks enough to pull that together?"

The arson case wouldn't likely be solved by then, but she still had to hedge her bets. The longer she waited, the greater the possibility that Olivia could go into labor, which would place her in a position to have her performance review with Grissom.

"I can do two weeks," Sierra replied, hoping what she'd told Olivia about the investigation would lead to some kind of change. In the meantime, she would keep pushing forward. Even if she couldn't solve the whole thing, maybe she could serve up some big break in the case.

"Good," Olivia replied approvingly. "After I get a look at those, we'll schedule your performance review."

Chapter Sixteen

FORREST

"We gon' start this thing or what?" As usual, Frank Barnett looked utterly put out, more so after having been cornered by Dennis Peck after an innocent attempt to grab a slice at the pizza buffet. Last Forrest heard, Dennis was peppering him with dumb questions about work and trying to go deep on wild ginseng. Rule number one of poker night was keep the office at the office.

The other guys were milling around the upstairs lounge of the Green Valley firehouse, shooting the shit and grabbing eats in less predatory ways. They were minutes shy of their starting time. But Dennis wouldn't get off of Frank's dick.

"You dealin', Grizz, or am I?" Forrest pushed up from where he half-sat on the back of a leather sofa. A round dining table next to the open kitchen was where they played. The table next to their play table had been set up as half bank, half bar. Liquor bottles and mixers and glasses and a bucket of ice were set up on the right side. Cases full of poker chips were set up on the left. It was all done on the honor system: fix yourself a drink, then put your money in the box and take some chips to buy in.

"You deal this week." Grizz threw him a shit-talking look. "That way, you can't accuse me of cheating when you lose."

The guys started to move over. Forrest, Grizz, and Buck were the only ones from Fire. Wendell, Dennis, Clint, and Frank were all from the park. No one from the county sheriff was there. Forrest watched in pity as Frank chose a seat and Dennis was quick to fall in next to him. Dennis didn't appear to notice when Frank gave a little roll of his eyes. Forrest, meanwhile, took an extra chair from the table with the drinks and added it to the play table.

"Who's the eighth?" Frank wanted to know, cutting Dennis off from whatever he had been saying.

"Sierra might stop by."

Forrest grabbed three new decks off of the staging table and sat in one of the seats that faced the stairs.

"Sierra?" Three voices spoke in unison. Buck's was hopeful; Wendell's was curious; Dennis's was irritated, as if the very notion of her joining them for a few hands left a bad taste in his mouth.

"All right. Y'all just sounded way too surprised." Forrest began to open the decks.

"Who invited her?" That was from Dennis. Goddamn, was he obnoxious.

"Everyone's invited." As he said it, Grizz narrowed his eyes and pinned Dennis with a stern look.

"You think she'll bring some of those bacon bites?" Now it was Wendell who looked hopeful. He said it at the exact moment that Buck murmured, "I didn't know she played."

Seconds later, Forrest detected footsteps on the metal stairs. His hands paused their motion of bending the stiff cards in preparation for a good shuffle. By the time his gaze flew up to follow the sound, she had materialized.

Warm sensations flooded his every limb as he took in the sight of Sierra, who smirked at the men at the table from where she'd stopped at the top of the stairs. Out of uniform, she looked ten more kinds of gorgeous. He couldn't point to any specific change … only, everything about her seemed extra. Her bun was extra messy and her hair held an extra shine. Her breasts looked extra good in her scoop-neck white shirt. Forrest would bet all his chips that her ass also looked extra-good in those jeans. They were tighter—much tighter than uniform pants—and they cut off at three-quarters, drawing attention to calves that looked extra ready to be caressed.

"You talking about me already?" Her words issued from lips that looked extra kissable.

"Sierra!" Buck nearly knocked down his own chair in his haste to stand up and get her seated next to him. "I'm so glad you came! Here. Sit down."

Dennis didn't bother to greet her, but he tipped his head toward the paper bag she held in her hand—the kind they gave out at the liquor store. You could tell from its shape that it didn't hold a six-pack.

"What'd you bring? Some of that California Chardonnay?" he asked with a snide little laugh.

Sierra plucked the bag from the crook of her elbow and set it down on the table with a glassy thud. She proceeded to pull out a liquor bottle and angled it to show Dennis.

"Actually, I drink bourbon." She smiled neutrally at Dennis. "If I'd known you'd be here, I'd have picked up some of those peach wine coolers you like."

Before he could clap back, Frank cut in. "That's a good brand. You ever been to their distillery?"

Sierra shook her head.

"It's a good two hours over the Kentucky border, but it's worth the trip."

Dennis looked displeased as Sierra and Frank talked bourbon

while she got herself settled. Forrest shuffled and dealt the cards. And, just like that, the game was underway.

This many people in a game of Texas hold 'em meant a lot of rounds of betting, a lot of pontificating, and a game that was bound to be slow. It made for halting conversation. On any given day, it could be about sports, about who around town had gotten into what trouble, or complaints about girlfriends and wives. Forrest hoped the boys kept it clean. He didn't want her to regret coming.

"How's that nephew of yours, Clint?" Frank wanted to know, two bourbons into the game. Forrest had just put down the flop. "You ain't talked about him in a while. He drop out of school or get some co-ed knocked up?"

Forrest studied Sierra as the others snickered. Her eyes stayed on her cards and she kept quiet. The five-dollar antes were in and now they were placing bets.

"Jesse's just fine. He'll be a senior next year." Clint, too, seemed engrossed in his cards. He was the first up to bet and quickly threw in another five.

"He's at NCU, isn't he?" Forrest knew the answer to the question but asked it for Sierra's benefit. He'd been doing the same for the past two hands—dropping little clues to give her context. She couldn't build rapport with the folks here if she didn't start getting straight on who was who and what was what.

And Frank was right about something: Clint did like to brag about Jesse and half the game had gone by without Clint doing it once. It was one thing that worried Forrest about the investigation—Clint seemed oddly checked out. It happened to plenty of men from time to time, usually owing to trouble at home. Clint was married, but it was well-known things between him and his wife were rocky. Forrest could sympathize with that. But whatever Clint's personal problems, Forrest didn't like that they were causing him to lose focus. They needed to solve the case.

"Yup. He sure is." Clint kept it at that. Buck folded and the others considered their bets.

It gave Forrest time to think about Jesse. Like Forrest, the boy had practically grown up in the park. Clint Grissom had been born a twin, only Quint had passed away some years before, killed in the line of duty. It had been a stupid accident, but tragic. Quint had gotten on the wrong side of a herd of buffalo and in running to save himself had run clean off of a cliff.

That was how Clint had come to half-raise the boy and why the longstanding park folk knew him. They all remembered Quint and had known Jesse as a young boy. For as jaded and political and just plain lazy as Clint had gotten these past years, he'd earned a lot of respect for doing right by his brother's boy.

"I'd imagine Jesse's considering law enforcement. It being the family business and all ..." Wendell mentioned this seconds before performing the impressive task of stuffing an entire loaded nacho into his mouth in a single bite.

"He's still thinking on it." Clint's tone was noncommittal, but one corner of his mouth lifted in a half-smile. "Getting a twenty-year-old kid to focus on anything but smoking doobies with his frat brothers and chasing tail is a lot harder than it seems."

The comment was met by chuckles.

"'Lot of us sitting here are second generation," Forrest calmly chimed in. Two references in two minutes to bedding women was enough. "Me and my dad; Clint and Jesse; Sierra and her dad. He was a detective, right?"

Wendell looked over with interest and he swallowed around a chip. "Shit, Sierra. All you ever said about your dad is he's retired. You never said he was a cop. You're from Oakland, right? Isn't that where MC Hammer is from?"

Buck looked up in confusion. "Who's MC Hammer?"

At least four pair of eyes looked over at him in disbelief.

Dennis snorted derisively. "Bet he had to deal with a lot of drive-by shootings and shit."

Sierra threw in a chip, calling the bet. Grizz bet, too, and it was time for Forrest to throw another card.

"Actually, I grew up farther north, in Sonoma County," Sierra replied.

"I've been up there once," Grizz chimed in. "Went in as relief crew on the Kincade Fire. Forrest was on that crew."

Sierra's gaze snapped up to Forrest. She completely ignored the turn. "Really?"

"That country's beautiful," Grizz continued. "Miles and miles of road with nothing but vineyard flying by. Shame to see so much of it burn."

As she looked between him and Grizz, Forrest thought he saw the shine of tears. The Kincade Fire had been catastrophic—worse than the Chimney Tops fire that had ripped through Tennessee three years back.

"So many departments came out to help us. It was … unforgettable. Thank you."

Forrest could see it on Grizz's face; it was the moment Sierra won him over. The moment left Forrest with something different. More like a dawning realization about the nature of his attraction to her. Feisty Sierra turned him on, but soft Sierra had heart. She cared about everybody and everything—from people to animals to all of the things that grew in the park. She cooked bacon bites every morning because she liked *taking* care of people, too. Sierra was selfless at a time when the world was in trouble. It needed people to care. How much she did kicked Forrest right in the feels.

"What the hell ever happens up there?" Count on Dennis to completely ruin the moment. "Uppity folks stealing other uppity folks' wine?"

Sierra turned to him with a smile so sweet and wicked, Forrest might've thought she was Southern.

"You mean agriculture theft?" Earlier, they'd all endured a solid five minutes of Dennis going on about his ginseng. "My dad didn't work on anything as trivial as that. He's the cop who caught the Orange Blossom Killer."

Now she had their attention. The gruesome murders had all been committed in California, but the story had been covered nationwide. Frank's jaw slacked. Grizz and Wendell nodded their heads, impressed. Dennis narrowed his eyes. Buck looked at Sierra as if it had been she, and not her father, who had solved the crimes.

Forrest laid down the turn—a three of clubs, basically junk, given the rest of what was on the table. Frank folded immediately. Dennis threw in two angry chips. As Grissom folded, all attention shifted to Sierra.

"Legendary case," Grizz finally said. "Didn't he go dark for, like, ten years?"

Sierra glanced at her cards and threw in two more chips. "Twelve. They assumed he'd died. Most murderers with a profile like his wouldn't have been able to stop."

Wendell folded. Forrest called. He wanted to see whether she was bluffing. Grizz had folded just before him.

"Who says he did?" Dennis challenged, throwing in five ten-dollar chips. Wide eyes swung to Sierra, who threw in another three chips to call Dennis's bet. She spoke casually, as if the takes hadn't just gone up high. There had to be north of four hundred fifty dollars in the pot.

"My dad thinks he kept killing all along, and that all he did was change his style until he decided he wanted to come out of hiding."

Forrest folded. All he had was a straight. No card he turned over on the river could get him any better than that. And, it was clear by then, Dennis wouldn't back down.

"But why resurface?" Buck was all naive fascination, hanging on Sierra's every word.

Forrest didn't like Buck's flirting and turned over the river then. It was a queen of diamonds, which had the potential to change the game. There were two other diamonds on the table, a one-eyed jack and a ten. The only way either of them could win was with a flush.

All eyes went to Dennis, even though it was Sierra who had been asked the question. He threw in another five chips. All eyes swung to Sierra. They were the only two left in the game.

"For the attention." She looked around the table at her audience. "The act of killing was only part of the thrill. He missed the fear he'd created by people knowing he was on the loose. He missed the danger of getting caught."

Without looking at her chips, she grabbed exactly five, threw them into the pot and pinned her eyes on Dennis, jutting her chin at him before she said, "Call."

Dennis put down the eight and nine of diamonds and couldn't have looked more smug.

"Straight flush." He picked up his beer and took a long, satisfied sip, as if he were drinking from the chalice of victory itself.

But Forrest knew what Sierra was holding the second she allowed her facial expression to match Dennis's. He couldn't stop his laugh as she turned over the king and ace of diamonds.

Holy shit.

"Royal flush."

Chapter Seventeen
SIERRA

"You did good in there."

The poker game had broken up and Forrest had insisted upon walking Sierra back to her car. More like he'd saved her from a very eager Buck. When the latter had suggested that Sierra needed an escort, Forrest had swooped in from nowhere and said he was going her way. Sierra was fairly certain the blue metallic Explorer parked around the corner from the firehouse was his. From the looks of it, Buck knew it too. Sierra's car was still close to the middle of downtown. She'd dropped by the liquor store hours earlier, before walking over to the station.

They could have made it to her Prius in five minutes, but neither seemed invested in making good time. Forrest walked with his fingertips in his pockets. His gait was slow and he seemed relaxed and content. It was a change from the way he walked in the park. There, he was purposeful and commanding, with his sunglasses and his axe. Off-duty Forrest was gentle. And, away from the other guys, he seemed more subdued.

"You mean my poker skills or my social graces?" She made light of his compliment.

"Both." His voice was quiet and low. "Fish out of water, my ass. You knew how to wrangle them boys. And when it came to the poker end of things ..." He blew out a long breath between his lips. "You were a shark."

Sierra was glad that the cover of darkness might conceal just how pleased she was about her victory over Dennis. Beating him in any capacity felt better than good. She mentioned none of this. "You sound surprised."

"No, just impressed." His lips turned up in a smile. "I haven't seen anyone get their ass handed to them that bad since Richard Sherman took the Championship from the 49ers back in 2014."

Never mind. She wished it were light outside so he could fully appreciate her evil look. Sierra was seventy-five percent certain he only made himself out to be such a Seahawks fan so he could irritate her. Before she could tell him where he could take that Seahawks talk, he went on.

"It'd have been worse if you hadn't let him win that last hand. At one point, I thought smoke was gonna come out of his ears."

She winced at what he'd suggested. "Was it really that obvious?"

He gave another little smile. "Maybe not to other people. But I've learned your tells."

"If that was true, you'd have beaten me," she pointed out.

His smile became flirtatious. "Maybe I was having too much fun watching you teach Dennis a lesson."

Sierra laughed. "Or, maybe you're talking shit and you don't really know my tells."

"I'll admit, you're good at not reacting the moment you see your cards ..."

"But?" She was being baited. More and more, he liked to tease.

"But when you're on shaky ground, you pay attention. Size up the

146

other players and watch for their tells. It's when you've got a great hand that gives you away. When you know you can beat anything else that's on the table, you don't scrutinize the other guys. *That*, Sierra Betts, is your tell."

She lifted her chin proudly. "Either way, I think I'd better wait a while before I show my face in there again. Taking home such a big pot the first time you get invited to a game is generally poor taste. I just couldn't stop myself from taking it, every time I had the chance to beat Dennis."

"I don't know …" Forrest said lightly. "Frank sure did seem to enjoy it."

"Oh, yeah?" She was surprised. "I thought the three of them were some sort of trifecta: Clint kissing Frank's ass and Dennis kissing his …"

"Oh, you called it," Forrest confirmed. "Only, Frank prefers his ass to be kissed directly by Clint. I've never gotten the impression that Frank was a fan of Dennis."

His comment reminded her of how much she still had to learn about the politics. But even with all she didn't know, tonight had been a victory. Not every moment had been Sierra's idea of fun, but Forrest had been right: coming out more would make everything better.

"You were right, you know …" What she needed to say next was along those very lines. "It's good to get to know people at a personal level. I didn't know you'd ever been to California. Why didn't you ever tell me you fought the Kincade Fire?"

A glance at his face told her he was choosing his words. When he looked back over, his eyes were earnest, but kind.

"It's only recently that I've entered your good graces. Before a couple of weeks ago, you didn't want much to do with me."

His comment punched her in the gut at the same time as it held up a mirror, showing her what kind of person she had been. She'd gone to work and loved her job. She'd found her little tribe in Rick and

Olivia and some of the researchers she was friendly with in the park. But there were people she'd kept at arm's length.

She could see now how transparent her resentment of him had been. She could see even more how much she'd missed out on by shutting him out. Her first year moving to Tennessee had been difficult. It might have been easier with a friend like him.

Normally, Sierra wasn't too proud to apologize. And it wasn't pride that stopped her now. It was the way he made her feel—as if any honest emotion she showed him would lay her bare. She couldn't say out loud how big a mistake she'd made in keeping him out before. Even alluding to that might show him how desperately she wanted to let him in now.

"So I'm late to the party," she conceded. "Tell me all the things I ought to know about Forrest Winters that I have somehow missed."

It came out flirty—sultry somehow—but she liked the way he smiled.

"I think that might take a long time," he warned.

"Start me off easy."

By then, they were approaching Main Street, which bustled a little, even for a Monday night.

"I know all the secret places." He stopped to face her squarely. He was close enough that she could really breathe in his scent. The night was not young, but the air was cool and she could smell the leather of his jacket, and the sharp freshness of cedar against the sweetness of beer.

"*All* the secret places?" she repeated, her throat suddenly dry, too clueless or swept up to know what he meant. Maybe it was nighttime that made his eyes look the color of slate.

"The wildflower meadow? The one you can see from the trail on the way to Hen Wallow Falls?"

It was her favorite place in the park. Of course Sierra knew it. But how did he? It was the second time he'd mentioned it to her.

"I love that place," she confessed.

"You ever been down to sit in the field?" he asked.

Sierra shook her head. "They say there's a hidden trail, but I've never found it."

The road had long since cleared for them to cross, but they made no move from the street corner. Forrest leaned forward, all the better for her to breathe him in even more.

"Like I said, I know all the secret places. Let me take you there."

Chapter Eighteen

FORREST

"No wonder I never found this place," Sierra commented as Forrest parked his truck on an unmarked turnout. Being in an official vehicle had its privileges. It meant he could park where he wanted.

"This'll just get us closer." Forrest killed the engine. Everest sniffed up at the cracked window with interest. "We can bushwhack it to Old Settlers Trail and pick it up at about the two-and-a-half-mile mark. Another mile and we'll be at the spot."

In this case, Forrest didn't want to save too much time. He wanted at least half a day with Sierra. Starting at the trailhead would have meant a longer hike. Instead, he wanted to spend most of that in the wildflower field. The place was magical. Knowing she was so enchanted by it was another one of the hundred little things he was beginning to love about her.

As they set out into the forest in the quiet of the morning, Forrest loved everything about it. He loved that this was her idea of fun. Plenty of women he'd been interested in lacked an appreciation for the outdoors. He loved that she could handle a strenuous hike and wasn't skittish about going off-trail. He loved their companionable silence. Nature space was sacred space that did not always need to be filled with words, though—sometimes—talking could be nice.

It was early enough that they'd beaten the day hikers and had the whole of Old Settlers Trail. After getting them to the main trail, he'd let her lead. In another three-quarters of a mile, Forrest would have to switch places—with him leading and getting them to the hidden path that would take them to the wildflowers. Her civilian hiking outfits were fitted, and he was rather enjoying the rear view for now.

"How'd you know I knew about this place anyway?" she asked at random, after they'd been hiking in silence for some minutes. Forrest didn't mention that he'd happened upon her, twice, sitting under a tree off-trail and staring down at the meadow. Both times, she'd looked pensive and he hadn't disturbed her peace. Since telling the girl you liked that you watched her was creepy as hell, he went with the other true explanation.

"I overheard you asking a researcher about it one day."

"Huh," she tutted thoughtfully. "I didn't know you ever went to the research institute. Do they do fire research or something?"

"No ... but Kevin does nachos on Tuesday afternoons. You know I like to make my rounds."

She looked back at him. "Are you serious? You base which part of the park you're in, on what day, on who has what food, and when?"

"It's not a crime to head to Cade's Cove for some of that special coffee. Or to head up to Crosby on pound cake day ... but the best are the Greenbrier bacon bites."

She stopped in her tracks and looked back to give him a look. "You are unbelievable, Forrest Winters. Where else do you go to scavenge?"

He just shrugged and answered cryptically. "Places."

By happenstance, she had stopped near the unmarked tree that he knew only by sight. Sierra had gone several steps beyond it on the trail, which had begun to slope up toward the place where the meadow was visible from points above.

"It's here. This is the turnoff."

Everest had trotted forth, but came back once she saw Sierra wasn't following.

The path was unassuming—hard to follow unless you knew where to look; useless unless you knew there was something there. In the map of his mind, the way in didn't much make sense. From above, the trail path that overlooked the meadow ran west to east and faced south over it. But, when you looked down on it, it seemed like any path in should be from the east.

Right then, they were coming in from the west. The path would take them beneath ancient trees that formed an odd canopy that gave the sensation you were walking through a tunnel. With every step, the path became more cavernous, its slope seeming to deliver them more deeply into the earth. Then the moment came—the one he'd been waiting for, the one when they turned the corner and the canopied path gave way, abruptly, to the bursting meadow.

Ignoring the landscape, Forrest took in Sierra's face. Everest ran ahead, frolicking in the tall-growing meadows with flowers that reached her haunches. Wood sorrel and aster and Turk's-cap lilies and even flame azaleas created a rainbow of color, completed by the blue-bells and purple rhododendron that were white in the middle and lavender at the tips.

Sierra's face registered unbridled wonder as she walked in several yards and gave a slow spin. Something clenched at Forrest's heart when her wide eyes closed and her lips melted into a satisfied smile, all at the same time as she breathed in the fragrance of the flowers.

For the first time, Forrest went beyond merely wondering what it might be like to kiss her and thought specifically about where they might share their first. If he'd thought it was welcome, he might have kissed her right then. They weren't quite at that point, but he buoyed himself with confidence that she was interested. Sierra was interested, all right.

"Tell Olivia I quit," she breathed when she opened her eyes and smiled over at Forrest. "This is ..." She struggled for words. "Beyond. I feel like I could just lie down here forever and never get up."

"There's a great place where we can sit. Come on."

The flowers in the field grew so high that they were nice for standing but nearly impossible to sit. Hidden out of sight from the trail's overlook was a clearing under a tree.

Forrest reached into his pack and grabbed his picnic blanket. It was waterproof on the bottom, fleece on the top and it compacted well. It had left plenty of room in his pack for food. If she could make bacon bites to share around the office, he could provide the picnic for their hike. He wanted to impress her with his sandwiches.

"Do you know what some folks call this place?" he asked after they'd settled in—after he'd handed her his masterpiece of bacon and bread. He'd gone all the way to Knoxville to get good sourdough, used heirloom tomatoes, and spread on a tangy paprika mayo. He'd even brought a baggie full of plain bacon for Everest, even though the strips on their sandwiches had been maple baked. They ate in companionable silence. Forrest enjoyed Sierra's proximity and the warm, fragrant breeze coming off of the field.

Sierra looked toward him and shook her head.

"They call it the Elysian Fields. You know? From Greek mythology?"

"I've heard the name ..." Sierra trailed off. Forrest couldn't help being jealous of Everest, who had quickly finished her bacon and now rested her head on Sierra's lap, enjoying loving scratches and rubs.

"In that system of beliefs …" he began slowly, "the Elysian Fields were the final resting place of the souls of the heroic. It's been portrayed differently over the years in art. Sometimes, it's depicted with people. More often, it's depicted as a verdant landscape … always summer, always in bloom."

"Like this place," Sierra concluded.

"Exactly like this place." He nodded. "Rhododendron doesn't grow at this elevation anywhere else in the park, let alone at this time of year."

"Neither does bluebell," she observed. "That's what I always called this place in my mind—Bluebell Fields. The rhododendrons are gorgeous, but the bluebells are my favorites."

It took everything inside him not to lean over the edge of the blanket, find the perfect bluebell and cut it clean with the sharp blade of his axe before leaning back over and presenting it to her. But just because he was itching to show her how he felt didn't mean she was ready. And he'd waited too long to ruin it now.

"Know what else they say about this place?"

He liked that she'd taken off her sunglasses. He didn't like being cut off from seeing her eyes. They were dark brown indoors, but in the sun, they lightened to acorn.

"They say the reason why this place blooms is because it's hallowed ground—a resting place too ancient to date, but hidden away by magic from the rest of the park. And they say no one has ever found the way in on their own. Legend has it, you have to be shown."

"So who showed you?"

"My mom. She was like me—she grew up in the park. Back in those days parental supervision wasn't a thing."

"Who showed her?" Sierra wanted to know.

"Her father, my grandfather. And his father before him."

"Have you ever run into anybody, sitting up here?"

Forrest shook his head. "Never. Not even once. Even from a distance, I don't think anyone's ever seen me."

Sierra seemed to be trying to wrap her head around the legends. "So how many people have you brought up here?"

"One," he said honestly. "Just you."

Chapter Nineteen

SIERRA

T he passing of time was hard to keep track of. It could have been the wildflowers, hypnotizing Sierra with their magic as they swayed in the breeze. It could have been that she and Forrest had actually gotten to talking, conversation that meandered through topics —everything from how each of them had come to their professions, to which cooking shows they liked best, to what Sierra's family was like.

Forrest didn't ask the usual questions. Most men who found out she grew up with a high-profile cop for a dad forgot about Sierra and asked about him. Forrest asked deeper questions. He wanted to know what her mother did for a living and what Sierra had been into as a kid. She told him what it had been like to grow up with identical triplet brothers—from their high jinks to their protective love to the loneliness she sometimes felt at being the only girl and the only singleton. She told him how her father was a quiet man and how her love affair with the forest had come from the solo hikes her dad took her on to get away from the craziness of her brothers and their loud house.

"What about your family?" Sierra asked. "You said you had a sister. I'm guessing that'd be Naomi Winters, the librarian."

Sierra thought of the woman who she'd only seen at a distance and had studiously ignored in recent weeks as she'd conducted intermittent research. Did Forrest know anything about her hours spent in the archives room? As with Jake Stapleton, the fact of her solo research was one Sierra kept to herself. She'd never seen him and Naomi together or heard anything about them being close. But friendships and alliances in Green Valley were still a mystery to her, and Forrest seemed to have them everywhere.

"Naomi's not my sister. She's my first cousin. So are Beverly Townsend and Scotia Simmons. The three of them are sisters. Naomi's the youngest—closest to my age, but we never grew up together. They grew up a ways away, in Cedar Gap."

"Who's your actual sister, then?"

"Her name's Marlena. She's a rocket scientist." Forrest grinned and said it with pride.

"A rocket scientist?" Sierra laughed.

"Yup. An aerospace engineer for Lockheed-Martin. She lives down in Huntsville with her husband. My parents moved there three years ago to help with my nephew. She and my brother-in-law, Brandon, both work full-time so they watch Colton during the day."

For the first time all day, Forrest unpocketed his phone and thumbed around on the screen, scooting in closer to her as he did. Sierra tried to be subtle as she angled her nose to get a better whiff of his scent. An hourlong hike had done nothing to neutralize the cedar and spice of his aroma. It was all the better to enjoy, the closer he came.

"This is my mom and dad."

She wasn't surprised when he stopped his swiping and turned the screen toward her, revealing two older people equally as beautiful as him. His smoky, gray eyes, he got from his mother, but his father's were also striking—a bright, cornflower blue. His father had also passed down his strong jaw. His parents were both graying, his father the sort of salt-and-pepper that foreshadowed that Forrest, too, would age well. She imagined the elder Mr. Winters had been just as much of a troublemaker as Forrest in his day. The two shared the same half-playful, half-wicked smirk.

"You look just like them."

"Wait 'til you see Marlena."

He swiped forward, not stopping until he reached the image of another dark-haired, gray-eyed beauty, holding her wide-brimmed straw hat in place with her hand, laughing at something off camera from her seat in what looked to be a boat.

"When we were little, people thought we were twins. Even on days when my mom didn't dress us alike."

Sierra tried to imagine little Forrest in a little plaid shirt. "That sounds cute."

"Now my nephew is my little buddy," Forrest said, his voice tinged with excitement as he began to swipe his screen once again. "My mama gets me on FaceTime with him once or twice a week. I make it down to Huntsville about once a month. This is us gone camping for Memorial Day."

Speaking of little people in little plaid shirts ...

Sierra couldn't decide whether to laugh out loud or let her heart melt when she got an eyeful of Colton and Uncle Forrest, the former sitting happily on the latter's lap. They sat on a fallen tree trunk so large it was seat-height to the hulking Forrest. It looked to be late afternoon, with tents and a campfire visible in the back. Forrest looked at the camera, eyes crinkled and beaming, one steadying arm planted on the log, and the other around Colton's waist, holding him up so that he wouldn't slide off. Colton was in profile, rosy-cheeked and laughing, gazing at Forrest as if he hung the moon. In his chubby hand and slung over his shoulder was a tiny axe.

"He is absolutely adorable." Sierra said what had to be said. "And you are absolutely obsessed. Let me guess—that axe was a gift from you."

Forrest beamed down at the photo, smiling as widely as she'd ever seen him do. It was obvious he loved the little boy.

"Daggone right it was," he said with pride, taking one last look before thumbing off his phone and replacing it in his pocket. "I made that axe myself. Pear wood handle. Ten and a half inches on a five-inch aspen blade. It's just carved wood painted silver. I'll get my blacksmith to make him his first real one when he's about ten. To be used only under strict supervision, of course."

"You have your own blacksmith?"

Forrest didn't move back to where he had been seated a minute before, even though they were done with the pictures. He smirked. "You don't?"

Sierra's heart skipped again. It was the same kind of witty come-back Forrest always made—the same words that would've come out of his mouth six months or a year ago when they met. Only, now, when he said the kinds of things he always had, it felt like flirtation. And it hadn't escaped her notice he'd started sitting closer, too, or that there was something new—something *invitational*—in his tone.

"I'll bet you sleep with that thing …" Sierra quipped. If she let the silence take hold, quiet truths would show on her face.

"Leaned right up next to my bed."

"Do you shower with it, too? Polish its handle and sharpen its blade while you're watching TV?"

"Make fun all you want." He was unperturbed. "The axe is the single most useful tool ever invented."

"Tell that to my Papa Bear." Sierra leaned away long enough to reach her day pack and unclip her own knife. "I could survive in the wilderness with this bad boy for weeks."

The sheathed blade measured a good ten inches from end to

end. Sierra bounced it lightly in her hand. Forrest let out a long whistle, then stopped her motion with a warm, callused hand upon her arm.

"That is one serious blade." He sounded impressed. "May I? That is, unless you get nervous when a man wants to handle your knife ..."

Sierra hummed in mock indignance but handed it over. She half-expected him to come through with more snark, but Forrest quieted. He sat a little straighter and carefully unsheathed the blade.

"Scar Blades makes this one, right?"

It was Sierra's turn to be impressed. "And here I thought you only knew axes."

He didn't spare a glance when he replied, "I know a lot of things."

He took in all the markings and features at the same time he spouted off stats.

"Quarter-inch thick high-carbon steel ... six-inch blade ... aggressive pommel ... front finger grip ... what is that, a Tidex sheath? It looks customized."

"The fire-starter element comes in handy in my line of work."

He flipped the knife between his fingers to return it to her, handle first, then gave her back her sheath. "That is one badass knife, Sierra Betts."

She blushed, not so much from his praise as from the rumble of his voice when he took it reverent and low. But she tried to keep things light. "The pink sheath was a dead giveaway, huh?"

"Doesn't matter what it looks like. Just matters what it can do. I'll admit, if you had to survive, that knife would do you a lot of good."

"Then why do I hear a 'but'?" She slid her knife back where it belonged and fastened it to her bag.

"A good knife will keep your heart beating—food in your belly and a little protection. But an axe will keep you warm."

Sierra might have laughed if Forrest's face hadn't been so earnest.

"You said it stayed on the *side* of your bed."

Thoughts about Forrest and beds and being kept warm infiltrated her mind.

"Your knife can cut small things. And a blade like that is long enough and thick enough for you to get a good baton. But it can't cut you a big log, or build a real shelter, or butcher whatever you catch. It can't do the same thing as Old Faithful here ..."

Forrest reached toward the side of his blanket to pick up his tool.

"Please tell me you didn't name your axe."

"I name all my axes. It makes them feel special."

Sierra laughed again. "You have given this entirely too much thought."

"Go ahead. Make fun. But you'd change your mind if you were ever out in the wilderness with me. I'd have us living in the lap of luxury."

Forrest's big talk got her imagining again. Her mind flashed to the two of them, stranded alone in the woods, surviving together, making their own fire, catching their own food, and staying even warmer from body heat.

"You said you majored in psych," she baited with a sly smile. "Have you ever considered the deeper significance to why you carry that big axe everywhere?"

His eyes twinkled and the chuckle he let out was rich and deep. "Maybe," he admitted. "Have *you* ever considered the deeper significance to why you keep up that tough-girl routine? About how you want me and everyone else to think you're some sort of ball-breaker?"

She didn't answer. She wished she had. Her silence prompted him to keep talking—to say all manner of thing she wasn't ready to hear.

"I've got your number, Sierra Betts. I see what you don't want anyone to see—the part of you that's soft, that cares so much. It's beautiful."

I see what you don't want anyone to see ...

She wanted to scoff and look away and dream up some flip response. Only, his gray gaze kept her in his thrall. His irises were light in that moment, the hue of clouds after a storm chasing the darkness away with the light of the sun. They were earnest and wise and they made her want to tell him things. Some part of her wanted to tell him about Shasta and about Jake Stapleton. But a bigger part of her was just plain scared.

With her next blink, she looked away, head turned and gaze set back out on the gorgeous vista. The heat of his attention warmed her face. When he, too, turned his head and fixed his gaze back on their surroundings, she thought the moment had passed. It hadn't. His voice was softer when he spoke again.

"The first time I ever saw you was on Little Pigeon Creek, on the part that splits off after the falls. It was last summer, a few weeks after the Fourth of July."

Sierra remembered the day she'd seen him there, at the narrowest stretch of the creek. It was an off-trail shortcut park workers used to cross between different sides.

"That wasn't until September. Just before Labor Day," she corrected gently. "I never ran into you at the creek until fall."

"I said the first time I *saw* you—not the first time we met."

Heat prickled her nose. This was a confession.

"I've taken a shortcut across that creek twenty times. But when I came up on you helping that cub, I just … stopped."

Goose bumps rose on Sierra's flesh. What she had done that day had been extreme. She'd never mentioned it to a single soul. It had also been the right thing to do. A bear cub had gotten caught in fishing netting that had floated its way down the creek from some point upstream. And the cub couldn't disentangle himself.

But that hadn't been the dangerous part—the dangerous part had been the fully-grown mother bear, who saw that her cub needed help but whose every instinct should have been to keep other animals away from her baby.

Understanding the mama bear's predicament, Sierra had been cautious. She had approached slowly—carefully—hidden the knife in her pocket until she'd absolutely needed to use it to cut away the net. She'd approached the cub carefully and slowly. But when it had been time to set him free, she'd made quick work of cutting him loose.

"At first, I stayed back out of caution," Forrest continued. "I didn't want to spook the mama bear. But I got my tranq gun on her right away. I was aimed and ready to fire. And I'll admit, I was spitting mad—rehearsing in my head the earful I was gonna give you about pulling a stunt like that, alone. But then I saw how gentle you were, and how you somehow got that mama bear to believe you weren't gonna hurt her baby … it was magic. I knew then, crazy or not, I wanted to know you."

Sierra's nose prickled even more and some emotion she couldn't identify welled within her—whatever it was called when you felt completely laid bare.

"Why didn't you announce yourself, after I freed the cub and he went back to his mother?"

"Honestly? I didn't want to intrude on any of it. There was something sacred about it. But I did follow you back. You looked shaky, afterward. I wanted to make sure you got back to the station okay."

"Look," he said in a way that made her lift her gaze. "I like you, Sierra. And now that you don't hate me so much anymore, I'm hoping I've got a shot at you liking me back."

"I never hated you," she corrected. It was easier than responding to what he'd said.

His expression changed, his eyes crinkling at the corners and his lips subtly turning up.

"Then maybe you'll say yes if I ask you out on a date."

Chapter Twenty

FORREST

The dull thud of his lunch cooler bumping against the seat of his Explorer caused Forrest to look over at it for a third time. Whenever Forrest did drive the Explorer, he tended to enjoy the quiet. Compared to the creaks and rattles of his old service truck, riding in his Explorer was tranquil and luxurious. But right then, the jostling of his cooler on that front seat—and what it represented—felt loud.

I've never tried this hard. Ever.

The sentiment repeated itself in Forrest's mind, just as it had that morning when he'd been in town for a hot-towel shave and to pick up a bag of gourmet dog biscuits from Donner Bakery. He'd said it to himself three hours before, when he'd driven to the other side of the park and hiked in to pick her favorite wildflowers. And he'd sure as hell thought it an hour earlier when he'd stood inside his closet for minutes wondering what look Sierra might like.

Not that Forrest dated much, but when he did, the courting part was easy. Taking a shower, throwing on some clean clothes and picking a woman up to show her a good time had always been straightforward enough. It was the chemistry that had proven more difficult. Kelly Brighton was the closest he'd ever come to being in love. Things had ended between them when she'd left Tennessee to get her master's. That had been a full four years ago.

For the women he'd dated since, the physical part had been most of the attraction. And the promise of sex was what had gotten his heart racing when he'd thought about spending time with them. Forrest wasn't anywhere near that point with Sierra. But the thought of spending even five minutes with her—or even seeing her in passing at Greenbrier—made his smitten heart race in ways it never had.

The flip side of that was what had him worried. Going on a date with her would be a slice of heaven. Only, Forrest wanted the whole cake. For the first time in his life, he honestly didn't know whether he had a real shot. Her not being from around here meant he had no idea what kind of guy she liked to date.

It hadn't been his finest hour, but when Forrest had done a Google image search on "hot California men" no one was dark-haired and clear-eyed or bearded like him. They stood on beaches. They looked bohemian and blond. Some of them had shaggy cuts that were either obscenely expensive or born of extreme neglect. Some of them had dreads and other styles he couldn't name.

It played on another fear: California had variety in every respect; what if Sierra didn't date white guys? Their chemistry was becoming more reactive. But what if that wasn't enough? It was a positive sign she'd agreed to a date. But he felt far from winning her over.

So impress her, dumbass, he chided himself again as he turned on to the road to her cabin. It was an unsettling, unfamiliar feeling—the notion that he might not measure up. He'd never been rejected by a woman he cared deeply about. And he hadn't cared deeply about many women.

When he parked in front of her house, jitters about impressing her were replaced by anticipation of seeing her face. He opened his cooler and pulled out the flowers he'd gathered. He hadn't been able to find anything as pretty as a ribbon to tie the bunch he'd picked, but he'd found some basic twine and tried to tie it in a way that looked artistic.

Stowing the cooler in the back, he got out of the car and made his way toward the door. As he stepped up onto the porch, he heard Everest's tags. Before he could raise a hand to knock, the door swung open. And there Sierra was.

Damn.

He'd been hoping she would wear her hair down. Today, her mane sprang outward, a beautiful mess of shiny, spiral curls. It cascaded down to touch her smooth shoulders, but spared her elegant neck. Forrest already wanted to nuzzle it, just to breathe in her scent. Her eyes were dark and lovely and she wore some sort of gloss on her lips that made him want to kiss her that instant. In place of its usual smirk, her mouth was turned up in a shy smile. Her dress was made out of a gauzy fabric and had gray-on-gray leopard print. He tried to look-without-looking at the way the dip of the dress in the front flattered her bosom.

"You're as pretty as a picture."

He bent in a shallow bow at the same moment he brought her hand to his lips to kiss the tops of her fingers. He was sorry to have to let it go as he reached back to his other hand to bring forth her flowers.

"These are for you."

He watched for her reaction and saw the moment her eyes registered recognition.

"Are these from the Elysian Fields?"

It had been a week since they had been there together. A week since he'd asked her out on a date, and one of the longest weeks of his life. He'd been crazy busy closing cases in order to inch closer to the superintendent's demands. He had so many ideas, he'd jumped the gun on an outline of his drone proposal. Sierra had been busy, too, covering some of Wendell's territory during his vacation and working on her research project. It meant that Forrest had hardly seen her these past few days.

Her face broke into a wide smile as she took the proffered bouquet. The hike had been worth his time. But he just shrugged. "A woman deserves her favorite flowers."

He bent to his knee to present his final gift, which already had Everest nosing around. "These are for you, girl. I know you've got refined tastes, just like your momma."

He took the time to give Everest a proper pet and rub. She was smart and playful, and sweeter and sweeter the more he got to know her. He'd come to look forward to seeing her whenever he came to visit Sierra.

The latter waved him inside and began to move around. She untied the flowers, opening a cabinet and standing tall to retrieve a large mason jar from the top shelf. Being bent to one knee lowered Forrest's vantage point, enhancing his experience of observing her reach. The skirt of her outfit—which stopped naturally at her thigh —rode up.

No scale or measure in the world went high enough to describe how much he liked her in that dress. The pretty silver sandals she wore showed off lickable ankles and strong, lean calves he wanted to touch. In his mind, he ran the backs of his fingers up her smooth calves, ghosted their tips behind her knee, and got his palm involved by the time he made it up to her thigh, reaching beneath her skirt to give her ass a good squeeze. The impulse to abandon the date he'd worked so hard to orchestrate nearly overcame him as he indulged visions of throwing her over his shoulder and carrying her to her bedroom, caveman-style.

JFC, Forrest. Focus.

* * *

Daytime dates were underrated—thought of as inferior by those who failed to understand the art. The superiority of the 7:00 PM pickup was a common misconception. The later a man wanted to pick you up, the more likely he could only stand you in small doses. Or—if you wanted to get down to it—the more likely he was only willing to wine and dine you for so long to get to the main event.

But daytime dates were expansive. They were teeming with possibility. They knew that, if you really liked someone, what you wanted most with them was time. Forrest would take letting the day, then the evening, unfold with the right woman any time over a swift, punctuated end.

Forrest *needed* time with Sierra. For one, it took her time to drop her guard. He wasn't sure what had her so tense. It could be the investigation and what was at stake for her at work. It could be that she hadn't totally warmed up to him. Usually, an hour into their time together was when they hit their stride.

They were about an hour into their date when they arrived at Chase's farm. Forrest hadn't seen his friend in more than a year. There were no hard feelings, but they both knew why. Chase had been on the crew in Southern California. He, too, had been close to Forrest's best friend, Todd. When Forrest had called in a favor to get last-minute seats at one of Chase's famed dinners, they'd had a long overdue talk.

"What *is* this place?" Sierra asked. They had turned onto a private driveway flanked by peach tree orchards on both sides. It was late in the season, but some trees still bore fruit. They'd just driven past Chase's farmhouse, which was situated two-thirds of a mile in. It stood inside the V of a fork in the road. Forrest knew to go left, in the direction of the barn. Half a mile down, the road had been blocked off, their cue to park next to a few other cars. The stopping point was next to an old fruit stand that didn't look like much. It was the first part of the experience. Chase's dinners were extraordinarily well-done.

"You ever been to a supper club?"

Sierra shook her head.

He announced with excitement, "This is The Noble Pig."

He extricated himself from the driver's side, then jogged around to open her door, offering his hand to help her out. He put his palm on the small of her back as he walked them toward the stand. It sat at the head of a wide walking path that bisected rows of planted trees and ran perpendicular to the road where he'd left his car.

The covered shed was the kind he remembered from his childhood —open in the front with a counter separating the person buying the fruit and the person selling their wares. Only, the inside was abandoned and the shelves were bare. The counter held an octagonal, glass dispenser full of an icy drink with upturned mason jars set on a colorful kitchen towel beside. A tiny chalkboard sign next to the dispenser announced it as blood orangeade.

"This reminds me of home." Sierra smiled with delight as he poured them orangeade. He passed her her glass and they began a slow walk down the lane. Trees still heavy with fruit lent a sweet smell to the warm afternoon breeze. There wasn't another person in sight. Forrest liked how well this place felt removed from the outside world.

"Did you grow up on a farm?"

Forrest was conscious of how much he still didn't know about her. He'd gobbled up every breadcrumb she'd laid down, but he was hungry for more.

"No. But, in Sonoma County, there are farms everywhere. Vineyards. Orchards. Dairies. Even walnut groves. I used to belong to a co-op. I'd work a certain number of hours each month and then go there each week to pick up my vegetables. There was another place I went for fresh yogurt and small-batch ice cream."

He liked the reminiscent smile that brightened her face as she talked about her home. California sounded like culinary heaven. He listened intently as she told him about eating fresh oysters at outdoor tables at a fishery right on the coast; about a pig farm that sold a bacon sausage she was sure Forrest would like; and about how plenty of folks headed to local farms in the spring and summer to help with the harvest.

"We've got peach orchards in California," she was saying, bringing it full circle. "When we were little, my mom would take us picking. But I have to admit—the peaches in the South taste better."

"You must miss California," he observed.

She half-smiled. "Some things more than others. I miss In-N-Out Burger, that's for sure. I miss my family a lot. But it's good to get away. You know—to live other places and to see a bit more of the world. Do you travel?" She looked up at him as they made their slow stroll.

"Yes and no. Most of what I've seen of the U.S. has been through the window of a fire truck. I've volunteered on relief crews at least a dozen times. It's taken me to California, Washington, Kansas, Arizona, New Mexico, Colorado … I've seen those landscapes, but it's not the same as exploring a place. It's been a couple years now since I took a trip just for myself."

"Where did you go?"

His smile at the memory of the trip was bittersweet. "New Zealand. I stayed there for a month. Rented a camper van. Went to Tongariro National Park. It's one of the most beautiful places I've ever been. Before that I went to Costa Rica to see Arenal, and Hawaii to see Kilauea."

She seemed amused. "So the fire marshal is a volcanophile."

"Yeah, I've got a thing for volcanoes," he laughingly admitted. "And a bucket list for a whole lotta national parks."

She stopped in her tracks and squinted up at him. "For real?"

He blinked. "Hell yeah. I wrote out an actual list. Ngorongoro Crater, Nahuel Huapi, Tassili n'Ajjer ..."

She shook her head and smiled and wrinkled her nose all at the same time. It was cute and quirky and made him want to kiss her already.

"I wrote out an actual list, too ... of all the parks around the world that *I* want to see."

Forrest had heard people talk about their whole lives flashing before their eyes—seeing everything that had or would happen in a single, suspended moment. It had never happened to him. He'd never completely believed it had really happened to anyone else until he saw it clearly, right then and there: his life with Sierra.

In flashes in his mind's eye, they sat together at airport gates, bumped along in the back of Land Rovers in game parks, and stood, arms around one another, taking in majestic vistas. He saw them hiking in the Great Smokies, Forrest with a baby backpack on, and a chubby-armed, fat-cheeked toddler with golden-brown skin peeking out from her perch. He even saw beyond that to a bigger family—a vision of him and Sierra with three kids. He saw yet another park and a family photo, them asking a ranger in an unfamiliar uniform to photograph them for a change.

"What places are on your list?" he managed to ask through his internal chaos. The visions had finally cinched it—the sum of everything he'd been feeling for her added up to one undeniable thing. Forrest was in love with Sierra, and not the footloose and fancy-free kind of being in love. The kind where everything was at stake, because you were sure you'd found the one.

"Well, I've always wanted to go to the Azores and the Bolivian salt flats. The park in Zernez is definitely on my list."

"I've been wanting to go to Switzerland," Forrest agreed. "People say it's the cleanest air they've ever breathed."

It was subtle, but a confirming look passed over her face, as if something between them had just changed for her, too.

It didn't mean he wouldn't go slow. She was getting closer to accepting their crackling chemistry. But something told him she still wasn't ready to take everything he was ready to give.

"Why'd you stop traveling?" she wanted to know.

He ached to hold her hand as they resumed their walk. He put that thought on pause when he heard her question.

He'd thought a lot about Todd that past week. Reminiscing with Chase like that marked the first time he'd been able to think about their friend without an edge of abject pain. He wanted Sierra to know about Todd—wanted her to see that part of who he was. Still, it was too soon to bring him up.

"I used to travel with my buddy," he said simply. "His circumstances changed. And I'd rather travel with someone than go anywhere alone."

She hummed in understanding.

"A friend of mine is a travel writer," she said at the tail end of a sip of her drink. "We have an ongoing debate. He wrote this famous book on solo travel. He's this big, six-foot-tall white guy from Kansas. He waxes poetic about the self-discovery of solitary journeys. But traveling alone—and having it be safe—is a privilege I just don't have."

They reached an intersection within the orchard—another wide road like the one they were on. Before Forrest could respond, Sierra turned to the crossroad and her face transformed. The scene that Forrest had remembered didn't fail to impress.

A long, reclaimed wood dining table between a light brown and light gray in hue was set up in line with the road. The white china with silver details, vintage cutlery, and enough glassware for every form of libation sparkled in the sunlight, and the center line of the table was bursting with color thanks to vase after vase of flowers.

The table seated at least twenty. Some of their dining companions had already arrived. On the far side of the table, a bar had been set up. Folks milled around with frosty cocktails and noshed on small bites set out at bistro tables.

"Forrest, this is ..."

He was secretly pleased when she couldn't finish the sentence.

"For once, I've rendered you speechless."

But she was still too transfixed to return his snark.

Something Forrest didn't know he'd been holding, released. He did something he'd waited weeks to do: he took her hand.

Chapter Twenty-One

SIERRA

T *his feels like home.*

Sierra couldn't stop thinking and rethinking the phrase that repeated itself like a mantra as she sat next to Forrest at dinner, laughing and chatting it up with a couple they'd met who already felt like fast friends. Going to dinner parties was something Sierra had done all the time when she'd lived in California. Feeling like she was in the right place—with a whole group of people where she belonged—was something she hadn't felt in a long time.

It showed her how much she was missing—things she'd longed for so dearly, she'd never admitted how much. It made her think about the difference between a lifeline and a life. Jaya and Rick provided the former. But Forrest made her feel like she had a shot at everything else.

The heads of the table were empty but they sat right at the end, on the far side away from the bar. At some point, it became clear they had the very best seats. From their western-facing vantage point, they had an idyllic view of the sun setting over the orchard, its trajectory in perfect alignment with the road.

Dinner itself had been a languid, luxurious affair, with plate after small-plate of culinary delights. They'd been—as the name *The Noble Pig* had foreshadowed—heavy on things like short ribs, pork belly, and bacon.

The right amount of time had been allotted between each course to relax and digest. Each course was served with its own libation. Every drink had been perfectly paired with the food. Just after the host who had been emceeing the affair announced the conclusion of the meal and invited guests to proceed down the road past the bar, a man as tall and as built as Forrest came out of nowhere and patted Forrest on the back.

"Hey, man. Glad you could make it," the other man said.

The man engulfed Forrest in a tight hug. When they pulled back, they shared a long, meaningful look.

"You must be Sierra," the man finally said, turning his gaze upon her—he had striking golden eyes that seemed to light from within. Even in profile, she'd noted that he was good-looking. Standing next to Forrest now, there was a sameness about them. The dark hair, the trimmed beards, the light eyes and the fact that both men were strikingly handsome ... it was like they belonged to the same hot guy club.

"Enjoying everything so far?" He extended his hand and regarded her warmly. He wore a clean apron over black pants and a stylish version of a chef's jacket—this one short-sleeved black denim. "Forrest let me know you were a big fan of bacon. I tried to integrate it into the menu."

Sierra shot a surprised look at Forrest, still shaking the strange man's hand.

"Everything was incredible. I can't remember the last time I ate anything so good."

"I'll take that as a compliment," the man continued easily. "Forrest said you'd be hard to impress. I hear you like to cook?"

"More like Forrest likes to eat ..."

"You sure got that right," the man said. All three of them laughed.

"Sierra, this is my buddy, Chase. We go way back. And it's a good thing I know him. If I didn't, it would've taken a good six months to get into this place."

"It's about damn time you made it out here for dinner," Chase cut in. "I thought I'd have to send an engraved invitation. He came here once for a wedding a few years back, before I turned this place into what it is."

"Maybe I was waiting for the right person," Forrest put in casually at the same moment he slid his arm around Sierra's waist. It felt like that was where it belonged.

"Well, I hope y'all left room. It's sour cream pound cake with a peach wine reduction for dessert. I'll try to catch y'all later. In the meantime, enjoy."

Chase left Sierra with a congenial shoulder squeeze and gave Forrest a bro handshake with his free hand. A second later, he was gone.

"Shall we?" Forrest asked.

The other guests had begun walking, leaving them to bring up the rear.

"Do you know *everybody* in Tennessee?" she wanted to know.

They resumed their slow stroll down the lane. She didn't want to leave the pocket of his arms but liked the way he took her hand immediately as soon as he had to let her go.

"No, not everyone. Me and him grew up together. Then, we worked together. Chase is a legendary firefighter. He would've beat me out for Fire Marshal if he'd stayed in."

"Why did he decide to get out?"

Forrest looked out at the orchard in the fading light. The way he paused told her there was a story.

"Well, for one, he loves cooking. Probably should've gone to culinary school to begin with. When he got out of the fire service, that's just what he did. Even without that, it's a tough job—hard on your body, hard to maintain a relationship. And it does a real job on you, when you lose friends."

Oh.

Sierra hadn't thought of that. Some part of her still found it hard to wrap her head around—the fact that Forrest knew how to fight fires. She'd only seen him in his marshal uniform, which was similar to hers but for its color. Her most frequent reminder was the axe he carried around.

"Is that why you became a marshal?" she suddenly wanted to know.

"Indirectly, I guess ... Not from the trauma of losing people, necessarily. But because I saw better ways to fight fires—more strategic ways to approach them and to run incident command. Better ways to set up the whole system to save lives."

Sierra only had a vague understanding of how the fire service hierarchy worked. The parks system was complicated enough.

"Can you do that as a marshal or is this just a temporary stop to something bigger?"

"Something bigger," he answered easily. "The guys who do what I want to do don't have titles. They're called in wherever they're needed to write policy, develop standards, and solve the biggest problems. I don't have all the experience I need, but if things go right, I'll end up as a highly specialized internal consultant."

She replied without hesitation. "Sounds perfect for you."

She liked the sound of his chuckle. "It does?"

The sun was setting behind them and the sky was getting dark.

"Of course it does. To be a problem-solver, you have to be tenacious. Circumspect. Persistent. Willing to stick your nose everywhere it doesn't belong."

He laughed again. "Sierra Betts, if I didn't know better, I might think you were calling me a pain in the neck."

"Your words, not mine."

"Say whatever you want. My persistence got me here with you."

Sierra rolled her eyes but said nothing.

"And it was worth the wait." His voice took on a deeper note. "I've been wanting to go out with you for a long time."

His words triggered her buried longing to be uniquely desired. Some part of her had lost hope that she would ever meet a man who would make her feel treasured, and seen. It was so hard meeting men, period, a part of her had resisted growing feelings. At first, Forrest's little compliments had been hard to take because she didn't know whether she believed them. They were harder now because she did.

"I'm surprised you didn't take me axe throwing or something," she quipped instead of telling him that she'd started to feel the same about him—like she needed to see him more and more.

"Axe throwing was supposed to be our second date."

She laughed out loud because he was serious.

"What's our third date going to be?" she quizzed.

"I was thinking Dollywood. It's a real experience, especially if you've never been."

Sierra had, indeed, not been to Dollywood, though it sounded just kitschy enough that she wanted to go. She recalled something he'd said minutes earlier: some things just needed the right person or else it wasn't worth it at all.

"Sounds like you've thought this through. Do you have a whole sequence of dates for all your girls?"

He stopped in his tracks, which prompted her to do the same, then got close in a way that made her heart flutter.

"What other girls, Sierra? There's only you."

* * *

Sierra perceived the golden glow coming from above the orchard trees before they came upon the barn. Tiny lanterns lit a path between the illuminated building and the end of the lane. The twilight sky was darkening and the moon rose over wild-grown woods that stretched beyond. Music could be heard from inside.

Sierra had never thought herself underwhelmed when it came to going on actual dates. She'd been wined and dined by men she liked. She'd been yachted and hot-air-ballooned by suitors who weren't slouches, even though their appeal hadn't stuck. But nothing held a candle to dinner at sunset in the middle of an orchard. Nothing she'd ever seen was as romantic as this barn.

The approach to the double-tall, wide-open doors was strung with white lights that hung from trees, creating a canopy of magic. Inside the barn, cocktail tables took up half the floor. Place cards marked where each guest was meant to sit. Past a dance floor up on a stage sat a band.

"You like bluegrass?" Forrest helped her into her seat and pulled his own chair closer to hers.

She nodded and glanced at the band. "But I don't know it well."

Most bluegrass she was used to was up-tempo. She liked the liveliness and the sound of the fiddles and she especially liked it when people clogged. But the music the current band played was mellow. Their chairs being so close made it easy for Forrest to tuck Sierra under his arm once again. The angle should have been awkward, but she melted into him, lounging as her back was to his chest.

He told her about his father's strained relationship with his family and Sierra listened quietly. He spoke of his religious grandfather, and the rift that his own father's rebellion had caused. He told her about how the only times he ever remembered his father and grandfather not fighting was the two of them on his grandfather's porch, playing bluegrass music.

"So your father was a rebel?" Sierra asked when he came to the end of his story. She liked the vibration of his chest and she wanted him to talk again. Everything about being close to him like this felt right.

"According to my granddad, marrying an Episcopalian was the worst my dad could've done. For years before I was born, they didn't even speak. My sister being born was behind why they ever reunited. My grandma wanted to know her grandbabies."

"Your dad sounds like a romantic."

Forrest kissed her temple. "Oh, he is. Growing up, I remember him bringing my mom flowers, and them dancing in the kitchen. He'll still tell ya … marrying my momma's the best decision he ever made. Having the patience to wait for the right person is one of the biggest lessons he taught me."

"I learned the same lesson for the opposite reason." Sierra wasn't sure she had ever said this out loud. "My parents are still together, but they never really got along."

He angled himself to look down at her. "Not at all?"

"They function like a business team. They're, like, these really efficient companions who like each other. But there's no romance."

What she also hadn't said out loud was how adamant she was to not end up like her parents. And how, the older she got, the firmer she was in her decision not to settle. In her heart of hearts, she hoped it could happen for her one day like it did in the movies. Her biggest fear was tepidly ever after.

"Hey. You want to get out of here?" Sierra didn't mind his subject change. Mention of her parents had turned her thoughts dark. "Unless you want dessert …" he hedged.

"I'm stuffed like a turkey," she admitted.

"There's a place I used to go when I was a kid. If we're lucky, there'll still be lightning bugs. I bet our dessert'll be waiting right here for us when we come back."

When they emerged from the barn on the other side, the air was a degree cooler. Sierra's dress was light and Forrest seemed to sense she had a chill. They walked at a pace that allowed for a comfortable stroll, even with his arm around her. As they walked down a path that said "Private," Sierra started to see lightning bugs here and there.

They hadn't strayed too far from the barn when they reached a tall oak that sat at the border of a pond. The sun behind them was almost set and the oak tree had a swing. The chirruping of crickets overtook the faintest hints of bluegrass still floating in the air. Forrest stopped just short of the swing.

"We don't have lightning bugs on the West Coast," Sierra said in a whisper, as if speaking loudly would ward them away. The more her eyes adjusted to the darkness, the more dots of glowing light came into view. She looked around herself as they seemed to float into all of the space around them. Delight prickled her cheeks and she felt herself smile. When she brought her gaze back up to Forrest's, his was fixed upon her.

"They're magical."

She half-expected him to come in again with his low, quiet voice —to tell her another story about growing up in Tennessee—maybe even to tell her a story about having been a kid catching fireflies on this very pond. Only, he didn't have a talking look. And that smirk he sometimes wore had disappeared.

"I want more with you, Sierra."

He took a step closer and she forgot to breathe. He threaded his fingers in hers.

"One night isn't enough … I haven't even kissed you yet and—"

His eyes smoldered. She had known this moment was coming. A kiss had hung between them, suspended and waiting, all night.

"Why don't you?"

Sierra remembered her own high standards. Every cell in her body had screamed all night that she belonged with Forrest Winters, but she needed a man who could kiss. Not an okay kisser or a passable kisser.

Someone who kissed so good, she'd want to kiss him for the rest of her life.

Forrest wasted no time circling a possessive arm around her waist, as if the night itself would steal her if he didn't hold on. His beard was soft as it grazed her cheek. But there was something raw and animalistic about the way he avoided her lips at first, nipping her shoulder and inhaling deeply as he ran his nose up the column of her neck.

"Sierra ..." he whispered.

Only, it wasn't really a whisper, except for the fact that it was quiet. It was desperate and hungry and it held an undeniable truth. It was abundantly clear in the seconds before his lips touched hers that she had been wrong about everything. She had sorely underestimated what existed between her and this man.

God, yes, all the good parts inside her murmured when his lips touched hers.

Forrest Winters didn't just kiss with his lips—he kissed with his whole body, holding her in a way that pressed them together, some-how, from head to toe. Forrest had been easy with her that night—gentlemanly—making clear his own affections but letting things go at her pace, conscious of some unspoken boundary that whatever happened, happened when she was ready.

But now that she'd made it clear that she was ready for that kiss, he didn't hold back in giving it to her. Forrest's kiss was hungry, like no matter how much he drank her in, he couldn't get his fill. His tongue stroked hers slowly and deeply, pulling her impossibly closer with the arm that was at her back. It made her feel utterly content and like she was crawling out of her skin all at the same time.

The half of her that didn't want to be cocooned in his fold forever wanted to untuck his shirt from his jeans and bring her fingers up to fan out over what she was sure were fantastic abs. The short moan he let out a second before they pulled apart was nearly as sexy as the kiss itself.

"Sweetest thing I've tasted all night," he murmured, a little out of breath.

It was a very Forrest thing to say. Only, his face didn't register the playful look he got when he made light. In all her years of kissing, Sierra had never shared a kiss like this. Something told her that Forrest hadn't either.

"Got room for seconds?" she asked, aware in some distant corner of her mind that tomorrow would bring a reckoning. Admitting how actively and desperately she wanted something with Forrest was an overdue task. But right then, right there, she had him in the flesh. Right then was a time for action.

"Hell, yeah," he agreed before swooping in for another.

* * *

Tell me everything. Spare no detail.

Sierra burst out laughing the moment she got an eye full of Rick's text, then second-thought the outburst after realizing that she was quite hung over. She had the day off, an ideal circumstance given that it had been a late night. After kissing under the big oak tree for a good, long while, she and Forrest had made their way back to the barn, where they ran into Chase again.

Sierra had always assumed the guys she saw Forrest with around town and around the park were his friends, but she'd seen a different side of him the night before. He and Chase were close. Hearing them talk had clued her into dimensions of Forrest's life she had never imagined. Undoubtedly, Sierra would spend her day off not only recalling every lick of his kiss and every sweet and sumptuous moment of their date, but every tiny little brushstroke that had painted a more complete picture of him.

He passed the kissing test.

The memory of said kissing gave her body a tingle. She bit her lip against a smile as she tapped the message out. It was a swollen lip, by the way. That was how much they'd enjoyed themselves. It was another mark in his favor: not only did his timing and technique make Forrest a master of the lost art—she could tell that he really liked doing it.

What other tests did he pass?

Even though they were just texting, she could hear Rick's voice in her mind. She had a good guess, too, as to the expression on his face.

He got an A in seeing me home safely and bidding me goodbye at the door like a gentleman.

Rick's response was three eye roll emojis. The bouncing dots that had begun on the next line of the chat window told her he was typing again.

All right. Just remember. That "no sex 'til the third date" crap is for people who secretly hate themselves and resent their bodies.

Now it was Sierra's turn to roll her eyes. Rick was the poster child for sex-positivity.

She tapped back, *I'll keep that in mind. Call me this week for drinks.*

With that, she got out of bed, brushed her teeth, made her coffee, and swallowed three Advil down. As she went through all the motions, she couldn't help but relive every moment of what could never be erased in her mind as the perfect date.

You got what you wanted, a voice inside her whispered. It was an unfamiliar voice. The one that often spoke to her was grim—some inner manifestation of all her fears. It felt as if—for months—petty annoyances and disappointments had loomed. Only, this new voice inside her rang of hope.

Sierra was half a cup of coffee into meditating on that thought, seated outside on her back patio, looking at the creek below. When her phone rang, her heart gave a flip. Instantly, she hoped it was Forrest.

"Hey, Jaya ..." she answered after the caller ID confirmed that it wasn't. Her friend didn't bother with a greeting. Jaya's excitement was as palpable as the enthusiasm in Rick's texts.

"Well? How'd it go? Where'd he take you? Tell me you took my advice and wore the gray romper. It makes your boobs look hot."

The table in the orchards had been so picturesque, Sierra hadn't been able to resist snapping a picture. Forrest had already texted Sierra the selfie he'd taken of both of them in the barn. It had captured a perfect view of the dessert table and the band setting up the stage beyond.

"Hang on ..." she instructed Jaya, and took a second to send over both. "All right ... I just texted you pictures."

Sierra had to hold her phone away from her ear a minute later when Jaya screamed, "Holy shit! He took you to The Noble Pig?"

"You've heard of it?" Sierra was surprised.

"You haven't?"

"His friend owns the place. I mean, he's the chef and that's his orchard. His name is Chase. He used to be a firefighter."

If Sierra wasn't mistaken, the words that issued from under Jaya's breath were, "Lucky bitch."

"So ... what was he like? Was it awkward?" Jaya asked.

That had been Sierra's fear—that however flirtatious their banter in the park, it wouldn't translate out of the office. She couldn't admit how wrong she had been. After only a brief period of awkwardness once they'd got to talking, she'd felt like she could talk to him forever.

"Just the opposite," she told Jaya. "Forrest is funny. He's been places and done things and has all these strange, interesting hobbies. Like, he goes ice caving. You know, where you go snow hiking and instead of bringing a tent, you bring a shovel, then you dig out an ice cave to sleep?"

"Sounds awesome." Jaya's voice had gone a bit flat, as if ice caving didn't sound awesome. Only it did sound awesome.

"Yeah. I know," Sierra answered dreamily.

"So … how'd you leave things?" Jaya prodded.

"He told me he'd call."

"Uh-uh," Jaya protested. "No waiting around for him to call you. This is the twenty-first century. If you want to see him, make it happen."

Jaya and Rick had a lot of opinions for friends who didn't totally have their own love lives figured out. Sierra was about to say as much when a call came in on the other line.

"Shit. I gotta go. Call you later?"

"It's him, isn't it?" Jaya demanded.

"I'll call you back," Sierra said hastily so she could click over before missing the call. Just before she did, she thought she heard Jaya murmur "lucky bitch" again.

"Hey …"

Her voice was much softer than it had been just seconds earlier, with Jaya.

"Hey, gorgeous," came his deep voice, playful and flirtatious as ever, but sincere. "You sleep all right?"

She realized with alarm that she'd never talked to him on the phone. They'd texted before but that was it. As she listened to the deep richness of his disembodied voice, she tried to imagine his physical surroundings, what his house might be like, and what he might be doing.

"Like a rock. Though, I don't think I'll need to eat again for a month."

"That's a shame …" he said in a slow drawl. "I was hoping to entice you. Let me take you out again."

Chapter Twenty-Two

FORREST

"Are you sure we shouldn't be taking the lesson?"

Sierra eyed the group of new throwers who stood a few lanes over from her and Forrest at Knoxville Axe. An instructor stood with his back to the targets and a dozen people crowded around him as he spoke.

"Not for you," she said quickly. "Obviously, for me ..."

When he turned back to her, she looked nervous and held the store-issued axe awkwardly.

"I mean, what if I rear back wrong and hit my spine with the blade?"

Forrest put his hand on the small of her back and circled her in a way that turned the angle of her body away from the primer they weren't taking.

"Me not wanting you to develop bad habits is exactly why we're not over there with them. You'll get your first axe-throwing lesson from me."

From what Forrest could tell, lessons of the date-night variety were dumbed down to the simplest terms. But Sierra deserved an expert lesson and Forrest was just the one to help her build the foundations of a strong technique. There was something else he didn't like about the group lesson: Forrest had seen that instructor in action; he didn't want that guy's paws all over her.

He lined her up to the target. "Now, here's how to hold your stance."

Forrest didn't mind coming in close to her and touching her body —squaring her hips and showing her exactly where her throw should be coming from: her core.

"If you're throwing with two hands, you take two steps. One hand gets one step. You'll know you've arched back the right amount when you feel it in your abs. If you always check your blade side and take it back slowly, then you're never gonna hit anything you shouldn't."

Forrest stepped back then to let her try her first throw. The narrowing of her eyes told him that she'd focused. He didn't continue to coach her—just let her come into it in her own time. When she threw, she put muscle behind it, and the axe spun fast.

Instead of watching where the axe flew, he kept his gaze upon her face. From her posture and alignment alone, he'd bet that she'd hit within the target. What he wanted to see was the moment when she realized she'd nailed it.

He couldn't help but laugh when her eyes lit up and she clapped her hands together, bouncing on her feet a little as she took in where the axe had hit. His chest got tight in the best kind of way when she looked back over at him to see his reaction.

"Did you see that?" She motioned to the target and beckoned him to look. He was impressed to find that she'd made it into the circle second-closest to center. Stepping into his space, she circled her arms around his waist and leaned up to kiss his chin.

"See? You're a natural." He brought her closer with the arm that wasn't holding his axe.

Sierra stayed there for a second that felt too short, looking between him and her handiwork before giving him a squeeze and beginning to walk forth. It frightened him a little—how quickly he'd grown addicted to pulling her body close. It felt like she belonged in his arms.

"Here, let me show you the safest way to take that out."

In the few steps it took them to get to the target, Forrest thought ahead to more times like this. He couldn't wait to get Sierra her first axe. He knew just what style would suit her for her everyday tool and he had ideas about specialty models. Not for the first time, he'd gotten carried away at the thought of matching axes with engraved handles: his and hers.

"It's a little unfair, don't you think?" Sierra mused after they'd unseated the axe and were making their way back to the throwing line. "You're kind of a ringer. Shouldn't they handicap your score?"

After the lesson, there would be a tournament, couple against couple.

"Don't be fooled." Forrest looked back toward the people taking the lesson. "My guess would be some of them boys have thrown an axe once or twice. No man comes axe throwing unless he thinks he can look good in front of his girl."

"You trying to impress me?"

She slid her free arm around his waist and he leaned down to kiss the tip of her nose.

"Always."

* * *

The next few days took Forrest to the Carolina side, where he also had jurisdiction. In focusing on the arson investigation, he'd neglected the southernmost areas of the park. What they had unearthed thus far—particularly the lead about someone buying fire retardant from Eager Beaver's and the proximity of the fires to certain roads—pointed to whoever was doing this coming from the Tennessee side.

Forrest had paid Stokes a visit—asking him officially as the fire marshal to notify him of anyone who came in to buy fire retardant of any kind. He'd also asked Stokes to look back on his point-of-sale system to see whether anyone who had bought it recently had paid with credit. Records showed all transactions had been in cash. The purchase dates were all over the place but were still in range for the crimes. Stokes said he didn't recognize anyone who had bought as being from Green Valley.

By the time Thursday rolled around, having a day off felt good. He'd scheduled his to line up with Sierra's. Given that weekends were prime tourist time, she only had every third one free. It meant if they wanted to see one another, it would be in the evening or at odd times of day.

"This isn't Dollywood," Sierra quipped as he helped her out of the car in front of an industrial building in the artistic area of Knoxville.

"Dollywood's gonna have to wait." He closed his car door and kept hold of her hand as he walked her in. The sign wasn't visible from the street, but as they approached the door via a long ramp connected to the sidewalk, it finally came into view: a chalkboard easel that said, "Welcome to Blow this Bitch Glassworks."

The owner, Samantha Mandell, was a noted artist in Knoxville. In every photo he'd ever seen, she wore a heavy apron and bare arms that showed off her tattoos. Samantha Mandell also took commissions and had an outstanding portfolio. The second he'd gotten the idea to have something one of a kind made for Sierra, Samantha and her store had come to mind.

As they made their way inside, Sierra took her fill of their surroundings—all the various ovens and kilns. The place looked empty at first glance. Forrest scanned the space for Samantha, whom he'd spoken with twice.

"You must be Sierra," came a voice from behind.

"Sierra, this is Samantha." Forrest still hadn't filled her in, but Sierra shook Samantha's hand and went along, exchanging pleasantries. There was some energy about them that felt the same. They were both confident women who wore their power like a badge. You could feel it the second they walked into a room.

Forrest was still gratified by shreds of evidence that he'd earned Sierra's trust. It had only been two weeks since they'd sat together in a meadow and he'd asked her out on a date. Things were moving quickly—faster than he'd dared to hope after so many months trying to get her to at least not hate him. People said the honeymoon never lasted, but the way she made him feel didn't feel like it would ever end.

"I told Samantha I broke your bear statue. The one I offered to replace. You said it was one of a kind. I can't un-break it, but I thought you might like something new."

It had been months since he'd brought it up, but every time he had, she'd shot it down. He'd once thought it was pride, but maybe it was habit. Sierra was so busy taking care of the animals in her territory, the park visitors, Everest ... she wasn't used to people doing for her.

She'd better get used to it.

The quiet way she thanked him with her eyes felt like progress, as did the squeeze of her hand. Samantha motioned for them to follow her by stepping farther inside.

"I can show you my book of past designs. Or, if you tell me why you might like, I can tell you what I think I can do."

Sierra didn't hesitate. "This may be a tall order, but could you do another bear?"

Sierra and Samantha sat at a table. Samantha sketched and they both created and conceptualized. They had determined that the figure would be clear glass with the color of the bear represented in ribboned threads.

"I'm guessing you want the bear to be black?" Samantha looked up from her sketch to confirm.

"Actually … the original bear was a grizzly. It's the state animal of California. Back home, most of the bears are brown. I know there are only black bears in the Great Smoky Mountains National Park."

"You know …" Samantha mused. "I wouldn't have to do just one color. I could ribbon in either color, or both."

Sierra seemed to like the idea. Forrest liked it, too. He didn't want to think about her ever going back to California, but, if she did, he liked the idea that her figurine would be half black bear.

A few minutes later, the design plan was set and their only job was to watch Samantha work. They stayed at a distance as she talked them calmly through each step. Sierra stood, her back to his front, with his arms around her waist as they watched the spellbinding process of Samantha shaping and cutting the glass, spinning and molding and tweezing until before them stood a gorgeous bear.

Watching Samantha's artistry wasn't the only thing that had Forrest under a spell. Sierra was magnetic. Spending every free moment in surrender had become an addiction. Increasingly, he needed her nearby to feel balanced and complete. Only, each day they spent together nagged at something more. Each day, their bodies whispered insistently to one another. It thrummed between them, even there.

He wanted to turn her in his arms and kiss her then, with all the love and passion he had not yet spoken aloud. Even as Samantha delivered the bear carefully to the final kiln, and told Sierra to pick it up in no sooner than three days—the time it needed to cool—the current he felt between them didn't break.

"You like your bear?" His arm was slung around her as they stepped back into fresh air and walked together down the ramp.

"Forrest … I love it. I don't even know how to thank you for a gift like this."

He stopped just short of his Explorer and switched to the voice he used when he wanted her to know he was serious.

"Me breaking your statue was weighing on me. I want things between us to be clear."

"My statue had sentimental value," she admitted at the same moment they reached his Explorer. He had arrived at her side and she leaned with her back against the door. "It was kind of a good luck charm. But it only cost about fifteen bucks. Samantha's work … I'm afraid to ask."

Forrest came in so close he nearly had her pressed up against the car. He was listening, but it couldn't hurt to get her in position for a kiss.

"The money's not the important part. The important part is not having anything come between us. That's how I want to treat you, Sierra. You're special to me."

* * *

Back in Green Valley and in the park, no one had caught on to the fact that they were dating. Forrest preferred it that way. Such things had to be handled carefully at work. It wasn't himself he was worried about. Office romances played out differently for women than they did for men. It was something they'd have to talk about, once things were more defined.

At the moment, they were still in the "see each other as much as possible and neck like teenagers" phase. They'd gone to the poker game that Tuesday, kept up the ruse all night, then indulged in a marathon make-out session after he'd seen her back to her car. She had undoubtedly caught on to the effect her body had on his. The night before, on her sofa, she'd brought him within an inch of his restraint. It was possible she was trying to kill him.

It was supposed to have just been takeout and movies. The "pajamas" she'd worn had been gray cotton shorts with a cut that showed a hint of the curve of her cheeks. The delicate white and gray camouflage V-neck tee that she'd had on was made of a sheer fabric you could practically see through.

Forrest was beginning to think the outfits she wore were meant to entice him. He didn't want to be presumptuous, but … damn. If she wanted his attention, she had it. At that very moment, his attention should have been on Superintendent Ed Ellis, who sat three seats down from him at the conference table. Wednesday morning was when he met with his leadership team. As usual, pressing matters of park safety and efficiency were under discussion.

Laptops were open. The superintendent ran through performance statistics on the screen. He was all business—a far cry from the Ed Ellis who showed up when Forrest took him out for fishing on his boat. Flash memories of being horizontal on Sierra's sofa the night before with her body pressed against his were making it hard to follow along.

"How's your incident rate?" Ed wanted to know.

The question was directed to Frank. Forrest should have been mentally rehearsing his own answers for the moment he would be called on—a moment that would come too soon. Difficult, when thoughts of Sierra inhabited every corner of his mind. He couldn't even resist chatting with her intermittently, right there in the middle of his meeting, as they volleyed back and forth flirtatious texts.

We should make movie night a regular thing.

The message from Sierra had popped up on his desktop through his messaging app. It wasn't unusual for Forrest to jot down notes. Feigning a desire to note whatever statistic Ed had just popped off, he wrote back to Sierra.

Maybe next time we'll even watch the movie.

Forrest commanded his face to remain neutral as he issued the response. He shifted his attention to Frank, who was going on about his budget woes.

"I don't even have the right amount of budget to begin with," Frank argued for the second time in two weeks. "The multiplier on my baseline is *official* visitors. What's using up my resources now are the people who don't even get counted. The ones who come in illegally, at night, to misuse the resources in the park."

"How's the arson investigation coming?" Ed asked next.

Forrest's ears perked up to hear Frank's answer. And it didn't escape him, the language Ed had used in mentioning it. Ed had called it arson. Forrest wondered whether Frank would correct Ed and say out loud that he had overruled Forrest's finding. It was a detail Ed would have been privy to if he'd read the report. But who knew whether he had?

"Grissom's running the investigation. No leads, but it's been hard to profile suspects in the absence of witnesses. At this point, five weeks have passed since the last fire. It's positive that we've gone a spell without any more."

"You seeing anything out there, Forrest?" Ed wanted to know.

"Like Frank said, nothing new. I've lent a little support as people on Frank's team have come to me with questions."

"Good." Ed looked back at Frank. "Wildfires are still the biggest issue for the guys upstairs. You want budget? You get me that arsonist. Then we'll talk."

No sooner did Ed move on to Q4 planning than did Forrest's pocket vibrate, sending his gaze flying to his laptop screen to read his next text.

Last night was just the previews.

Forrest had been walking around with a semi for most of the morning, but her text made him twitch.

I'd watch that trailer again, he tapped back with a quickness that matched his eagerness to be all wrapped up in her.

You bring the popcorn, I'll bring the candy, she came back.

His pants became even tighter and he was glad the meeting was far from over. It would take more than a few minutes to calm himself down.

When's showtime? I'll be there, he wrote back, praying she didn't have plans with Jaya or Ricky or anyone else.

Tonight. Drop by any time.

* * *

"You are in so much trouble."

Forrest practically growled the words the second Sierra opened the door. He was cleaned up and showered, his hair still a little wet given a combination of his haste to get out the door and the speed with which he'd taken the drive. Before leaving, he'd plucked from his shelf a jar of dry popcorn kernels. As he stood at her door, it sat cradled in his hand.

He saw the second he laid eyes on her that her flirtation hadn't been just flirtation—that her afternoon banter hadn't been a tease. Somehow, he was glad it hadn't happened the night before. Lots of things seemed like a good idea in the heat of the moment, when one thing led to another. But he liked that it would happen this way, liked that with each taste after delicious taste, neither could get their fill.

What he wanted to do was divest each of them of their clothing as soon as possible, leaving a trail en route to her bed. There were other possibilities, in case they didn't make it that far: the zig-zag rug in front of her fireplace … with her up on the kitchen counter … bent over the sofa … against the wall. Yes, Forrest had thought about this moment, many, many times.

If things went as he hoped, they would claim every surface in both of their houses. But, for the time being, he was too far gone for that level of creativity. The bed seemed like the very best place to splay her out—to drink her in with his eyes, and touch, and taste every unexplored inch of her body.

Forrest put the popcorn kernels down on the key table next to the entryway at the same time he used one arm to sweep her up behind her thighs, leaving her jackknifed over his shoulder. She let out a surprised little hoot as he kicked the door closed behind them, made the short walk to her room and deposited her onto the bed.

Far be it from Sierra to take anything lying down. Though he'd set her down on her back, Forrest got only a second or two of that vision: her chest heaving and her organized mess of coils splayed out to halo her face. Soon enough, she was on her knees on the mattress, beginning to undress him.

He was already on the edge of overwhelming sensation when her fingers clawed at his shirt. Her palms grazed his hips, then his ribs, to take the garment off. Something stronger than pride swelled within him when she full-out paused to feast on his midsection—to run her fingers from the top of his happy trail to his chest. It was a slow, tactile perusal, one she indulged in for seconds after she'd let his shirt fall away.

Her warm breath fanned over his chest a second before her teeth teased his nipple. His head lolled back and he let out a short groan. He reached forward to brace himself by cuffing his hands around her slender shoulders. When he did, she lifted her gaze. They hadn't even kissed and she made no attempt to. She also had yet to speak a word.

Forrest *couldn't* speak given what she was doing. Her hands had made their way back downward and she was unzipping his pants. Still standing, he did a little shimmy to help them fall. He was still kicking off his shoes and toeing off his pants when her hand smoothed over his erection. From outside of his boxer briefs, she began to stroke his cock.

What happened next was some version of what had been happening between them from the beginning—something playful and competitive and satisfying that went back and forth. Each pushed the other to the edge with some sly, sexy maneuver, only to be one-upped in short order.

From her stroking him had come him flipping her around, relieving her of her shirt and shorts, getting her on her hands and knees and stroking down her back. Among things he had figured out about her was that her spine was an erogenous zone. She practically purred with his featherlight touches. He could smell her arousal when, near the end of his teasing, he'd bent to kiss the twin divots near the small of her back, just above her panty line.

Forrest knew she was his match in every way when she pulled an advanced maneuver, flipping them over in some swift, singular move-ment that found her straddling his hips. His legs were bent at the knee and his feet dangled off the side of the bed. She was reverse on him, her back to his front. Her pulling his cock out of his briefs and bringing it into her mouth for a long, deep kiss while giving him a close-up view of her backside was the sexiest thing that had ever happened to him in his life.

He was so much closer than he wanted to be to blowing that he only let that go on for a minute. Soon, he sat upright on the bed. She turned to face him as they kissed and necked intensely, her legs wrapped around his waist. Quiet moans and pants from each of them punctuated the motion of their bodies and drew at the tension in the room.

"Half of everything I want to do with you next involves a condom," he growled into her ear.

She pressed them together harder.

"Only half?"

Her remark was all it took for him to lift her off of his lap and shuck his final garment: his boxers. By the time he turned back to

Sierra, her clothes were off, too. He wished that there were three of him—one to palm her heavy breasts and suck her nipples, one to bury his face between her legs and one to ply her from one position to the next as he buried his cock inside.

He must have been slow to the uptake, because she took the condom out of his hand, ripped open the foil wrapper and began to roll it on. Her hand smoothing over his shaft repeatedly as her opposite fingers held the tip secure made him delirious with lust.

At that point, both had migrated back to the middle of the bed and faced one another on their knees. How did he want her right then? More importantly, how did she want him? He hooked an arm across her lower back, pulled their bodies together and bent in for a searing kiss.

When they broke apart, she whispered, "Dealer's choice ..."

Chapter Twenty-Three

SIERRA

T he unusual sensation of someone climbing into bed with her coaxed Sierra from a pleasant state of half-sleep, encouraging her to wonder how Everest had learned how to pull the covers aside. When she was tucked under a beefy arm and pulled close, she remembered the night before.

Forrest.

Her mind remembering led to her body remembering, which led to her notice of a very pleasant ache between her legs, half-sore from use, half-throbbing for even more.

Still incomplete in her coherence, she snuggled closer on instinct and smiled at the sensation of a kiss to her forehead. What time was it? More importantly, did she have to work today?

When she cracked an eye open, the first thing she saw was a smooth, amazing bicep. It catapulted her memory to a far less innocent series of thoughts. She and Forrest in her bedroom. That same bicep as his arms had held on to her headboard and she'd ridden him from above. That bicep across her chest, holding her in place in some variation of reverse cowgirl.

"Morning," she murmured, finally peering up at him. It was past dawn but the sky through the window hadn't quite achieved the full light of day.

"Mornin', sunshine," he greeted.

Moving her body enough to look at the clock would have meant leaving his protective hold.

"What time is it?"

"Almost seven," he replied. It was an hour and a half past when she normally woke up. "I think I tired you out."

Shit. Everest.

"I gotta feed—"

"Your dog. Already walked her. Coffee's on. Say the word and I'll put breakfast on the griddle."

"Either you're the perfect man or you're an overachiever," she quipped.

"Just strategic." He kissed her temple again. "It'll leave us time for another round."

His words were all it took for Sierra to fully awaken—for the rest of her senses to remember the details. Only, the way he said it took her mind to a different place. Not to what part of hers had been the perfect fit with what part of his, and what had felt like the perfect friction. It was the deeper parts that stuck out to her then.

The desperation in his voice as he'd whispered her name ... how tightly he'd held on to her when he came ... light-gray eyes that smoldered like hot charcoal with a layer of ash—calming from the looks of it but hot and dangerous inside ...

True, it had been a long time. But not so long that Sierra had forgotten the difference between sex starvation and something more. Something sacred had passed between them. It felt insane to even think it.

She and Forrest were falling in love.

This time, when he kissed her, his lips were no less hungry, but they did take their time exploring her skin. He brushed her wild hair aside and worshipped her neck, her arms, her shoulders. As he spooned her from behind, he used one smart finger, stroking her from inside, but keeping her at the edge, extending things for her, even though his erection was insistent.

By the time he slid the condom on, she was close to begging him to let her come. He flipped them so that he was on bottom and lifted her above him like she weighed nothing, positioning himself at her entrance. They both let out sighs of relief as she sank down.

Everything about Forrest was hot. He was long and thick and rock hard. He made the manliest, sexiest sounds and sometimes he cursed. It was clear that something about Sierra made him war with his self-control. Watching it slip and seeing him shatter to pieces was a beautiful thing to watch.

* * *

"Do I get to see you later?" Forrest asked fifteen minutes after they had collapsed back onto the bed, once again exhausted and spent. Forrest didn't have to clock in, per se, but Sierra did. The moment was drawing near when they would have to get up.

"Today's my weekly with Olivia. She's gonna ask whether there are any leads on the fire. I feel like I'm running out of things to say. I'm starting to think Frank's right. Maybe this guy's just too hard to catch."

"Giving up isn't an option."

There was an unexpected sort of edge to his voice—a resoluteness she didn't expect while lounging with him like this. Sierra knew the case meant a lot to him, and he'd told her about his grant. But she was starting to think it was time they both came up with a Plan B.

"Well …" Sierra trailed off. "If we still have no leads, we might not have a choice."

"There are more stones to turn. I still haven't talked to the Wraiths."

"You haven't?"

She'd thought he would have by then. She'd figured he just hadn't told her about it, lest it lead to another fight. She was certain, if he turned up anything, he'd tell her about it and deal with her sour grapes. He'd always struck her as the "ask for forgiveness, not permission" type.

"No …" he began slowly. "I haven't talked to the Wraiths. Remember? You asked me not to. I figured I'd wait. See if anything else panned out. But now that it hasn't, it's time."

"So we turn over the last stone," she agreed, not wanting to end a night as perfect as the one they'd spent together by bringing up logistics. "And if nothing's underneath, we figure out our next move."

Forrest quieted, which she took for acquiescence. Aware that their time was winding down, she let herself melt more deeply into his arms.

"I used to have a friend …" Forrest began a minute later in a voice so cryptic she couldn't help but to tease.

"A lady friend?" she asked in a playful voice.

His returning tone was graver than the one he'd used before.

"A best friend. His name was Todd," he said after a long second and in a choked sort of voice that chased all playfulness away. "You asked me once why this is so serious for me."

The relaxation she'd felt moments before was replaced with a sort of instant sadness. His palm came around to stroke her hair and he kissed her forehead, as if he sensed her distress.

"I'm doing this because of him. Two years ago, I lost him in Southern California. I lost him in an arson fire."

Forrest had to be referring to the ones that had burned in Ojai. They had blazed so hot and so long and so high, they'd leveled four hundred square miles. Homes had been destroyed. Lives had been lost, both from fire service and civilians. It was booked as Southern California's deadliest fire on record.

Extricating herself from her ensconced position, Sierra sat up and turned to face him. She was certain pity was the last thing he wanted. But she felt for him, and those fires had been recent enough that his grief would still be fresh.

"Oh, Forrest ... I'm so sorry."

He took her hand in his, playing with her fingers for a minute before drawing it to his lips and kissing the back of her hand.

"It's time to get more aggressive," he stated. "Do a few things we wouldn't have been willing to do before. We can't let this guy go."

She nodded. "Okay."

"Are you with me on this?" When he finally flipped his gaze back up to hers, his eyes were as soft and light as the gray of a dove.

She choked back her own tears before saying, "Yes."

* * *

Sierra had been thoughtful all morning as she took her walk in the woods, making good time despite her mental haze. Reliving every hot, delicious moment with Forrest took up no small amount of her energy. Neither did Forrest's story about Todd. It explained his motivations, from getting funding for his ideas, to finding the arsonist, to teaming up with the one other person with a sense of urgency around finding the culprit. Hearing that story renewed her sense of purpose, even though there hadn't been a break in the case.

That was part of why she found herself trekking again toward Jake's camp. She'd been less worried about his safety the week before last, when they'd seen some rain. But the fire level warning had gone up again that morning. The only thing she'd made less progress at than solving the case was in getting Jake Stapleton out of the park.

"You've been avoiding me," she accused lightly, approaching

from a roundabout way. Even with that, Jake had heard her coming. He'd been nowhere to be found the last three times she'd looked for him over the past week, though the condition of the campsite spoke of his well-being and health.

Jake looked around himself and motioned to all the markings of his camp, giving a small, crooked little smile.

"Technically, I've been avoiding everybody."

Something struck her then—a thing that hadn't before: Jake Stapleton had charm. It was understated and expressed in an entirely teenage way. Maybe that was why Sierra hadn't seen it. His handy answers and calm manner had disarmed her—turned her into a sympathizer. She still was. Only, she'd given him too much leeway. And her not knowing his whole story had to stop and it had to stop now.

"I need you to tell me what you're really doing here."

Sierra said it bluntly. No pussyfooting. No messing around.

"I can't tell you." It was said with a resolve that surpassed his years. "I can't tell anyone."

This was the part that always got to Sierra—the part that might even have explained why she went so soft on Jake: there wasn't an ounce of pretense in anything he said. If anything, his proclamations were raw—and wrenching. They made her trust the judgment of an eighteen-year-old boy more than she should.

"I've always respected your privacy," Sierra pointed out. "I've brought you food and looked in to make sure you're okay. I should've reported you weeks ago, but I didn't. I took a risk on you, at the peril of it costing me my job."

"And I'm grateful," he came right back. "But I didn't ask you to do any of those things."

She didn't mention that he'd wheedled his way out of half a dozen requests for him to find a different situation. The thing was, coming up against this wall with him didn't make her want to throttle him like it usually did when she locked horns with everyone else. It made her want to give him a hug.

"Look," she said instead. "I know what it means to feel alone. But there's a difference between feeling alone and truly being it. Alone would be you needing a safe place and nobody coming to your corner. It would be me using my authority to make things worse instead of protecting you. You never asked me directly to help. But you and I both know you're not allowed to be in this park. I'm sorry you can't see me for what I'm trying to do. I covered for you because I care— because I think you wouldn't be here if you weren't better off here than in town. I've stood behind you—and in support of you—all along."

When Sierra came to the end of her statement, she was slightly out of breath—because the speech she'd just delivered to Jake was a speech that could have been delivered to Sierra, herself. It could have been a speech delivered to her straight from Forrest's lips. Sierra had been just as stubborn in accepting his help and in seeing him as a benevolent force. The déja vu of it all gave her a moment of pause.

"Did you commit a crime?" Her voice was pleading when she finally chimed in with another question. He hadn't answered her earlier ones out loud. "If there's something you think you can't tell me —because I'm a park ranger—I grant you temporary immunity."

This was where things got tricky. Because Sierra didn't believe Jake Stapleton had committed a crime, and she needed the truth in order to figure out his presence inside the park. The problem was, if he *had* committed a crime—and he admitted it—she would have to choose between how to help him personally versus how to see through to the letter of the law.

"I'm waiting on someone," he finally relented. "I'm waiting for *the* one, actually," he revised with emphasis. His hands found their way into his pockets and suddenly he looked vulnerable. If only preliminarily, Sierra put something together.

"You're in love."

It explained more than one peculiarity and answered some basic questions—like how he'd gotten that big cooler and some of the other, larger, equipment into the woods. It explained how he'd stayed so well-provisioned if he was avoiding town. It explained the double sleeping bag and even all the books.

"That's right." He smiled crookedly, sadly. "Only, the person I'm waiting on can't get out for another week."

Relief washed over Sierra. It was an odd reason to be living in the woods, to be sure. But it explained why he'd left town without really leaving. It also corroborated what she already half-knew about his situation and it made a lot of sense. Jake Stapleton did plan to leave Green Valley. And in a week, he would.

"I take it there's a reason why you wouldn't just wait so the two of you could go together ..."

He looked away, some bitterness coming over his face. "You know I grew up in the Wraiths. There's no wide-open exit door you can go through any time. When I saw an out, I took it. He has to be more cautious. But the plan is in motion. And when he gets out ..." Jake shook his head and cut himself off. "He's got some money coming—the minute it comes through and not a second longer, we're leaving this place."

"You don't know how glad I am to hear that." Sierra actually smiled.

He rolled his eyes and responded, "I know, I know. I can't stay ..."

"Not that," Sierra said. "It gives you a soft alibi."

"And why would I need one of those?"

"Because they're looking for a suspect in all these controlled fires. A suspect who fits your description."

"A suspect?" he said in a voice louder, stronger and more

emotion-filled than she'd ever heard him use. "Uh-uh. They're not gonna pin this on me."

Good. He's scared, Sierra thought. She had him right where she wanted him: balking at the idea of having to save his own skin and more motivated than ever to leave.

"You're not stupid, Jake. Not every cop is good. Some of them dig deep and find the person who actually committed a crime. Other ones round up the usual suspects, point a finger and call it a day."

"You know I didn't set those fires." His jaw was tight.

"I know you didn't. But your best shot at taking suspicion off of you is to put it on someone else. Please, Jake," she pleaded. "Federal arson is a serious crime. If you know who's doing this, tell me."

PART III

Chapter Twenty-Four

FORREST

"Sonofabitch," Forrest mumbled to no one in particular, considering he was riding alone in his car. There was no one to see him smile, but he did that, too. It had to be divine providence that the woman who had woken up in his arms for the very first time that morning—the one who he couldn't get off of his mind—should randomly and suddenly appear to him during the course of his shift.

By then he could spot Sierra's truck at fifty feet, even though it was identical to the trucks of the other rangers. The telltale "036" painted on the back of the tailgate was all he needed to know to tell him the truck was hers. He sped up and turned on the flashing lights on the top of his own truck, thinking to have a little fun.

The sex appeal in the notion of pulling Sierra over wasn't lost on him. He wanted to do a lot more than flag her down. He would resist the urge to pull out the blanket he always kept in the back of his own truck and put it down in the bed of her truck, strip them both naked and ravage her again in the afternoon sun. But kissing her … Now that was something Forrest could definitely do. Even if she was busy on her shift, she could take a minute for this.

She pulled over at the flashing lights and Forrest jumped out, striding toward her car quickly. Knowing Sierra, she'd be looking through the side mirror to see him coming. He wondered whether she would go full role-play with him. If she did, that would just be more proof they were at the beginning of what would be a very fun relationship.

"You know how fast you were going back there, ma'am?" he asked in his best cop voice. She hadn't bothered to stay in the car. She'd gotten out and leaned her hip against her truck, where she stood smiling up at him.

"You gonna give me a ticket?" she asked.

"No. But I do take bribes." When he reached her, he circled his arms around her waist. "You promise not to do it again and I'll let you off with a kiss."

Reaching up toward her temple, he pushed her sunglasses off of her eyes until they sat on top of her head. But the look in her eyes was different than he'd expected—a mixture of exhilaration, and recollection and sadness.

Whatever it was that troubled her, it didn't stop her from leaning into his kiss. A second before their lips touched, he wondered whether she was having doubts. Sleeping with someone was something he didn't take lightly. But he could feel it—last night had meant something to both of them.

Don't you feel how right this is?

Forrest poured his every emotion into that kiss, wanting her to know it had certainly not been some one-night stand, or the start of some meaningless fling to him or anything else she might be thinking. Not now, when they were on shift, but soon, Forrest would cop to what needed to be said. He was absolutely, indisputably falling in love with her.

He smiled into her lips as she hummed into the kiss. It caused him to press his body against hers. He didn't exactly mean to, but when he finally came up for air, their position had changed—his fingers were in her hair and he'd flattened her against the truck.

"God, you're good at that," he breathed, unable to control his filter and uncaring that he could not. He bent his head to breathe her in and nipped at her neck.

"Forrest," she nearly panted. It didn't help his situation. His tongue was hungry to taste her again and he was rock hard.

"Forrest," she said again. "We have to talk."

Fuck.

It took him effort to process her words—which didn't sound good —to step away and push sex out of his brain. He would've bet money she was about to spout off some reason why they weren't perfect for one another. Forrest cracked his mental knuckles and prepared to argue otherwise.

"All right ..." he said disarmingly. "Tell me what's going on."

"We've got a break in the case. I'm just coming from talking to someone who saw something."

A rush of relief that she didn't want them to stop what they were doing paired with exhilaration at the news. "Holy hell. We got a break in the case?"

Sierra nodded and bit her lip, seeming suspiciously unhappy for a woman who he'd seen talk about little else for a good three weeks.

"Well, are you gonna tell me what you found out?"

"Yes." She frowned. "I'll tell you. But ..." She sighed. "You're not gonna like all that you find out."

"So rip off the Band-Aid," he said as gently as possible, though something in the way she was setting this up felt wrong. And Forrest didn't want a lot of preamble. He wanted her to spit it out.

"I talked to someone today who says he knows who's starting the fires. He gave me the names of two Wraiths. He says he ran into them in the forest a couple of times. He says they've been dealing magic mushrooms that they've been foraging in the park. That after they harvest the mushrooms, they burn the patches up."

Forrest took a step back into the deserted road, the quiet of the forest stretching between them for a long moment. Questions hit him, one after the other. Who was this *someone* Sierra had talked to? How did they know so much about the Wraiths? And why would any Wraith make a random someone who wasn't involved privy to that kind of information?

"Who is this person?"

Sierra hesitated to answer. Now Forrest's hackles were fully up. Something was very wrong.

"Jake Stapleton," Sierra reported in a voice that seemed artificially light.

"I didn't know he was back in town. Where'd you run into him? Down at the Piggly Wiggly or something?"

Sierra did something with her hands that straddled the line between wringing them and fidgeting her fingers. She shook her head. "I saw him in the park."

Forrest's initial theory—of her running into him in town—was a weak one to begin with. It wasn't as if she and Jake would stop each other in the produce section and get to chatting. Frankly, Forrest was surprised that Sierra even knew who Jake was, seeing as how she was so new to town.

"That explains how he knew something about the Wraiths," Forrest mused. "He *is* a Wraith."

"No." Sierra shook her head. "He's not. He took his chance to get out of the Wraiths. That's why he left town."

"Sounds like he didn't really leave if you ran into him in the park …" Forrest baited, knowing instinctively that she knew more, and that —whatever it was she knew—needed drawing out to say.

"I didn't just run into him, Forrest," she admitted in a way that told him she was finally about to come clean. "I've been talking to him for weeks. He's been living here in the park."

Forrest took another step back at the same time he was stolen of breath. An instant sense of betrayal set in, though—as he tried to process it—he couldn't pinpoint which part of this was worse. No one "lived" in the park. Campers camped and they needed permits to do it. If he'd been there for weeks, he'd been there illegally, as a squatter.

"Are you kidding me, Sierra?" When he spoke again, all calm was gone from his voice and its volume was louder than he wanted it to be. "Why would you not tell me Jake Stapleton was living in the park?"

She came back in a heated whisper. "Oh, I don't know—maybe because it's illegal?"

"You know goddamned well that someone who fits our profile is relevant to this investigation. Jake Stapleton is the definition of a troubled youth."

But Sierra came back with her own fire. "Jake Stapleton was born into a bad situation. He can't help that he was brought up in the Wraiths. And it's to his credit that he took his chance to get out."

"Jake Stapleton's got a rap sheet, Sierra, which has nothing to do with what he was born into and who brought him up."

Sierra blinked and shot him a disbelieving look. "Are you serious right now? You're trying to tell me that growing up in an environment like that didn't predispose him to trouble with the law?"

But Forrest doubled down. "Don't make this about something that it's not. I'm sure there's a reason why he is the way he is. But the 'why' of things doesn't change the 'what.' Jake Stapleton's been in trouble with the law. He fits the profile and he's living in the park. That makes him a suspect."

Sierra stepped toward Forrest and got in his space, only this time it didn't turn him on. For the first time, he looked down at her angry, lovely face and didn't know who she was.

"*Jake Stapleton*," she began again with emphasis, "is a kid who has always had the odds stacked against him. Has it ever occurred to you that any trouble he's been in hasn't been because he was the one who did it—he was just the one who got blamed? Do you think Jake Stapleton's ever gotten the benefit of the doubt when it was his word against someone else's, when the *someone else* was thought of as an upstanding member of the community?"

"*That's not what this is about*," Forrest ground out through clenched teeth.

"Then what is it about, Forrest? Because I thought it was about figuring out who set those fires. I just served up a damned good lead from a kid who didn't have to tell me anything, and you're so busy vilifying an eighteen-year-old you don't even want to pursue it."

"Oh, I'll pursue it." Forrest didn't back down. "And don't think I don't want to know all about those Wraiths he said did it. But I've got a few questions to ask Jake, myself. And I still haven't heard any good answers from you."

"What is that supposed to mean?"

"It means you lied to me," he practically roared. "Not just Fire Marshal Winters, your partner in the investigation. You lied to *me*, Forrest Winters, the man who thought you trusted him, and who cares more about you than he should."

"There's a difference between lying and waiting until the right time. Did you think the second we started working together on the investigation, I would bare my soul?"

"No, not your soul. Just things I needed to know. I thought we were together in this, Sierra. You let me think we were a team. I thought—"

But Forrest cut himself off, unable to finish the thought out loud.

I thought you'd finally let me in.

It hurt to even think it.

"I guess I thought wrong."

Chapter Twenty-Five

SIERRA

You're late, bitch.

The text from Jaya came through at the exact moment Sierra was paying for her bakery purchases. Cookies 'n cream cupcakes alone wouldn't suffice. She needed red velvet today. While she was at it, a chocolate marshmallow couldn't hurt and she also wouldn't mind a carrot. Some cream cheese frosting right about now might just hit the spot.

But Jaya's text sent her crashing down from whatever sugar high she'd been set to go on. Forgetting their dinner plans in Knoxville, she'd done everything in reverse. She'd gone straight from the park to the bakery, intending to double back to her house and stay in for the night. Everest was with her, her leash tied to a post in front of the store as she munched happily on a courtesy dog biscuit. How soon she had forgotten the girl-talk dinner she'd organized herself just that morning.

At least Jaya had been running errands out that way, regardless of their dinner plans. If Jaya had gone to Knoxville just to meet her and Sierra was a no-show, she would have felt even worse.

Sorry. Everything went wrong today. I'm still in Green Valley and I'm not even dressed. Some things happened. They're not good.

Seconds after Sierra pressed "send," bouncing bubbles took over her phone screen and indicated Jaya's reply.

Clint Grissom? Jaya wanted to know.

It was a logical guess. Things had been going so well with Forrest, the only one she'd vented to Jaya about lately was Grissom. Every good-faith attempt she'd made to help on the fire investigation, he'd shot down. He'd even taken to scrutinizing her other work. Just that morning, he'd shown up at Greenbrier, unannounced, and grilled her about her watering system pilot. With the questions he asked and the way he asked them, she got the distinct impression he wanted to shut it down.

Things went sideways with Forrest, she wrote back, instead of explaining any of that. It deepened the ache in her chest to write the words. Jaya's response came in right away.

I'll order takeout. Meet me at my place in an hour.

Just forty minutes later, parked outside of Jaya's place, Sierra sat in her idling car, eating cupcakes with Everest next to her. Her dog didn't seem to judge her for the sad songs playlist but she did seem grateful that Sierra had cranked the air-conditioning up. With every delicious bite, Sierra mulled over how things had gone upside down so quickly. When she'd called Jaya that morning, she'd had visions of boy talk over dinner, of finally admitting there was something serious happening between her and Forrest, and giggling through post-game replays of how good he was in bed.

How hard the fall, she thought miserably, folding up the spent paper of the red velvet and mulling over which one she ought to try next. She knew Jaya would be back with dinner, and Jaya always picked something good. But the siren call of the chocolate marsh-mallow was proving to be too loud.

I really should've gotten some milk, Sierra was busy thinking as she bit into chocolate goodness, closing her eyes to better experience the ecstasy of the first bite. When a hard knock sounded on the driver's-side window, she nearly jumped out of her skin.

"Holy hell," she said around a mouth full of cupcake when she set her eyes on Jaya's face, which managed to achieve a half-alarmed, half-wacky look.

"Okay … What are you doing?" Jaya wanted to know the second Sierra stepped out of her car. It took Sierra a minute to brush off all the crumbs. Some of the gooier, chocolatier crumbs smudged on her uniform shirt in a way that would stain if she didn't stay on top of washing it. Apparently, today was her day.

"Eating my feelings," Sierra admitted miserably, holding up the half-dozen cupcake box which only had three left.

"C'mon," Jaya coaxed, leading her into her home, which was really Jennifer Winston's mother's home. Jaya was renting it as an Airbnb. As they walked deeper inside, Sierra was calmed by the aroma of something tangy and something fried. Hand it to Jaya to know what to do.

"You got any bourbon?"

"That depends," said Jaya. "Are you sleeping here tonight?"

"As in, get drunk and pass out? Probably."

"What the hell happened?" Jaya demanded, beginning to pull takeout boxes out of the bag. "This morning you made it sound like something happened. Something good. I thought you guys did the deed. Are you already broken up?"

Sierra flopped onto a barstool and groaned. "I don't know. I mean, were we ever really together? Was whatever we were doing really defined?"

"No talking in code. Tell me what happened."

Sierra sighed. "He caught me in a lie."

Over scallion pancakes, Sierra spilled most of the sordid tale, about Jake Stapleton and how it was conceivable that he could have been viewed as a suspect. Over fried rice, she talked about telling Forrest, and how he'd reacted when he found out. Over kung pao chicken, she speculated on what Forrest would do next. He'd asked her for the coordinates of Jake's camp and said he would "pay Jake a visit" in the morning. That seemed like code for something bad.

"I know I shouldn't care so much. I mean, I obviously can't be with this guy. He and I are just too different. It doesn't matter in our own little world, when the boundaries of our existence are the park, but in the real world, when there's something important at stake, it does.

"He looks at Jake Stapleton and he sees a bad egg, without even knowing him personally. I look at Jake Stapleton and I see a kid whose real story is worth me finding out. I think I didn't tell Forrest because, on some level, I knew Forrest would turn suspicion right on him."

"You think Forrest is pro-establishment," Jaya concluded.

It made Sierra miserable to admit. "Don't you?"

"If he was as bad as you're making it sound, you wouldn't have even let him get this close. What is this really about?"

Sierra paused. Speaking the only logical conclusion would solidify what she had to do.

"It's about being realistic. I don't want to have to fight about this for the rest of my life."

Jaya's eyes widened and she stopped chewing. "The rest of your what now?"

Sierra waved it off. "You know what I mean."

"Yeah …" Jaya murmured. "I actually do."

Before Sierra could backpedal, Jaya wiped her hands on her napkin and pinned Sierra with a "tough love" kind of look.

"Look," Jaya began. "I'm not saying the guy's woke, but he cares about you. If he didn't, he wouldn't have been so hurt."

"He wasn't hurt. He was *mad*."

Jaya shook her head. "He's hurt. Anger and sadness are two sides of the same coin, just like love and hate are parallel emotions. One gone wrong creates the capacity for the other."

Sierra scowled, some part of her wanting to stay good and mad at Forrest, but she saw the reason in Jaya's words. And if she got past her own anger at how quick Forrest had been to blame Jake, she could admit that what Jaya had said was true.

"So what do I tell him?"

"The truth. That you couldn't tell him about Jake because it would have forced you to come to terms with your feelings. And that you weren't ready to do that because you were scared. Tell him the fact that you wanted to tell him so badly was what scared you the most."

Sierra's lip trembled. "But what if—what if he doesn't feel the same? I mean, I know he likes me, but this is Forrest. He's always been a showboater and a flirt. He's got charisma coming out of his ears. Charming people is what he does."

Jaya threw her a pitying smile, as if she were the daftest creature on earth. "I won't deny that everyone likes Forrest. But he doesn't lavish his attention on everyone the same. When are you going to wake up and realize the only person he flirts with is you?"

Sierra did feel dense. Maybe all the fatty calories from the cupcakes and the Chinese had gummed up the gears in her mind. But she tried her best to think. It was true; she'd never actually seen him flirt with anyone else. But they were usually in the company of men.

"I've asked around," Jaya continued. "He's not a dog. Forrest is one of the most eligible bachelors in Green Valley. Hard to land, and many have tried. He doesn't date much, but when he does, he's known to treat a woman right."

"You've asked around?" Sierra asked incredulously.

Jaya waved her hand. "Please. This has been brewing for weeks."

Sierra quieted long enough to process this new information. "All right. So I apologize. I tell him I've grown feelings. I tell him no more secrets. I come clean about Jake."

"As a start." Jaya nodded. "Then you go home and think about why you've been keeping him at arm's length all along."

Chapter Twenty-Six

FORREST

It was to Forrest's credit that he knew how to be so quiet in the woods. All the better to get him close to Jake Stapleton, undetected. Forrest's eyesight was just fine. Still, he took out his binoculars and let his eyes wash over every inch of the camp as he came upon it. Any tiny detail could be a clue.

An eight-person tent in plain beige. A camo tarp tied between the tent and the tree, constructed in a way that made side flaps fall down. A woodpile with enough dry, split logs to last three or four nights. The stake-style camping grill hovering over a buried, smoldering cooking pit came complete with a kettle hook apparatus. Forrest had seen the model in catalogs. It cost at least $300.

"Just a kid," he muttered to himself, still furious with Sierra for not telling him she was trifling with one of the Wraiths. Jake Stapleton hadn't been a kid for a very long time. This was the campsite of an experienced outdoorsman who knew his weapons and had survived for weeks in the woods. The axe against his woodpile and the knife that sat on a log near the cooking pit were proof of that.

Forrest spent that final minute studying the man himself. Jake lounged in a hammock, unaware that he was being watched, reading some sort of graphic novel. He didn't appear to have any weapons on his person, but ascertaining whether he did would be Forrest's first order of business. Forrest's plan hinged on Jake believing that Forrest wasn't working with—and maybe didn't even know—Sierra. But he had to calm the hell down if he was going to do this right.

"'S'cuse me, sir."

Stepping loudly now, Forrest made himself known, breaking twigs with his boots and clearing branches as he made his noisy way. He had stowed his binoculars in his bag, taken out his phone and set it to begin recording a voice memo. If nothing else, he would walk away from this conversation with leverage. If things went sideways, he would need anything he could get his hands on to protect Sierra.

"Sir ..." he repeated, as Jake struggled not to fall out of the hammock. When Forrest had issued his "'S'cuse me," Jake had jumped in surprise. By the time Forrest was upon him, Jake was on his feet and the book was caught and twisted in the hammock, which had bunched back up. Given Forrest's bulk and his height, he usually threw new people a kind word and a disarming smile. Today's default would be his intimidating glare and his menacing voice.

"This is an off-trail, unauthorized campsite. You are not allowed to camp here, sir, let alone build a fire in an area of thick brush."

Forrest motioned to the cooking pit, careful not to appear to study Jake's face too hard.

"I'm gonna need to see your fire permit," Forrest continued. "And while I'm looking at that, I'm gonna need you to extinguish your coals."

"I don't have a fire permit, sir."

Forrest looked straight at him then, leveling a hard glare before narrowing his eyes. He feigned dawning recognition.

"You're Jake Stapleton."

"Yessir."

"What the hell are you doing up here, boy?"

"Camping, sir."

Forrest paused for effect, pretending to be puzzled.

"I thought you left town."

"I did."

"How long you been up here?"

This was it—Forrest's first indicator of what role Jake really played in this thing. This was Jake's first chance to tell a big lie.

"Six weeks, sir."

Jake's honesty gave Forrest pause. Teenagers could be the worst kind of liars. Trying to not get caught for the laundry list of things their parents wouldn't approve of made the lies just roll off their tongues.

Not only was Jake not lying—he didn't seem too irreverent. Like a good Southern boy, he called his elder "sir." Only, most kids who grew up in the Wraiths didn't have such impeccable manners. It could be that Jake was kissing up—playing the respectful youth to curry favor. But Forrest didn't get that vibe.

"Six weeks doesn't sound like camping. It sounds like living."

"Yessir," Jake replied, but he didn't say anything else.

Forrest went a different route. "Do you know who I am?"

Jake nodded. "'Course I do. You're Forrest Winters."

"Do you know what I do?"

Jake nodded again. "You're a firefighter. Just like your daddy."

"Wrong." Forrest threw a small glare—a baby glare in the grand scheme of things. He would start the intimidation off small. "I'm not a firefighter. I'm a federal fire marshal. Do you know what that means?"

Jake shook his head. "No."

"It means I'm in charge of investigating any and all fire activity that happens in this park. It's my job to decide whether the fires were set intentionally. And to charge anyone who set them with a federal crime."

That last part wasn't quite truthful but it had the intended effect. Jake Stapleton looked rightly and acutely afraid. Forrest needed him to be. It was the ones who were cocky and overconfident who turned out to be a pain in the ass in situations like these. But a suspect who was afraid would give him what he needed.

"Are you aware that a series of suspicious fires has sprung up over the past two months, right along this creek?"

It was another big chance for Jake to tell a lie. He'd already admitted to camping illegally and setting fires without the permit, and the length of time he'd admitted to being there constituted squatting in the park. If he lied about this piece, Forrest could be sure he was connected to the fires. Maybe Sierra's hunch was right—that he hadn't set them. But he might have played another role in all of this. Innocent people had nothing to hide.

"I heard about some fires."

It wasn't a lie, but it was vague—a contrast to the straightforward "yessir" and "no, sir" answers he'd given up until that point.

"How'd you know about 'em?" Forrest wouldn't let it go.

"I have a walkie," Jake said. "I've heard transmissions from other through-hikers and campers. It's how I get a lot of my information about the park."

Interesting. A lie of omission, Forrest noted right away. He also noted that Jake had spared Sierra. The riskiest part of Forrest recording all of this was that Jake could say something that would incriminate her. When given the chance to say that he had been here for weeks under a federal park ranger who had knowledge that he was squatting, he had chosen not to throw Sierra under the bus.

It was the only fact that could have ingratiated Jake to Forrest in that moment. But Forrest was still the fire marshal and he still had to be sure. Which was why he had to keep playing hardball until he was.

"Three things are gonna happen right now," Forrest commanded, leaving no room for pushback. "First, I'm gonna search this camp. Second, I'm gonna escort you out of this park. Third, I'm gonna need information about where you're going next and the contact information for three friends who know how to find you."

"I don't have three friends." Again, Jake's voice was earnest. "And I didn't have anything to do with those fires."

Jake had answered the one question Forrest hadn't asked. Forrest didn't like his hunch—his strong inclination to believe Jake without even having inspected his campsite. Now, he understood better why Sierra had believed him. Without seeming slick, something about him was convincing.

"Do you have any weapons in this camp? Firearms? Knives? Anything that could be wielded in attack or self-defense?"

Forrest went down the list of standard questions he would ask any camper at an unauthorized site. The ones he found off-trail were usually the most dangerous, with the most to hide. After Jake had surrendered his weapons—two more knives and a hatchet, apart from the axe and survival knife Forrest had already seen—he leaned against the tree where Forrest had asked him to stand.

Clandestinely, Forrest stopped recording on his phone and took pictures of what he found as he went through, partially to prove he'd seen Jake and what was there, but also for the intimidation factor.

Jake didn't seem like a stupid kid. Photographing him and his things proved that he was camping illegally. The cooking pit proved he had broken a law. Even minor charges were a threat to someone with a record. If he found a gun, that would be another charge. And if he found anything he could pin to the fires, Forrest would have him in handcuffs within the hour.

What would you tell them? some voice inside him asked. If Jake had anything to do with the fires, Forrest couldn't let him go. But turning him in would force Forrest to write a report describing what led to Jake being found and brought into custody. This was the complicated part. It was why he'd been so furious with Sierra. Because if he lied to protect her, and Jake eventually talked, both of them could get fired.

There was nothing interesting in the tent—just a sleeping bag, air mattress, clothes, a lantern, and a hell of a lot more books than Forrest had ever seen in any tent. Much of the space was unused and sparse. The only other detail of note was that the sleeping bag was a double.

"Anyone staying up here with you?" Forrest hollered from inside, where he'd lowered the inside window flap to be sure that he could keep an eye on Jake as he searched.

"Every once in a while, a friend brings me supplies."

It sounded like another half-truth, one Forrest wouldn't pursue just then. After taking his photos, Forrest went to the final, unknown place. If there was anything incriminating to be found, this was where he would find it: the mysterious, covered area underneath thirty square feet of tarp.

"Anything under here you want to tell me about?"

No one in law enforcement liked surprises. Situations could go south, quickly. Some criminals kept up appearances so well, terrifying discoveries sometimes abounded.

"It's just where I keep my food … and things I use to maintain the site."

Forrest whipped up the side of the tarp to reveal the kinds of things Jake had admitted to having. After a painstaking ten-minute inspection, Forrest found nothing more. A Yeti cooler full of food and surprisingly fresh ice. A bucket and a shovel. Toilet paper. Toothpaste. A couple of towels. A bathing suit. Biodegradable soap.

"Start packing up," Forrest finally ordered after he took his last picture, some of the fight already drained from his voice. "I'll check to make sure your cooking pit is extinguished safely."

Jake said nothing and obeyed. It wasn't until Jake had disappeared into his tent that Forrest let go of the stress his body had been holding. He stood a minute with his hands on his hips, trying to slow the pounding in his heart and deep breathing into his relief.

Sierra was right, he thought to himself. He thought back to how he had chewed her out—how he hadn't trusted her instincts, or her judgment. Forrest didn't like that she'd lied to him. But he wasn't proud of the way he'd reacted. Before nightfall, he'd go to her. He had to make it right.

But Forrest still had questions. None of this exonerated Jake. And his half-truths caused Forrest to believe that Jake was guilty of something. He had expensive equipment, and lots of it. How was it that he could afford so much gear but had no place to stay? Money enough to buy this kind of stuff could've gotten him an apartment.

It took Jake a solid hour to pack up his camp. After tending to the cooling embers, Forrest helped. Both men were silent and efficient. It took two trips to get everything from Jake's camp to Forrest's truck. As they made their final twenty-minute trek, Forrest calculated his next move.

"I'm not gonna arrest you," Forrest finally said as they got into the truck. "I'm not gonna levy a fine or give you a ticket. Though— just to be clear—you're guilty of at least three crimes on federal land."

"What are you gonna do?" Jake wanted to know.

"I'm gonna ask for your honesty in exchange for my kindness. We're gonna go for a little drive. The two of us need to have a man-to-man."

Chapter Twenty-Seven

FORREST

"First thing you're gonna tell me is where you got that equipment."

Forrest's voice was quiet and low. He waited until they'd been on the road ten minutes before he asked. Forrest wasn't sure yet where they were going—only that he and Jake needed a long drive. Bypassing the road to Green Valley, where they might be seen, he took them on a different road, this one closer to the exit near Bandit Lake.

Several aspects of Jake's situation were odd—but only one fact rose to the level of suspicious. People who committed crimes had money they couldn't explain. Jake Stapleton was eighteen years old with no job. The stock boy job he'd once maintained at the Piggly Wiggly was low wage. So what was he doing with $3,000 worth of gear?

"I borrowed it from a friend."

"Your friend must be well-off. I counted about five hundred dollars' worth of gear in tactical knives alone. Add in that Yeti cooler, that nice tent and that nice fishing rod, I'm thinking over two thousand. Must be some good friend to lend you all that nice gear in the middle of summer."

Jake sighed and Forrest gave him time to answer. He'd given Jake the score. Sometimes people just needed a few minutes to accept their fate.

"The one who lent me his gear … He's not just a friend. He's my boyfriend. His stuff is only so nice 'cause his parents are rich."

"So why isn't he camping with you?"

"Because he's still seventeen. He won't turn eighteen 'til Sunday. I turned eighteen July fourth. I was camping in the woods until he could get away—you know, until we could run away together."

Wow.

"This guy have a name?" Forrest hadn't expected this. His mind raced to cross-reference this new information with earlier details of Jake's alibi to figure out whether this might actually make sense.

"He does have a name." Jake's voice had become steely—even bold. "But it's not my place to push anyone out of the closet."

"Fair enough," Forrest came, unable to argue with that. "What about you? Are you out?"

Jake turned his head and stared out the window. "Not to many people. And I'd appreciate it if you kept it that way."

Forrest sighed, believing for the second time that Jake was inno-cent, but still needing more to go on than he had. If the trail were ever to lead anyone else to Jake, Forrest needed a good reason for why he'd let him go.

"Look, kid. I'm not trying to bust your balls. I'm trying to under-stand your situation. This would be a lot easier if you just told me what the fuck was going on."

Jake sighed heavily and shook his head. "My dad kicked me out two days before my eighteenth birthday. He caught me and—" Jake stopped short of saying a name. "Me and my guy. From the way he treated me before that, I'd always thought he suspected. Turns out he hated me for reasons all his own. But finding out I'm gay ... I guess it was the last straw. The thing you gotta understand is, he didn't just kick me out of the house. He made it so I'm excommunicated from the Wraiths."

"So you wanted to be a Wraith?" Forrest quizzed, trying to ignore the pang of guilt he felt over him and Sierra fighting over this very point.

"Hell no," Jake practically shouted. "The thing you gotta understand about the Wraiths is, we're one big, dysfunctional family. Cutting me off means cutting off any good chance I had."

"I take it no one's supposed to talk to you?"

"Let alone take me in. Let alone help me in any way. I'm an embarrassment to him. He wants my ties to Green Valley cut, and he wants me gone. He even gave me a piece of money on the condition that I completely disappear. That's the other reason why I can't be seen in town."

Forrest didn't know what to say to all of this. It occurred to him that maybe Sierra knew—that she'd refused to out Jake much like Jake had refused to out his mystery man. Mostly, he thought about what it must be like to be shunned by your own father. Forrest's own dad hadn't been around all the time and Forrest had resented him for that. But there were moments when his dad had made him proud. Even without the criminal record to mar his reputation, Mortar seemed like a real piece of shit.

"So what is your plan exactly? You and this guy of yours? Where are the two of you going to go?" Forrest didn't want to force Jake to dwell on his father's rejection.

"Head west," Jake answered simply. "We're gonna move to Austin—see how we like things there. He's got a truck. That'll be our transportation. Both of us have been saving up. We've had it planned for more than a year."

Forrest nodded. Put into context, it made a lot of sense. It also explained why Jake Stapleton was deep in the woods with everything he owned.

"So here's what I still can't figure out," Forrest said after a long silence. "For someone looking to start fresh, to wait for the man you love and ride off into the sunset together, you sure felt fine about taking on a bunch of risk. If you've been listening to the walkie and you know about the fires, why would you want to stay? What made you so sure you'd be safe?"

Forrest watched from the corner of his eye as Jake pursed his lips.

"Where are you taking me?" Jake commanded to know, his voice coming through firm and determined.

Forrest had been thinking about that.

"I told you—it's up to you. You tell me the truth and I'll take you where you think you need to go, to lie low. If you don't have any place, I have a place on Bandit Lake where no one will come looking. But if you lie to me, I'll bring you up on charges and you'll go to jail."

Jake blinked over in surprise.

"You'd let me use your place?" The tone of Jake's voice sounded hopeful and relieved. It only made Forrest believe him more. If this kid really had something to hide and Forrest was offering him an out, he'd take his chance to get away.

"With conditions," Forrest said. "No guests, and just for a little while. But, yeah, I'd let you use it 'til you and your man can leave town. I may not look it, kid, but I was young once. Far be it from me to stand in the way of true love."

Forrest took his eyes off the road long enough to throw Jake a small smile. Instead of returning the gesture, Jake's eyes took on a suspicious shine. Forrest thought about what Sierra had said and felt sick with the idea that maybe Jake was only so emotional because he'd never been treated by law enforcement like a human being.

"You don't know how good that sounds …" Jake finally choked

out before turning his body toward Forrest and regarding him squarely. "But what could happen if I tell you the truth is worse than jail. I know how much time they'll give me for anything you could charge me with. And—trust me—time served isn't worse than delivering me back to the Wraiths."

Jake's fear was palpable. It only raised Forrest's hackles. His intention going into this questioning had only been to find out the identities of the Wraiths growing mushrooms and starting fires. But how big was this thing? How many details were there that Sierra didn't know?

"What do the Wraiths have to do with you knowing you'd be safe in that park?"

Jake shook his head, seeming to realize in that moment that his own phrasing had given something away.

"If I tell you, I need you to make sure I stay gone. As in, nobody can know I'm staying out at your cabin. And as soon as both of us are ready to leave this place, I'm gone. I can tell you who's starting those fires. And I can give you enough on them that you'll be able to go off and prove it yourself. But I won't stick around, or testify in court."

Forrest had to hand it to him—Jake Stapleton was savvy to the ways of the law. And Forrest was a man of his word.

"You have my promise. You tell me the truth about those fires and I'll leave you alone. Even small fires are dangerous—they can blaze out of control real fast. I'm not some cop looking to round up the usual suspects and get 'em in the paddy wagon just because I can. It's my job to protect this park and all the plant and animal species in it from fires. I need to find who's doing this. And I need to get them to stop."

Jake looked straight ahead and then started in on a sigh. Forrest sat straighter in his seat. This was it.

"I ran into an old buddy," Jake began. "He was one of the people I mentioned before—one of the ones who wasn't supposed to be talking to me. But he stumbled upon my camp."

"Little far off-path, don't you think?" Forrest prodded gently.

"My thoughts exactly. I'd chosen a spot where I knew I was unlikely to be found. The only reason why these guys found it is 'cause they were following the river."

"How many were there, total?"

"Just two. They were as surprised to see me as I was to see them, but we were always cool. I asked them what the hell they were doing all the way out there. They said they had a side-hustle, growing mushrooms in the woods."

"As in *magic* mushrooms?" Forrest played along.

Jake hummed his confirmation. "They knew how to track where they grow. That's why they were following the creek. They told me all about their growing operation. They were sort of bragging, you know? That's how I found out about the fires. They heard someplace that when you burn up a patch, it does something to refresh the soil and makes it so they grow back better the following year."

"Fire-fallow cultivation," Forrest mused. "It puts nutrients back in the soil and revitalizes the land. Smart strategy. Profitable, too. These guys sound like pros."

Forrest didn't mention the one problem with the plan: that the heavy use of chemicals to start and put out the fires would poison the land. Forrest would be shocked if anything grew there the following year at all.

"That was the weird thing about it ..." Jake trailed off, turning his head once again to look at Forrest. "No offense to Two-Buck Chuck. They were my buddies and all, but not the sharpest tools in the shed. There's no way the two of them could've come up with it alone. I'm guessing they're the brawn and that Catfish or Gears are the brains."

"Two-Buck Chuck?" Forrest asked. "Who the hell is that?"

"Buck's the one guy. Chuck's the other. They're always together, so …" He trailed off.

Forrest just blinked. "So you didn't know anything about it when you were in the Wraiths?"

Jake shook his head. "Like I said, I was never in. I never wanted to be. And even if I had, I would have been cut off from a lot of information. Even after you go through formal initiation, it's still just the top guys and their lieutenants who ever fully know what's going on."

* * *

Forty-five minutes later, Forrest was three-quarters of the way through a tour of his cabin, which—as cabins went—was pretty luxe. It was a hybrid of timber and log with a grand entrance and angled rooves arranged appealingly in rustic configuration. The inside was all high ceilings and hammer beam trusses and grand windows that looked out at the lake. Medium-toned leather furniture in browns and grays complemented the stonework of the grand fireplace in the great room's far side. Next to the great room was an open kitchen with an equally stunning view. A furnished deck and a short runway of additional backyard stretched between his house and his private dock. Three of the five bedrooms upstairs had a lake view.

They'd stopped at the general store in an unincorporated enclave right near Bandit Lake. Best as Forrest could tell, Jake had been well-fed but living a bit rough on the fish he caught and food from the cooler, like beans and franks. The second they'd walked into the store, Jake had made a beeline for cold soda, a bag of oranges and fresh milk.

The rest of their ride had been mostly silent. Forrest knew he ought to be using this wealth of new information to solve the case. But he couldn't stop thinking about Sierra—about how he'd thought about driving this very road with her, how he'd fantasized about having her up to the cabin for a romantic retreat. He thought about what he would say to her when he saw her, how he would apologize and make sure they talked—really worked out whatever had gone wrong. Forrest was no relationship expert. And Sierra Betts was one complicated woman. But he'd never felt so sick over anything in his life as he felt now about fighting with her.

"You got a phone?" Forrest wanted to know.

Jake nodded and reached into his pocket. "I'll turn it on now. I mostly kept it off. Searching for signal burns up juice."

Forrest unpocketed his own phone and thumbed on his screen. "I'm gonna need that number. I'll give you mine, in case you need to get in touch with me."

Even before Forrest could get his sentence out, Jake's phone had begun to chime furiously and in sequence, as if he had missed a dozen or more alerts.

"What the hell?" he murmured under his breath. Forrest only half-paid attention as he turned his phone off of Do Not Disturb to find his own barrage of missed calls. He had put it in that mode earlier so an incoming call wouldn't cut off whatever he was recording.

"There's a fire in the park." Jake's voice was panicked. Forrest heard his words at the very same moment he saw a missed call from incident command. Such a call could only mean one of two things: either there was a small fire in the park and someone had thought to give Forrest a call as a courtesy and an FYI, or things were bad enough, they wanted Forrest to come in.

Sierra.

She was working today. And, even if she wasn't, she lived inside the park. She'd be in danger if the fire was in her territory, up by her house, or anywhere in between.

"I gotta go," Forrest announced, his feet already moving. "I'll call when this is over. You lie low. Everything will be fine."

Forrest had his hand on the doorknob when he felt Jake hot on his heels.

"No it won't!" Jake exclaimed in a voice so shrill, Forrest turned back and looked. The stoic teenager who had just spent more than an hour keeping Forrest at arm's length had tears streaming down his face.

"Eddie thinks I'm still in there! When he couldn't reach me, he went to look for me in the park!"

Chapter Twenty-Eight

SIERRA

"I'm never drinking again," Sierra vowed out loud to whatever hangover gods might be listening, in the vain hope for mercy and the divine alleviation of pain. The ginger ale she had guzzled on her way back into the park had made the nausea marginally better; the three Advil she'd swallowed had taken some of the edge off of her headache; and a shower and a thorough toothbrushing had made her feel half-human again. Still, there was no good to come of walking her patrol—of making good time on moderate to hard trails—hung over, in punishing heat.

At least today was a light-ish day. She would check in on her red-cheeked salamanders. She would perform some maintenance on the westernmost parts of her trail. She would log conditions in three risky areas and reserve paperwork for the hottest part of the day. Knowing that Forrest would have gone to see Jake by then, to make his own assessment. She would give them their time in the morning, make her other rounds now, then follow up herself with Jake in the afternoon.

And what about tonight? she asked herself unhelpfully, because it still hurt her head to think, and it still hurt her heart to know she was so unsure of where things stood with Forrest. They had bickered like champions, but this was their first honest-to-goodness fight. She didn't know whether he liked to clear the air quickly, or whether he needed time to stew, or whether a fight like that meant you didn't make up at all.

"Dispatch to four-one-five. Over." Rick's voice crackled over her walkie and the labor she felt in performing the small act of unfastening it from her belt and bringing it to her mouth told Sierra she needed a rest. The day was already too warm and she'd avoided lunch, thanks to her roiling stomach. She'd forced herself to drink her Gatorade, but it sloshed uncomfortably in her stomach as she walked. Maybe real food in her stomach and a fifteen-minute lie-down would do her good.

"This is four-one-five," Sierra replied. "I'm ready with my coordinates for your check. Over."

Looking at her watch to read said coordinates, Sierra noticed something: the always-on-time-for-his-checks Rick was putting in his call a full twenty-three minutes early. It wasn't like him at all.

"I'm calling to report a fire in your territory, four-one-five, and to pass on an order for you to vacate your patrol. Fire crews are on their way and rangers on campsite duty are handling those evacuations. Research facilities on your patrol have been notified. Your orders are to report to Sugarlands. Over."

"What is the location of the fire, dispatch? Over."

"The fire is in the vicinity of Greenbrier Cove, in the western area of your territory, by Little Pigeon Creek, away from most of the campsites, thank God. Over."

Suddenly, Sierra was cold all over, despite the heat. It was the exact area where Jake was camped. Only, Sierra had no way of knowing whether he knew about the fires and had gotten out. The only way she could be sure was to check.

"There may be a camper in the area," Sierra said vaguely, barely knowing how she was going to explain all of this at the end of the day. "An unauthorized camper I found yesterday and asked to move on. Over," she lied.

"You got a description? Over," Rick asked.

"Young adult male, Caucasian, nearly six feet tall, straight, black hair, blue eyes. Over," she rattled off.

"I'll let Fire know," Rick said. Even through the walkie, she could hear him clicking away at his keys. "And I'll take your coordinates for a beacon test, now. Please read them off to me. Over."

Sierra did. After they had established her location and the in-range function of her device, Rick told her to be careful and got ready to sign off.

"Wait," she exclaimed before he could. "Have you heard anything from Forrest?"

"Forrest isn't on duty, honey. He's not even in the park. The GPS locator on his truck has him somewhere out by Bandit Lake. So don't you worry 'bout whether he's safe. We're trying to get a hold of him, to bring him in, but he's not stuck anywhere in the park. Over," Rick said.

The news filled Sierra with equal parts dread and relief. Forrest wasn't in danger if he wasn't in the park. But if Forrest wasn't at Jake's camp interrogating him, then Jake was the one in danger. Even more so if Forrest was off somewhere miles away. If Forrest was in the park and he knew about the fires, he would send a rescue party to Jake's location. But he wasn't, and he hadn't, which made Sierra the only person who knew to go in for Jake.

Sierra made a decision then—one she was sure would change her life and one that might just cost her her career. But it was her decisions that had placed Jake in greater danger. She should've kicked him out earlier—she should have escorted him out herself.

"I'm worried about the camper, dispatch. He was close to the area you described and I'm close enough to that area to check in. I logged the coordinates of his camp. I'll go in now to be sure he vacated. Over."

Sierra was already moving, walkie in hand. She brought it up to a jog, running a straight line into the wilderness as she went off-trail.

"Sierra …" Rick said with alarm. "Fire is fifteen minutes out. Your orders are to evacuate now. What the hell are you doing? Please confirm that you will follow orders. Over."

Sierra stopped long enough to tighten her pack fastenings around her chest and her waist and spoke her final words into the walkie. "Keeping campers safe is part of my job. I'll check on my camper and report back soon. Over and out."

* * *

Fifteen minutes later, Sierra had covered a mile and a half, managed not to throw up, and was making good time to Jake's campsite. She forced herself to run with full gear on; the smoke in the air and a wicked hangover was no match for the adrenaline that had seeped into her blood.

She'd turned down her radio, knowing that Rick would only try to talk her down from her decision—knowing that, if he did, he'd just be following protocol. Her insubordination would be known by now. She knew how this complicated things: placing herself in the middle of a fire against orders made her a victim. Some poor firefighter might have to risk his life to make sure Sierra got out.

That's why I'm gonna be quick, Sierra told herself. This wasn't like other search and rescue missions, where crews went to look for victims with only a vague idea of where they might be. She had given Jake instructions, and they'd practiced. If he had to leave his campsite, the shortest way out was the twenty-minute way she'd shown him through the woods.

In and out, she chanted again to herself as she reached a landmark on her route. Sierra's plan was to use the creek. She'd picked it up at a point she knew well—one without hazards she couldn't traverse at that time of year. From here, she would follow it upstream.

Not only was it the safest route, it was almost the most straightforward. And if the fires descended upon the area where she was, she'd be better off doused in water than anywhere else. She remembered from living in California, some of the wildfire survivors had made it out when the fires consumed their houses by creating makeshift air pockets and hiding in their pools.

Breathing was becoming harder, though it was hard to know whether it was from running or from the thickening smoke. Fatigue from her sustained jog was causing her to slow down. Exhaustion was her greatest enemy. The conditions would make it easy for her to run out of steam. She could go into heat exhaustion, then heatstroke, then go into shock. She could lose focus and trip over a root —get injured and end up stuck. She forced herself to slow down more.

Running creekside presented its own set of challenges. The banks varied in terrain and it was difficult to walk a clear path. Trees grew strangely and she had to weave around them in sporadic patterns to remain along the creek. Her only relief came during brief moments when rushing water from light rapids and little falls delivered bursts of air that were fresh and cool.

"Jake!" she shouted, recognizing that she was nearing the exact point of his camp but checking her GPS to be sure. Her nasal passages were irritated and her eyes had begun to sting. The thick tree canopy made it hard to gauge the darkness of the sky but the smoke was getting worse.

"Jake!" she shouted again as she ran the final fifty feet into his camp. Through the trees, she could see the clearing, his fire pit and his two upturned sitting logs. She didn't see his tent yet or his hammock or other telltale signs, but his camouflage had been strong.

So strong, it would have been difficult for a search party to find him —yet another reason why she was glad she had come herself.

She didn't expect Jake to be in the camp. Everything she knew about him told her he would have been vigilant and followed their plan. But, in the spirit of a good rescue, she'd shout for him all the same. Her best-case scenario was to find a hastily abandoned campsite. It would mean he'd gotten out. But what if he was hurt? Or asleep? She knew it from her own training: some people woke up at the smell of smoke. Others didn't.

"Jake?" she called again. As she ran in fully, more questions came hot on her heels. Questions like, why was the campsite so clean and deserted? And, where the hell had Jake gone? But this was definitely Jake's camp.

Even if the logs and the fire pit hadn't told the tale, Sierra still recognized it in its abandonment—the tree where the tarp had been anchored and the two where the hammocks had swung. She spun in a slow circle, sweating profusely and catching her breath. Her lungs hurt and her throat burned. She was sure already she would have some breathing problems to answer to tomorrow.

When her eye caught on something shiny, she walked toward what looked like a very wet patch—a wet patch that had a small heap with remnants of ice. His cooler. It was more proof of his abandonment. What she couldn't figure out was how he'd packed up and left so quickly. Melting ice was a sign he'd at least been there earlier that day. But she'd done what she'd gone there to do: ascertained that Jake himself was no longer at the campsite. The rest, she would figure out later.

"Dispatch, this is four-one-five, reporting from the site of the unauthorized camper, confirming that the camper has vacated the premises. I will now evacuate the area. I'm a twenty-minute hike from the Ramsey Cascades Trail. I'll hike to the park sign at Porter's

Creek fire road and request a pickup from that point. Over," Sierra said.

"Copy, four-one-five. You'll be picked up at the park sign for transport to Sugarlands. Over."

Rick was still the dispatcher. But the fact that he hadn't stopped to deliver a personal chastisement over the stunt she'd just pulled told Sierra that he was no longer alone. It foreshadowed how much trouble she was in.

Sierra began coughing before she even got her walkie back into her belt. Not a light cough, either—a long series of coughs that told her what she'd been avoiding. The air was getting smokier. Soon, her lungs would do more than just hurt. Soon, her breathing would be in trouble.

Unhooking her day pack, she brought it around her front and put it on in reverse, walking in the right direction at the same time as she rifled through her bag. She packed a fine particulate mask for exactly this sort of emergency. It would protect her from some of the smoke, but make breathing harder, which was why she hadn't used it during her run.

Now, the time had come. Conditions had changed. She would simply have to put on the mask and get out as fast as she could. No sooner had she done the former and gotten her pack back on the right way than did she hear the pained cry of a masculine voice.

"Help!"

Once again, Sierra's heartbeat spiked.

"Jake!"

Sierra didn't know who Jake's mother was, but she knew she didn't want to have to explain to any mom why she hadn't protected her kid.

"Over here! I'm hurt!"

The voice was off to the far left and somewhat behind her. Sierra had just traversed the creek. But the sound of the voice found her tracking back.

"Jake?" It felt to her in that moment like the only word she had ever said. Forgetting about her mask, she hadn't thought ahead to how muffled it would sound. In place of saying more, she followed the voice.

She spotted someone by the creek bank, fifty feet north of where she had crossed. He was in plain sight, propped up on one elbow, his eyes squinted shut and his face drawn in pain. He looked to be about Jake's age. Only, this kid wasn't skinny with jet-black hair that always flopped over his eye. This teenager was bulky, and blond.

"You're hurt," Sierra supplied unhelpfully as she jogged up to his side. His predicament was as clear as day. She didn't know how he'd managed it, but the bone sticking out of his shin confirmed a broken leg.

"I was running too fast … wasn't paying attention. If I was, I would have seen. It was one of Jake's game traps."

"You know Jake?"

The kid nodded, still wincing in pain as he held the top of his leg. He wasn't bleeding too badly, but, man, that had to hurt. Hastening to remove her pack and grab her first aid kit, Sierra made to talk to him as she stabilized his wound.

"I came to get him. I didn't know if he knew about the fires. I made it to his camp and was on my way back to my car. From the looks of it, he got out."

"How did you know about the fires?" Sierra was digging for information as much as she was also trying to distract. Examining his leg, let alone applying a temporary dressing, wasn't going to feel good.

"Police scanner." He looked a bit sheepish. She wasn't fooled by his quick subject change. "Hey, you don't have crutches in that bag of yours, do you?" he asked with a little laugh.

It was good that he was talking and seemed to have a clear recollection of events, but his eyelids lolled and he seemed somewhat disoriented despite his verbal skills. She was 95% sure that he was in shock. She needed to get both of them out of that fire, but her biggest concern at the moment was dressing his wound properly so that she could move him without him losing too much blood .

"What's your name?" she wanted to know.

"Eddie Claypool," he said. "House of Gryffindor."

Sensing she was about to lose him, she decided to keep it to the essentials.

"Eddie, you allergic to any medication?"

"I'm allergic to strawberries and latex, which makes things kind of complicated when it comes to flavored condoms."

Sierra couldn't help but chuckle, even as she cut at the leg of his hiking shorts, which nearly fell to his knee. She took off her pack, pulled out her first aid kit and spied one thing that could help—a tourniquet that could be placed above his knee. The problem with tourniquets was you needed a hospital right away or you could lose the limb.

"Too much information, Eddie," she replied. "And, don't worry— I'm gonna get you out of this."

"I know you will, Sierra," he said with a wan smile as his eyes lolled once again and he looked even more delirious.

"You know who I am?" She wanted to keep him awake for as long as possible.

"You're the one who's been helping him. Those bacon bites you make are awesome. Can you give my mom the recipe?" He smiled, even as his eyes closed.

Before she could promise she'd give him anything he wanted as soon as she got them out of this, Eddie Claypool clean passed out.

Chapter Twenty-Nine

FORREST

"I need a heat map against these coordinates. You ready?"

Forrest shouldn't have been talking on the phone and driving. Forrest really didn't care. He'd made it back inside the park in record time, though he was still a good ten-minute drive from the action. It had taken him twenty minutes to get from Bandit Lake to where he was. He'd used that time wisely to receive briefings from key players on the radio—from the chief, to the duty captain down at incident command.

But not before he'd tried Sierra on her cell. Not before he'd called dispatch to find out where she was. Not before he'd shouted a string of curses for a minute straight once he'd found out she'd gone in. Because, arguing or not, he could have taken thirty seconds to text her or give her a status update on Jake. This time, he was the one who had forgotten he was on a team.

"Ready for the coordinates," said Buck, who Forrest was thankful to have on duty. Forrest split his attention between the road and reading off the coordinates of Jake's camp. He'd said as little as possible in explaining the situation. All he'd said was that he'd escorted an unauthorized camper off of the premises earlier and that he had reason to believe the camper had a friend who was still inside.

Since this was still a fire-in-progress, Forrest wasn't the one in charge. Technically, he wasn't even on duty. If anything, he'd been called to be kept in the loop and to offer a helping hand. Everyone knew he had investigated the earlier fires. And everyone in the fire service knew Forrest had called it arson. As it pertained to the incident-in-progress, that made Forrest a key source.

Only this isn't like the other fires.

This one wasn't contained. For fires as small as the ones they'd seen before, Forrest wouldn't have been called in. Only an investigation would determine whether this one was related and why it was so big.

"It's closing in on that area," Buck reported grimly. "The ground crew is pushing the other side. If the wind doesn't change, you've got an hour to get in and get out without flames on touchdown. We can get a crew there, but they'd be twenty-five minutes out to reach the access point and half an hour to hike into those coordinates."

"I can get there sooner."

"You know it's not protocol …" Buck pointed out. Forrest didn't plan to explain himself. "But I'm glad it's you down there, going in after her. I'll cover you as best I can. Later, too, if you need it. Now you go on in and get your girl."

Your girl.

Sierra *was* his girl. No argument would change it. And, apparently, Buck knew. He could think about all of that tomorrow. Right now, his priority was getting to her and getting her out.

Focusing on that, Forrest stayed off his radio and his phone for the last ten minutes of the drive. Visibility had gotten exponentially worse. Driving in smoke this thick required two hundred percent attention. The closer he got to the blaze, the darker the sky became.

Being a marshal now, it had been a long time since Forrest had put on his turnout, though he always kept his full suit in the trunk. The last time he'd suited up like this had been in California, with Todd. Being this close brought back the least welcome of memories. Now, all he could do was pray his body's reactions wouldn't shut down his mission. This was personal. And he had a job to do.

Apart from the canopy of gray that obscured sun and clouds, ash rained down from the sky—so much so that he needed windshield wipers. Using a combination of his odometer and his GPS watch to navigate to the precise stretch where Jake had said Eddie parked, Forrest thought he was half a mile away. The vision that emerged suddenly and eerily from his gray surroundings made him come to a screeching halt.

Eddie's truck.

Jake had told him about Eddie's newer-model F-150. Though covered partially with ash, Forrest still detected hints of red. It was enough to convince him to get out and go. Jogging to the compartment that held his gear, Forrest hastened to suit up.

"This is eight-six-five to dispatch." Forrest spoke into his radio the second he'd put on his turnout. Already, he stalked into the woods. "I need you to get me a beacon on four-one-five. Over."

Forrest set off retracing the steps he'd walked only hours before. Smoke in the air cut the time Sierra or Eddie could survive out there, especially without equipment, like a mask.

"This is dispatch to eight-six-five. The first crew has already reached the western perimeter. Incident command has a second crew fifteen minutes out. They'll come in on the same side as four-one-five. Over."

"Backup is welcome, dispatch. But I'm going in. I need the beacon on four-one-five right away. It's getting thick out here. Over," Forrest said.

Whatever thoughts raced through his addled mind were grim. If he found Sierra, he would get her out right then, whether they had status on Eddie or not. It was a choice Forrest had never been in a position to make. If you'd asked him a month ago whether he could think of a circumstance in which he would leave a victim behind, he wouldn't have thought himself capable. Neither had he thought himself capable of his feelings for Sierra.

Rick read Forrest the coordinates. For once, he sounded scared. Was it because conditions were worsening or because Rick was afraid for his friend? With all forty-five pounds of his gear on his shoulder and the heat closing in, Forrest found his line and ran straight into oncoming smoke.

A strength that Forrest did not know he possessed propelled him forward at unprecedented speed, something more than adrenaline sparing the fatigue that should have slowed his pace. He flew through the woods, scanning with his eyes, jumping over roots and dodging branches, still half a mile away from the coordinates Rick had read out.

"Eight-six-five to dispatch. I need an update on four-one-five. Can you please confirm the new position of her beacon? Over."

Forrest needed to find her where she was and help her walk out. He'd lost track of time, but guessed it had been a few minutes already since he'd asked dispatch for her original position. He had to be getting closer, but needed her new beacon position just in case he wasn't walking in on the same straight line as she was walking out.

"Four-one-five's position hasn't changed. Please proceed to her location and report. Over."

Forrest's vision blurred. It explained even more why Rick sounded so distraught. Both men had been doing this long enough to know that not all stories ended well.

"How long?" He was breathless and drenched beneath his suit. He was just over a quarter of a mile away, now.

"Thirteen minutes," Rick choked out. "Over."

Forrest set aside fear of what he might see when he reached her and commanded his legs to work—to power through the burning of his quads and the chafing of his gear.

"Sierra!" he hollered, though much of the sound ricocheted back to his own ears given his full-face mask. He forced himself to slow down. The beacon had an error radius of 200 feet. Visibility was getting worse and he didn't want to miss her.

"Sierra!" he repeated, seeing that Little Pigeon Creek was nearly upon him and knowing that once he crossed it, he would be right near Jake's camp. He stopped at the bank to catch his breath. He couldn't see far, but he needed to stop, to look around.

This was it—the moment of quiet—the moment you took in any search operation to shut the hell up and listen for signs of life. The most haunting sound in the world after you called for someone was nothing. Forrest eased his breathing as much as he could, kept at bay the coughs that wanted to break through, and he prayed. For just a moment, he closed his eyes so he could really listen.

"Help! We're over here ..."

* * *

"I'm riding with her."

Forrest didn't wait for an answer to the proclamation he spoke as Sierra's gurney was being fastened into the truck. The Fire EMT was one who Forrest had seen before.

"Things are looking good for her, sir. It's probably just a little smoke inhalation," the EMT started in.

It was the mildest and most polite way to tell Forrest it wasn't protocol for a firefighter actively working a scene to escort a patient to the hospital.

Had Forrest been anyone other than a federal fire marshal and the highest authority in this park, the EMT would have given him a firm "no." But there was no time to go back and forth. There was also no time for Forrest to spin up some bullshit justification. He defaulted to the truth.

"I'm in love with this girl."

His voice held pleading and determination all at the same time. Come hell or high water, he was not leaving Sierra's side. "Don't worry about incident command. I'll take it up with him."

Getting on his radio and updating incident command on Eddie and Sierra's statuses while relaying other official details was exactly what he did next. He had already launched into his debrief by the time he climbed in after the EMT. As they sped out of the park, Forrest's eyes didn't leave Sierra's face and his two hands didn't stop holding her one.

Forrest had been in countless ambulances. He'd worked on the EMT side himself, long before he'd worked his way up the ranks of captain and chief. Everything the EMT was doing to treat her was by the book. Still, it was hard for Forrest to see her that way—unconscious with a nasal cannula feeding her oxygen, an IV dug into the top veins of her delicate hand. And it was terrifying for him to see a blood oxygen level reading of seventy-eight on her pulse oximeter. It would resolve itself with the right treatment, but smoke inhalation was more serious than people thought. Things could be touch and go for a good two days.

Once Sierra was stable, Forrest didn't fight it when the EMT held out a second pulse oximeter, took Forrest's reading, then handed him an oxygen mask. Only then did Forrest register that he remained in nearly full gear. Forrest accepted the treatment graciously. He needed his strength to be there for Sierra. While she lay up in the hospital, recuperating, he would need his strength for one more thing: getting her out of this mess.

Chapter Thirty
SIERRA

❧❦❧

S ierra awoke to the sensation of something—or someone—messing with her left arm. The appendage felt oddly burdened. She could tell that things were on it and that it was being held at a strange angle in relation to her body. It wasn't at her side, where it belonged.

Something on her right side was odd as well—something heavy that rested on her right thigh. She couldn't guess what. She didn't feel like she could guess at much of anything, with her brain as foggy as it was.

The peculiarity of her left arm's situation was displaced by sudden awareness of another sensation: Sierra's throat and chest hurt. There was something in her nose, her mouth felt dry and she couldn't seem to swallow. Now panicked, her eyes flew open. Her brain took just a second to tell her she was in a hospital room and to see the source of who had been messing with her arm. A smiling nurse stood by her side.

"You're awake!" the nurse whisper-shouted, her smile warm as she patted Sierra's shoulder. The touch was reassuring.

Sierra made to say something, but it felt like her throat and lungs were on fire.

"Don't try to speak yet. I'll start by telling you where you are and why you're here. You were brought in this afternoon following a woodland fire incident at Great Smoky Mountains National Park. You've suffered serious smoke inhalation and you've been intubated so that your breathing can get a little help. We've got you on the best regimen for treating it. It'll mean keeping you in the hospital for another day or so, but after that, you should be fine.

"Since you can't talk right now, I'm gonna have to ask you to blink for me. Two for yes, three for no. Is your name Daffy Duck?"

Sierra felt herself smile a little right before blinking three times.

"Good," the nurse praised. "Is your name Sierra Betts?"

Sierra blinked twice.

"Perfect. Do you have any allergies?"

Sierra blinked thrice.

"Even better." The nurse smiled again. "On a scale of one to ten, is your pain level above a five?"

The more aware Sierra had become of her body, the more she had noticed the pain. Once again, she blinked twice.

"All right," the nurse concluded. "No more questions. I'll give you another dose for the pain. It'll put you to sleep again for a while."

Even as she said it, the nurse was already fiddling with the drug-dispensing machine next to Sierra's bed.

"But don't worry—we'll be sure to let him know you woke up, and that you're fine."

Let who know?

The nurse jutted her chin across the space. For the first time since waking up, Sierra cast her glance to the right. That's when a mop of black hair came into view.

Holy shit.

Even in her fog, Sierra now understood the pressure on her right thigh. The bowling ball sitting in her lap was Forrest's head. Not only that, her fingers were threaded in his locks. Without giving it conscious thought, she began to stroke his hair.

"He hasn't left your side, except to go home and feed your dog."

Tears sprang to Sierra's eyes at the thought of Everest. But she was getting sleepy. And she really wished she could talk, then wished even harder that Forrest would wake up for just a minute—that he'd look at her the way he sometimes did with those smoky gray eyes. But she was rapidly succumbing to the meds.

"Oh, and I almost forgot. In fact, I should have told you this part first. The seventeen-year-old boy you saved in that fire? He's gonna be just fine."

Chapter Thirty-One

FORREST

"**H**ow's our patient doing?"

The nurse who strode into Sierra's room after shift change looked cheerful. Rested. Unlike Forrest, she must have gotten a full night's sleep. Forrest had dozed for a while but given up an hour earlier, then gone to get coffee. Sierra's room was small, but cheerful for a hospital room. Light streamed through tinted windows next to the right side of her bed. Cramped from sitting for too long and in too awkward a position, he stood.

"She's still sleeping." Forrest stated the obvious. "She woke up once overnight, but she's still groggy from the meds."

The nurse had one of those rolling stands that she could push around and take with her on rounds as she went from room to room. It was a simple device, just a standing desk with an iPad. She seemed efficient; the tips of her manicured nails made light clicking sounds on the surface of her tablet as she tapped away, charting notes on Sierra.

"Two out of the other three are awake, you know," the nurse

mentioned as she went to a small whiteboard on the wall, erased the name of the night nurse and wrote her own name in dry erase marker: Cathy.

The other three?

There was only one more. Eddie was stable and Forrest had already been in to check on him every couple of hours, at Jake's behest—easier said than done with Eddie's parents buzzing around.

In the sixteen hours since Sierra and Eddie had been brought in, Forrest had left for only ninety minutes: to take Everest to stay at his house with Jake, to get showered, and to get on his light-duty uniform. Seeming like he was there in an official capacity would give him an excuse to talk to Eddie and let him serve as a conduit between Eddie and Jake.

"Which two are awake?" Forrest fished. "I was in Eddie Claypool's room not too long ago and he was still out."

The nurse nodded. "He and Sierra had it the worst. The other two cases are milder. Neither of them thought they had it at first. They didn't come in 'til last night."

Forrest gritted his teeth as Cathy rapid-clicked a series of taps on her screen.

"They are ... Jesse Grissom and Sean Brady. Rooms 307 and 314."

Jesse fucking Grissom?

Forrest thought it so hard, he barely stopped it from coming out of his mouth. It was too much of a coincidence to ignore.

"Has any other law enforcement been by?" he asked.

Cathy looked back down at her charts, still executing what seemed like one long series of clicks.

"Not that I can tell from their charts; though, the closer I look ..." She trailed off, scrolling through for a minute. "This might be something else. Chart says they suffered smoke inhalation from a fire in one of their backyards. I swear, these kids ... they get dumber every year."

Cathy was still shaking her head when she finally tore herself away from her iPad. She strode to Sierra and fiddled with all of her tubes and wires.

"Maybe I'll pay those two a visit. Give 'em a little talk about fire safety. Whatever they got into, it sounds pretty reckless."

Cathy finally looked up at him, then motioned to Sierra's supine form. "Well, you've got plenty of time. This one's still out like a light."

* * *

Forrest sat in the stairwell, pulling himself together and calming his anger as he waited for an incoming text from Grizz. A call down to at the sheriff's office confirmed there had been no police calls to Jesse Grissom's house the day before, and that there was no record of someone by the name of Sean Brady living in Green Valley.

Grizz was getting back to him about whether the Green Valley Fire Department had answered any calls that matched the story. Forrest already knew what the text would say. Maybe it was instinct. Maybe it was his unconscious brain putting together a few things his conscious logic hadn't caught up with. Even with all the disorganized facts, a theory was starting to form.

Checked and double-checked. No calls that map to that description.

Grizz's text was all it took to find Forrest shooting to his feet and marching up the stairs. The part of his thoughts that hadn't been consumed by stringing together a theory had been taken up strategizing his approach. And it all came down to Sean Brady.

Forrest didn't bother to knock. He was glad they weren't alone.

Not Cathy, but a different nurse, fiddled with machines. Sean was hooked up to fewer than Sierra—just a nasal cannula, a blood pressure cuff, and a pulse oximeter. No ventilator. No IV.

"Sean?" Forrest used his interrogation voice—the one that warned anyone who he was about to question not to fuck with him. Whatever they said here would go on record. And confirming this kid's identity was the first step.

"Yeah?" That one phrase alone told Forrest this kid wasn't from the South. If he was, it would've been a "yessir," the proper greeting for anyone his age—the greeting for anyone dealing with a uniformed officer of the law. Forrest hoped he had a catheter in. The second he'd laid eyes on Forrest's uniform, the kid had looked about ready to wet his pants.

There wasn't much special about him, description-wise. Below the sleeve of his hospital gown, half a shoulder tattoo of three Greek letters peeked out. He looked like most of the other frat boy white kids Forrest had seen over the course of his career—probably much like Forrest had once looked himself. He was tallish and nondescript with brown hair and clear eyes. And he didn't look so cocky away from his bros.

"I'm Federal Fire Marshal Forrest Winters. I understand you're in here for smoke inhalation. I'd like to ask you a few questions about the fire that led to your current condition. Good morning, ma'am." After addressing Sean, Forrest turned to acknowledge the nurse. Because he *was* from the South.

"Mornin', marshal." She nodded back at him. This nurse looked to be in her fifties and had the air of someone who had seen patients receive visits from law enforcement before. "Do y'all need me to step out?"

Forrest threw her a charming smile. "That won't be necessary, ma'am. This'll only take a minute. But I do have one question: is this gentleman under the influence of any painkiller or other drugs that would impair his ability to answer questions?"

"No, sir. Just ibuprofen."

The lack of an IV drip made Forrest pretty certain of the answer but he needed this interview to be clean—for Sean's statement to leave no room for doubt.

"Thank you, ma'am." He turned to Sean. "First, can you tell me about the fire that led to your smoke inhalation? The location and the basic circumstances?"

Sean swallowed thickly and cleared his throat to speak. When he did, his voice was hoarse. Inhaling smoke from a kitchen or backyard fire gone wrong made your lungs hurt, for sure. But hoarseness like his was indicative of something much larger.

"I don't know the exact address. I was with my friend."

Nope, definitely not from the South. Forrest's best guess on his accent was the Northeast.

"Was it in Green Valley?"

"I think it might have been," the kid hedged. "I'm not from around here. I go to school at NCU. I don't know the exact address of his house."

"So this was a house fire …" Forrest repeated.

"Not inside the house." The kid fidgeted with his sheet. "It was the shed in his backyard …"

He kept eye contact with Forrest.

"Did you call the fire department?"

The kid looked miserable, and shook his head. "There wasn't time to do anything but put it out."

Forrest nodded and went a little easier since the kid was actually answering the questions. "You use an extinguisher to put it out, or water?"

"Just the hose. But there was a lot of smoke. We thought we were okay, but a few hours later, we started to feel pretty bad. So we came here, just to get checked out."

Forrest had been jotting down notes on a small pad he'd pulled out of his pocket. The kid was telling the truth about not having called Police or Fire. But the story about there being a shed fire and them putting it out with a hose didn't make sense.

Plenty of things people stored in garden sheds couldn't be extinguished with water. Oil-based paints and wood stain and gasoline were common on that front. Most people with woodshed fires needed help. Also, Forrest knew where Jesse's mother lived. It was a residential neighborhood. The houses were close enough together that, for a fire big enough to cause this level of smoke inhalation, a neighbor would have called.

"You did the right thing getting checked out," Forrest said, his voice a mix of praise and warning. This was the tricky part—making this kid think he was getting off with a slap on the wrist.

"But putting out fires is a serious thing. It ought to be left to the professionals. Any fire bigger than a wastepaper basket, you need to make a call. You said you're at NCU?"

The kid nodded again.

"All right …" Forrest softened his disapproving look. "Do I have your word you'll contact your local department and take a fire safety course?"

Sean just blinked. "Yes, sir," he said, surprise evident in his voice. Forrest glanced at the nurse, who also gave the kid a look of reproach.

"That'll be all, then."

Forrest pocketed his notepad, wished them a good day and walked out and down the hall clean past Room 314. He didn't want to involve Jesse—not just yet and not when he was this mad. For now, he had enough to place both boys under suspicion for the fires in the park. What he needed to find out was what Grissom had to do with all this.

If Grissom might have to put his own nephew in jail for arson and he really didn't know about any of this, Forrest wanted to do him every courtesy. No one in law enforcement liked it when the actions of a family member reflected badly upon them. But if things were the other way around—if Grissom was in on it somehow—well, then he was guilty too.

Chapter Thirty-Two

SIERRA

This time, when Sierra floated into consciousness, she remembered she was in a hospital. She wasn't sure how long she'd been there, but she'd roused herself a few times. It had been nighttime the first time; morning sun had filtered in from the window to her left the time they'd taken out her tube; the sun stronger on the right side now told her it was afternoon.

Her chest still hurt and her throat still felt dry. It was better than before, but she wanted to stay awake this time, which meant no asking for more drugs. She'd seen Forrest just that once—the top of his head, at least. The second time she'd awakened, he'd been gone.

The nurse had gone on about how he'd been in almost constantly and about how the biggest flower bouquet was from him, and how she didn't see a ring on Sierra's finger but all the nurses speculated that she would have one soon. Little did they know how precarious things were between them right then.

"Forrest."

She pried her eyes open upon speaking his name, but her voice was still too quiet. Even Sierra could hear that it was barely above a whisper.

"Have either of them had visitors or contacted family?" Forrest was asking the nurse.

The nurse tapped around on her screen. "No, it doesn't look like they have. Their charts say that each of them declined to call emergency contacts."

"Forrest," she said louder at the same moment she wondered who he could be talking about. Curiosity disappeared the second he met her eyes. Two seconds after that, her hand was in his and he stood right by her bed.

"I'll just leave you two alone," came the nurse's departing words. Sierra only registered them in the one tiny corner of her mind that wasn't focused on Forrest and the way he was looking at her.

And there it was—that sense of knowing that flowed between them in the quietest of moments. It told her he understood. It told her Forrest Winters knew her better than any other man ever had. It told her that he was sorry, too. It asked for her forgiveness and told her that she was forgiven and that he was there because she was precious to him. And if his bright, pained, loving eyes hadn't told her all of the worrying he'd done over her, the dark circles underneath them did.

"Forrest …" it was the only word her stupid, broken voice would actually say. That frustration only brought on a flood of tears. The more she tried to articulate herself, the more the jumble of sentiments clogged her burned throat. Instead of the half-pitying, half-mocking smile she was sure would come to tell her in not so many words that she was being ridiculous, Forrest's face fell and he shed a tear or two of his own.

"Sierra … baby, please don't cry." His voice shook and he took a sharp breath. "Everything's gonna be okay. I got you, girl. Everything's gonna be just fine."

But it only made her cry harder, which made Forrest get that look on his face that men sometimes get when a woman cries and they don't know how to make her stop. Before she knew what was happening, Forrest had pressed a button someplace and dropped the guard rail on the bed. Her IV was connected to her arm on the opposite side of where he stood and he picked her up like she weighed nothing to align her to the far side of the bed. Then, he climbed right in and tucked her under his shoulder.

She still didn't speak and her tears still fell, but she relaxed into him then, his comfort like a salve to her every aching part. What she still couldn't say out loud, she telegraphed to him in her mind.

Thank you for saving me.

I knew you'd come.

Thank you for saving Everest.

Thank you for getting Eddie out.

I want things to be right between us.

I'm falling in love with you.

He held her firmly, but carefully, pressing kisses to her forehead and in her hair, keeping the covers on her and his body against hers to make sure she was warm. The rest of her was somehow clean but her hair still smelled of fire. It had lingered in her senses all these hours. Now, with her face buried in his chest, she still got a good nose full of his scent, even hooked up to oxygen.

She must have dozed off again, but not for long. She awoke to the same sun, so high in the sky she was sure it remained early afternoon. Forrest was still with her—strong and steady as ever. It wasn't until she finally spoke and he inhaled sharply that she realized he had been dozing, too.

"I want to go home." Her voice was still scratchy but her tone was resolute.

"Come home with me," Forrest said, punctuating his words with another kiss to her temple. "You can recuperate at my place and I'll nurse you back to health. Besides ..." His voice was quiet and calm and he didn't make a move to let her out of his arms. "There've been some developments in the case."

* * *

The case.

Sierra had been so relieved that Jake and Eddie both made it out of the fire—that she herself had made it out of the fire—her brain hadn't gotten far enough to ask. The second she did, Forrest had clammed up. Back at the hospital, he'd been cagey—said there were reasons why he couldn't talk about it there. It had taken a full three hours to get her cleared to leave under Forrest's care, and to get checked out. She was bursting to know everything there was to be known the instant she got in the car.

"How many acres?" she demanded seconds after she strapped in —after he'd secured her many vases of flowers in the second row and jogged around to get himself into his truck.

"Seventy-seven."

She cursed under her breath.

"Any evidence to point to whether it's the same guys?"

She was almost sidesaddle in her seat, looking over at him as he began to drive. He looked tired, but something about him was starting to look fired up.

"Absolutely none. But you're never gonna believe what I stumbled upon." He threw her a brief look before beginning. "The only thing definitively linking the first three fires is the concentrated presence of fire retardant and the fact that they all happened along Little Pigeon Creek. With so many acres burned, there's no way for us to test the soil. Linking this one based on fire retardant is out.

"Now, it did start close to the creek and the wind gusts were stronger yesterday than on the dates of the other fires. That might explain it spreading, even if that wasn't the intent. But it's not quite enough to link the fires."

Sierra shook her head in confusion. "You said you stumbled on something."

"Two more hospital patients admitted for smoke inhalation. If they'd come in saying they were out hiking in the park and got caught in the smoke, I wouldn't have batted an eye."

"Where the hell else would they have been?"

"That's just it …" Forrest gave her a look that said the whole thing was suspicious as hell. "They said their backyard shed caught on fire. But the story didn't check out. They didn't call it in. And I took a ride over to the address where they said it happened. I found a burned-down shed, but the ash pile looked old by at least a month. Nothing about that fire was fresh. But it had something I couldn't ignore: a clear perimeter."

Something in Sierra went numb when Forrest revealed this information. She couldn't tell from joy or from pain. The answer seemed so straightforward. It should have been an unbridled victory to learn they'd probably gotten their guys. Only, it left a maddening question and the loosest of loose ends: what about the magic mushroom story they'd gotten from Jake?

Sierra went into detective mode, looking for anything she could either confirm or rule out. And she hoped to God that she could. She had vouched for Jake. He was taking care of Everest and staying in Forrest's house. But what if she should have doubted him? What if something more was going on? What if he had a dubious role in all of this?

"All right …" she began slowly. "Were there any reports of other fires they could have started, that they didn't want to take responsibility for?"

"I'm looking into it," Forrest confirmed, his eyes stuck to the road as he maneuvered a turn. "But we gotta be careful with this. We always had to be careful when we thought it was the Wraiths. Now we have to be completely under the radar. One of the kids in the hospital is Grissom's nephew."

"Shit."

Sierra shifted her body to face forward and she shifted her gaze out the window, no longer certain what she ought to think and painfully aware of how much more complicated this was getting. Now that her drug haze had worn off, she was also considering other practical matters, like who she would have to answer to for the stunt she pulled once she got back to work.

"Gut check," she said after long minutes had passed and signs began to tell her they were nearing Bandit Lake. "Evidence or no evidence, what do you think is really happening?"

She turned back toward him so she could study his face as he answered the question. The evening had set in and the sun was falling lower in the sky.

"Jake's story makes sense. They wouldn't be the first to go foraging for psychedelic mushrooms in this forest. People have been caught trying to take them out of the park and I've come across patches myself. Burning the patches is a dumb idea, especially in a national park. But no one ever accused petty criminals of being smart."

"All right ..." Sierra nodded and answered slowly. "You told me why Jake's theory makes sense. But you haven't told me what you think. And I was the one who asked you to believe him. Now, you've got him living in your house, taking care of my dog. But what if he threw us a red herring and he's in cahoots with Grissom's nephew? What if I knew the arsonist all along?"

"Uh-uh," Forrest started in quickly. "No one forced me to invite Jake Stapleton into my house. That was a decision I made on my own. And I didn't make it based off of logic—I made it because I believe him. And even if he does turn out to be our guy, I understand why you believed him, too. Jake Stapleton is very convincing."

Sierra nodded. It was charitable of him not to blame her for all of this, but every doubt she had just voiced was still alive.

"Besides ..." Forrest cut into her thoughts. "It's not like illegal drugs and frat houses don't go together. As a standalone theory, two frat boys harvesting mushrooms from the park to sell on campus is pretty damned plausible. People sure as hell sold mushrooms in my house when I was in school."

Forrest wasn't wrong about that. But something clicked hard in her mind before she could open her mouth to agree. And when she did speak, different words than she intended to came out.

"Morel Support," she breathed.

"What the hell is *Morel Support*?" Forrest wanted to know.

"The name of Jolene Peele's mushroom-lover's club."

"Those old ladies who walk around with the t-shirts?" he asked with no small measure of surprise. "You think *they're* the ones starting these fires?"

Sierra shook her head quickly, as if to shake away the dead-end theories that had floated around her brain in order for the good ones to take their place. "They're way too smart for that. But they do have a blog—a blog run by Jolene's college-aged nephew. One time I saw her, she said he was doing such good work, some of his fraternity brothers had taken an interest."

"You think the grandson's involved?"

"Maybe, maybe not. It could be that anyone reading that blog could figure out how to harvest mushrooms in the wild."

Forrest finished her thoughts. "Including the Wraiths."

No sooner had they edged out a theory than did they pull up at Forrest's house. He cut the engine and they stared at one another for a second or three. Forrest took her hand. She was still thinking and he stayed quiet, giving her time.

"We shouldn't talk about this in front of Jake," Sierra finally said. "We shouldn't talk to anyone until we have it all worked out. And, Forrest … I want you to know how much I trust you. I won't keep any secrets anymore. I know you're on my team."

She got the sense that something inside him lifted, as if her words had removed a weight. She was pleased when he threw her the hint of a playful smile.

"Teammates listen to one another, right?"

Sierra had the distinct sense that she was being set up.

"They released you from the hospital on the condition that you would rest."

Sierra sighed, the light burning in her chest good proof that she wasn't okay. She wouldn't admit it but, after one car ride, she was exhausted.

"I think you could use a little rest yourself."

"Fine, then. I'll wait. But tomorrow, I need to go see a Wraith I know …"

Chapter Thirty-Three

FORREST

T he sun rose over the horizon in that perfect way it always did on summer mornings on this side of the lake. Forrest's bed had an idyllic view. He'd configured the second-floor master bedroom with the express purpose of being able to take this in. Across all those splendid sunrises, he had never known a perfection like this. Sierra clung to his side, snuggled up, snoring lightly in his arms. Everest lay sleeping at her feet near the foot of the bed.

The night before had held all the potential to be fraught with awkward, with Sierra being there for the first time and being there to convalesce, still in some pain and too weak to do a few things on her own; with Sierra and Forrest at odds as they had been just two days before; with Jake Stapleton there, still mixed up, somehow, in a crime that needed solving; with Jake's own counterpart in Green Valley on the mend.

Hot on the heels of Everest's eager assault of Sierra the second they'd walked in the door, Jake's questions about Eddie had come in. He had been nearly frantic asking after Eddie's condition. Forrest had kept him posted via text from the hospital, but Jake was hungry for details. When were the doctors saying he could get out? How were his spirits and his general condition? And—most importantly—was he going to be implicated in any way around the fires?

That line of questioning took the conversation in an unexpected direction. Jake was ready to fall on his sword. As Forrest had stood at the stove making dinner, Jake had handed him a written confession. Jake's instructions were clear: were Eddie to be accused of having committed the crime, Jake wanted Forrest to turn it in and exonerate his man. It killed any lingering doubt to his innocence. Apart from that, it had earned Jake even more of Forrest's respect. The kid had pulled a boss move.

"You're thinking too hard," came the voice Forrest would never get tired of hearing. He didn't mind that Sierra's voice broke into his thoughts. At the same time as she spoke, her hand slid up his chest and her finger smoothed over his bottom lip. He pulled her closer and lowered both of his lips to hers.

"So give me something else to think about," he teased after brushing his lips over hers in a way that was entirely too tame. He wanted more—much more—but he didn't want to pounce on her while she was still recovering.

Instead of answering, she lowered her nose to nuzzle his bare chest, taking a deep inhale. "Why do you smell so good?"

She pulled herself tighter to him and he did the same.

"My pheromones are how I woo all the women I want to impress."

"All the women?"

"Well, really, there's just one. And I like her more than any other woman I've ever met."

He held his breath to hear her answer.

"Is that so? What are your plans with this woman?"

"Well, once I'm one hundred percent sure I'm back in her good graces, I'm gonna ask whether I can start something even bigger with her."

"Bigger? Like, how?"

"Like, go on an adventure together. You know, use the low season to take some time off … really get to know each other, away from all of this."

"She must be pretty special for you to want all of that with her."

He didn't say how much he wanted more.

"You're right about that. She is."

Forrest was telling the truth. "I love you" were words he hadn't ever said to any other woman. They were words he might say to her that very day if he could spend a languid morning with her in bed. When he said it to her, he wanted to show it to her, too—to consummate it again, and again and again.

But Monday was coming soon. And Forrest still needed to make a ruling on the case. He'd gotten cover from Buck and a few other guys on the team. But he was the fire marshal and he had yet to assess the damage himself. Given the amount of acreage destroyed, the superintendent had already called him twice. Chances were, Forrest would be out all day, photographing and documenting and writing his report and treading lightly around Grissom.

"Let me make you breakfast. Help you get back your strength."

She pushed back off of him enough to look up at his face. "I thought you only made sandwiches."

"That's what I was gonna make you—a bacon, egg, and cheese. I could make biscuits if you don't want it on a roll."

As if the very notion had caused her stomach to take notice, it growled on cue.

Forrest laughed and she blushed in that cute way she did and he wished he could stay with her all day. But she was hungry. So he gave her a final squeeze before starting out of bed.

"Come on."

* * *

"Sorry 'bout that …"

Teddy Blount closed the door behind himself and followed Forrest onto the porch, affording them some privacy from Thuy, his wife. When Forrest had knocked ten minutes earlier, not only had she answered—she'd insisted that he come in, give a status update on Sierra and tell her about the fires.

The fire was common knowledge in Green Valley by then. It had made the papers and the evening news. And there wasn't a soul in town who hadn't heard that Sierra had gone in or that it was she who had pulled Eddie out.

"No need to apologize. Thuy's sweet. And it sure was nice of her to give us this." Forrest held up the three fingers that hooked the heavy bag Thuy had pressed into his hand. "She cook for you like this every day?" Teddy kept them walking to the edge of the porch, then down the steps and toward Forrest's truck.

"Imperial rolls and pho are kind of her thing."

Thuy and Teddy shared the Blount family farm with Teddy's sister, Maddie. They lived in a little cabin and Maddie's young family lived in the main house. The property was expansive, complete with a greenhouse, livestock pastures, crop-growing fields and several sheds.

Technically, Teddy wasn't a Wraith anymore. But he'd once been known as "Drill." He'd gotten out of the business, which was exactly what made him such a good person to know. Forrest was discreet about it, but he wasn't the only member of law enforcement who had gone to Teddy since he'd gotten out. It had been long enough that there was no real expectation that he had information about current crimes. More often, he was able to provide context.

"You know why I'm here," Forrest began.

"I figured." It was one thing Forrest admired about Teddy—he took it in stride. Having been a Wraith, he and the local law enforcement hadn't been too friendly. But Forrest had known him since before he was a Wraith. Current business notwithstanding, reverting back to normal conversation felt good.

"Someone told me—and don't ask who—that the Wraiths are up to something in the park. Something that's causing the fires. This last one was just the worst. Before that, there were three. I have a hunch, but my theory's far-fetched."

"You have my attention," Teddy said, sounding half-intrigued, but only half. What Forrest had in mind was probably nothing to Teddy, considering all that he'd seen.

Forrest stopped at his truck, set the casserole Thuy had given him on his hood and turned back around to face Teddy.

"I need to know whether the Wraiths have anything to do with an illegal mushroom ring."

"Since when are mushrooms illegal?" Teddy asked with an I'm-just-fucking-with-you kind of vibe. Forrest had anticipated that Teddy's sense of humor would make an appearance.

"You know what kind of mushrooms I'm talking about. The ones that make you see things that aren't there. The kind that old Hash Brown used to sell."

Everyone who had gone to high school in Green Valley around the time they did knew Hash Brown Jones, the old hippie who sold drugs out of his RV. The harder Forrest reflected upon it, the more he wondered whether Hash Brown had foraged his supply from the park.

Teddy let out a hearty chuckle. "Wasn't nothing brown about that guy. He was lobster-red and platinum blond, even in the winter. What do you think ever happened to ol' Hash Brown?"

"Probably got beamed up to space with the aliens or some shit. You remember how he was always talking about his abduction?"

The two men joined in laughter for a bit.

"Look, man ..." Forrest finally said. "I'm at a dead end here. But I need to know who's behind some drug activity. And I thought you might have an idea."

Whatever amusement had lingered on Teddy's face after they'd laughed subsided when he saw that Forrest was serious.

"You think Catfish and Gears would ever get mixed up in that?"

"That's why I'm asking you. You ever hear anything about 'em farming those magic mushrooms inside the park?"

"And risk getting in trouble on federal land?" Teddy actually laughed at the notion, as if it were the richest thing he'd ever heard. "No one wants to go to federal prison. State penitentiaries are one thing, but the federal ones can leave you in a world of hurt. Just what is it you think they're doing?"

Forrest floated one of his theories. "I'm thinking they're doing the growing, maybe packing the raw materials and selling them to a middleman. If not that, they're doing the processing and selling themselves. Done right, it's a good investment. The street value of a single magic mushroom is pretty high."

"The street value of a lot of things is high," Teddy pointed out. "But that's not how they decide where to go into business. Believe it or not, Catfish knows a lot about risk. He's been away twice, which means he's fighting hard to stay out of jail. Half the guys in the Wraiths are on parole and a lot of them went away after last year. Whoever is doing this ain't as scared as they ought to be about what happens if they're caught."

Forrest thought a minute about how much he should say. But time was running out and he had to jump.

"Let's say someone already told me there were Wraiths involved, and someone gave me names …"

"Then it sounds like you have your answer."

"Only, if Catfish and Gears would never go for it …" Forrest prodded. This was the part that made no sense.

"Could be someone's got a little hustle on the side. Going against

Catfish would be very stupid. But it's been done before. No one ever accused everyone in the club of having good judgment."

Forrest looked out in the distance—out at the pastures on Teddy and Thuy's farm—and hoped the puzzle pieces in his mind would soon fit together. Jake's story was plausible. Only, Forrest still didn't understand how Buck and Chuck were connected to Jesse and Sean.

"You ever heard of Two-Buck Chuck?"

Forrest hadn't wanted to give identities away, but things had gotten too serious—the stakes too high if they didn't solve the case. And Forrest hadn't gone all the way out there to leave empty-handed.

"They both started right around the time I left. Both young—and eager to live the life, and hungry for more."

"More what?" Forrest wanted to know.

"More action," Teddy said, as if that part of things were obvious. "Being in when you're young with no clout is all grunt and no glory. You get the shittiest jobs, the shittiest pay, and plenty of people above you all too happy to push you around. It's temporary, but it sucks.

"Some people take it in stride but others don't take paying their dues well. I don't know much about Buck, but Chuck always struck me as the latter."

"All right …" A picture was beginning to form in Forrest's mind. "If they wanted to move product, but didn't want Catfish to know what they were mixed up in, do you think they might try to sell at colleges?"

By the time Forrest glanced back at Teddy, the man had crossed his arms and appeared to be thinking as hard as Forrest had been.

"Well, the problem with that'd be the Wraiths are already supplying to local schools. If the guys you're talking about really are underlings, chances are, one of Catfish's lieutenants would have caught on. The guys behind it might be the mules—the ones who deliver the goods and play mobster when the houses don't pay. But a guy at that level is under too much supervision for anything to get past Catfish. It takes a while before you pass the loyalty test.

"Now, if that were the case," Teddy continued, "and Catfish and Gears were to find out, they might kill the ones who did it. Them boys will do anything to keep themselves out of jail. Especially for something they're not even involved in. They don't want it to come back to them."

Possible scenarios still trotted through Forrest's mind. "Suppose I'm wrong and the guys I heard about aren't behind it. Do you think they would know who was?"

"Not if whoever was doing it was new, but, yeah—they like to know their competition.

"What do mushrooms have to do with the wildfires anyway?" Teddy had the presence of mind to ask. "Last time I checked, forest fires didn't go with psychotropic mushrooms."

"They do if you harvest illegally in the park, then set fires to cover your tracks."

Forrest had just given more away to Teddy Blount than he'd given to his own superiors, a fact that had to be rectified in the light of the next day.

"Honestly? These people sound like amateurs," Teddy confirmed. "Committing a federal crime by taking the mushrooms out of the park is enough. No one wants to get put away for federal arson. No one in their right mind would touch that with a ten-foot pole."

Chapter Thirty-Four

SIERRA

By nightfall, Sierra was tired and her chest hurt again, but she didn't want to take any more medication. She'd done enough of that earlier, and it was bound to put her to sleep. If she fell asleep then, she wouldn't be awake when Forrest returned. Not just for the case; she'd been itching to see him all day.

She'd made headway on her research and scoured the Morel Support blog for evidence as to whether it could have served as an instructional manual. To her relief, it was nothing so blatant as that. But if you were paying attention, there were clues. It described how to tell poisonous mushrooms from edible mushrooms from mushrooms that would "give you more than you bargained for." Reading that line, Sierra could practically hear Jolene's voice in her head.

Beyond that, it didn't take more than two hours with Google and YouTube for Sierra to receive an education on how to forage for magic mushrooms in the wild, how to process and dry them, and even how to burn the patches. No doubt, the guilty party's browser history would tell all. Sean and Jesse had been in the park, but were they the only guilty parties? How many others in their fraternity house were in on all of this?

"So I guess he told you?"

Jake's voice interrupted Sierra's thoughts. She sat at a barstool, drinking tea in Forrest's kitchen. Whereas she had always found Jake to be alert and quite on lookout every time she'd shown up at his camp, the new version of Jake Stapleton slept a lot.

Like many things Sierra was still processing, seeing a more complete picture of Jake had been both heartbreaking and rewarding. Only now, through his seemingly endless capacity for sleep, did she see a vigilance born of extreme stress. She was sure his inability to stay awake was his body reconciling itself after so many weeks spent in survival mode. It spoke of this place as somewhere he felt safe.

"You're asking whether Forrest told me about you and Eddie?" Sierra asked. "He didn't need to. I kind of guessed someone running into the fire to save you might be more than a friend."

Sierra loved seeing his goofy smile, another sign that he was finally relaxing.

"That boy is completely and totally in love with you, by the way. When I found him, he still wasn't sure whether you were okay. I was trying to get him out. He was fighting me to stay in, to look for you."

Jake's stupid-in-love grin faded and he shifted his gaze out the window, toward the lake, a forlorn expression taking hold.

"If either of you hadn't come out of there … I don't know what I would have done. I still can't believe either of you ran into a burning forest to save me."

"You were my responsibility. And I should've kicked you out weeks ago."

Jake shook his head. "I should've listened to you and gotten out of the park."

"Well, finding out about Eddie cleared up a few things. It explained what you were doing with so much nice equipment. His parents own The Happy Camper. He had what you needed to keep you straight for a long stay in the woods."

Jake nodded. "He's been stuck working there every summer since he was a kid, but he's got his license. Every day or two, he'd drive in for a visit, and bring supplies."

"What are the doctors saying?" Sierra asked. Forrest had been handling her with kid gloves, which was to say he hadn't given her many details. And most of what they'd talked about outside of Sierra's own health had been solving the case.

"He'll be in a cast for six weeks, but he can come home tomorrow. I called in one last favor. A friend's gonna go to his place, pick up his stuff, grab his truck and spring him from the hospital, day after tomorrow. Our friend will drive him here, and then we'll go."

"What if his parents come home while his friends are packing?"

"Oh no. It'll be in and out. Eddie's been packed and ready to go for a month."

Sierra opened her mouth as if to say something, then closed it again, not knowing what she meant to say. Jake saved her from having to continue.

"When I say we've been counting the days to his birthday, I mean we've been counting the days. His parents are terrible people. Me getting kicked out by my dad is easy compared to what he's been through. His parents did a real job on him. Sent him away three times to conversion therapy. They still think he can pray the gay away. Broken leg or not, it's time for us to get out."

If Sierra thought she'd been impressed by Jake Stapleton, survivalist in the woods, it was nothing compared to how she thought of him now. It was hard to imagine she would ever forget him, or his story. She suddenly wished she had a picture of him, or something tangible to remember him by.

"Sounds like you've got it all figured out."

Jake's serious look was back—not so much sullen as earnest.

"Actually …" Jake observed. "Every single thing that could have gone wrong, did. But good luck came on top of bad. And here I am—out of the park and living it up in a luxury cabin."

"Cheers to that."

Sierra lifted her glass of lemonade—all she was allowed given that she was still on painkillers. Though, after all she'd been through, she felt ready for the biggest sidecar in the world.

"Forrest is a good guy, you know."

The way Jake said the words held weight. He spoke as if he needed her to sit up and listen.

"I know he is," she agreed.

"Good. Because y'all have a pretty weird vibe. It's like, you're frenemies and you're always bossing each other around, but then you'll make the eyes at one another. I don't know. It's hard to explain."

"Yeah … it's still new. We're kind of working out the kinks."

"What's there to work out? While Eddie was busy running into a fire to save me, Forrest was busy running in there to save you."

* * *

The next morning, Sierra woke up in Forrest's arms once again. For the second morning in a row, there was kissing. This time, hands explored a bit more—gentle caresses rather than anything hot and heavy, which really was a disappointment.

Forrest had promised he would accept her insistence that she was "back to 95%" only after she went to the doctor. Her follow-up was scheduled for that afternoon. Procedurally, it was necessary for her doctor to sign off on normal activity like patrolling before she would be permitted to resume those aspects of her work.

What it meant for today was that she was on light duty—able to do desk work and respond to emails, but nothing that would require her to go onsite. That fact was what found her in the position she was in now. Forrest held the bag that contained her laptop out of her reach in the same annoying way her brothers used to hold things up and away from her once they'd gotten tall.

"If I give you this, you cannot abuse it," Forrest warned.

They stood in the laundry room, which separated his kitchen and his garage. Forrest had just retrieved said laptop bag from her truck.

"I rested yesterday, didn't I?" She stood taller on her toes, meaning to swipe it away from him. Unlikely, but it was worth a try. Only when he made his own decision to relent did Forrest hand Sierra the slim backpack she used for off the trail, but worry still colored his eyes.

"All right. I'll be back by noon, then I'll take you to your appointment."

Sierra rolled her eyes.

"I thought the whole point of Jake driving you to pick up my car yesterday was so that I could drive myself."

"The point of me and Jake picking up your car was so that your car wouldn't have to be towed and put into impound until you could pick it up. Trust me—that would've been a pain in the neck."

Sierra stood on her toes and gave him a peck on the lips as she plucked the laptop bag from his fingers.

"Thank you for taking care of me. Now, go before you drive me crazy."

But when she pulled away, he teased her back.

"You call that a kiss? We need to practice that. I'm gonna need more of that sugar to get me through my days."

She rolled her eyes, but her breath still caught as she leaned in for another. Forrest paused to smooth her hair and look down into her eyes for long seconds before he captured her lips. Comments like that had been small and random, but he'd definitely been making them.

Even before their blow-up, he'd been alluding to things getting serious between them for days.

Sierra took this thought with her as she closed the garage door after his truck had driven away. She took it with her as she sat down at one of the stools and set herself up in the kitchen. She let it distract her as she started up her computer, daydreaming for a minute instead of entering her password, about how her life might be different—no, better—if waking up in his arms was something that happened every day.

It took effort to push those thoughts aside and focus on things far less pleasant—like when she needed to go back to work and how she would explain her highly dangerous and generally frowned-upon defiance of direct orders. It only happened in the movies that foolish acts of heroism were rewarded as long as they turned out all right. In the real world, when you received direct orders to get out, you got out. Pulling tepid coffee toward her and taking a long sip, Sierra began composing an email to Olivia in her mind.

Over the weekend, her boss had texted her once or twice, both times to check on her health and wish her a speedy recovery. Sierra was sure she would get a talking-to and soon. Her first order of business would be explaining herself. She and Forrest had agreed on the story they would both stick to. It aligned to the statement Forrest had taken from Eddie: she had been in the area earlier and remembered seeing a day hiker, off-trail, in the woods.

When she finally logged on, Sierra scanned her inbox to find two messages from Olivia. One was an email. One was a meeting invitation. The former told Sierra to schedule time with Olivia after one in the afternoon. The latter was for the following Wednesday at 10:00 AM—its subject line read, *Performance Review*.

How this conversation would go—the one that would define the next few years of her career—was anybody's guess. For the first time in weeks, Sierra wished she could push it out farther. Forrest was meeting with Frank right then. But it would take him time to integrate new information about the case. Accusing the family member of a park official of anything had serious implications. Chances were, progress would be careful, and slow.

Sierra accepted the meeting invitation, then sent an invitation of her own. Olivia's calendar looked open at two. That gave Sierra a full six hours to figure out how she was going to explain. Because, at the same time as Forrest needed to tell Frank what he knew, Sierra needed to tell Olivia.

How much trouble am I in?

She texted Rick, whose water cooler game was strong, half owing to personality, half owing to working at Sugarlands. Since it was the main ranger station where the higher-ups sat—including Chief Barnett and Superintendent Ed Ellis—Rick would know the word on the street.

She sipped more coffee and perused the rest of her inbox as she awaited Rick's response. Only, the next sound she heard wasn't the chime of a text message coming through. It was a new message coming into her inbox.

Subject: Disciplinary Hearing + Performance Review

Sierra's breath stopped. Her shaky hand let her half-full coffee mug fall to the counter. It was a meeting invitation, this one from Clint Grissom. Clicking into the event, she saw that Frank Barnett and Ed Ellis were also invited. And the meeting was happening in one and a half hours.

Chapter Thirty-Five

FORREST

"A pologies for the fire drill, Frank."

Forrest pushed a pink pastry box with a small pile of napkins on top toward the opposite chair when Park Police Chief Frank Barnett breezed into his office. He had a beechwood desk littered with papers and files that Forrest had never seen the man sit behind. All of his talking got done at the conference table. The office was large enough to accommodate a matching round table that sat four.

Frank held a ceramic cup of coffee in his hand, an indicator that he'd only just been down the hall. He made a bit of a grumbling sound, but sat down and opened the box. Forrest leaned back far enough in his chair to reach out and close the office door. Frank pulled out a cruller. He raised an eyebrow as he observed Forrest's gesture, taking his first bite.

"It's as serious as that?" Frank asked around a mouthful. The office was practically empty at that hour. Apart from dispatch upstairs, they had a good hour before most other folks would clock in.

"Something's come up. On the arson investigation."

297

Frank set the doughnut down on one napkin and picked up another napkin to wipe his mouth.

"I know who's been setting the fires. I understand the motive. And I have enough evidence to make an arrest."

"Well, that's a damn relief." Barnett picked up his doughnut again. "'Cause Grissom's boy doesn't have shit and the superintendent's breathing down my neck."

"You're not gonna think it's a relief when you find out who it is."

Barnett put the doughnut down again, not even having taken another bite. "All right, then. Just spit it out."

"It's Jesse Grissom, Frank. Him and one of his friends from college. They've been setting the fires."

Barnett blinked, wiping his hands again. "Ho-ly-*shit*."

Knowing what questions would come, Forrest launched into an explanation. He reminded Frank about the fire retardant they'd found at all three scenes and told him Eager Beaver's had been bought out by boys described as college kids. He talked about them being admitted to County for smoke inhalation and Forrest following up to see whether their stories checked out.

"You know Jesse's the last person I want to have to pin this on. I've investigated quietly so far, hoping I was wrong, but I'm not. Jesse and Sean Brady are both suspects. We have enough to charge them with a crime."

Frank swept a hand across his face. "You still haven't given me motive. Are they some kind of pyros or something? Do either of them have a record for setting fires?"

Forrest didn't sugarcoat it. "The motive is profiteering. We think they were harvesting psychedelic mushrooms in the park."

"Who the hell is we?"

"I've been working on the case with Ranger Sierra Betts."

This was where things got tricky. Forrest had to give her just enough credit to earn her a commendation but not so much credit, the investigation seemed like her idea—like she was going over Gris-som's head. He also couldn't give the slightest inkling that anything Jake had told them came from anyone other than Teddy.

"She and I got to exchanging theories. Dennis Peck wasn't doing shit. When she found out the kids who showed up in the hospital were frat boys from NCU, she remembered a detail. Jolene Peele's grandson helps her run a blog for mushroom-lovers. The kid is in the Greek. Sierra put together that this kid might've given his fraternity brothers some inspiration to harvest mushrooms in the park. Her guess was some kids at NCU saw the blog and saw an opportunity."

"That still doesn't explain how you made a connection between them setting fires and them growing mushrooms."

"It connects to what I found out about the Wraiths." Forrest controlled his body language, so as not to let on, he was about to lie through his teeth. "I talked to Teddy Blount. He won't ever repeat it to you or testify, but he told me the score. Two of the younger guys in the club are probably in cahoots with Jesse and Sean."

"That's pretty damn circumstantial, Forrest. Sounds to me like all you can prove is that they had smoke inhalation and weren't where they said they were on the day of the fire."

"So get a search warrant. Have forensic testing done on the ash pile outside Jesse's house. I'm guessing you'd find the same chemical compounds that were present in the fires in the park."

"Y'all think Jolene's grandkid is involved?"

Sierra thought he wasn't, but Forrest wasn't sure. "Too early to say."

Frank took the lord's name in vain under his breath, then shook his head, looking ten times more put out than usual.

When he set his gaze back on Forrest, his eyes were intense and his voice was resolute. "I'm not accusing a family member of anyone on this team unless I'm absolutely sure."

Forrest nodded. "Agreed."

"You talked about a soil sample from Jesse's place. What else?"

"Get a warrant to search their phones and computers. See what research they've been doing on mushrooms and setting controlled fires."

"Before it gets to that point … what other pieces of this need to check out before I take it to Ed?"

"You could call university police—see if either of them has a record."

There were a few avenues Forrest hadn't pursued because he wasn't a cop—avenues that a fire marshal wouldn't typically go down alone.

"Don't forget, Frank. These aren't hardened criminals. That Sean Brady kid sure hadn't thought it through well enough to cover his ass. There's a chance you can get what you need the old-fashioned way. You could always just question the guy."

Chapter Thirty-Six

SIERRA

B y the time Sierra's truck screeched into an Official Personnel Only parking space at Sugarlands, she was certain of three things: Grissom was actively sabotaging her; he'd found out about the investigation; and his best weapon against her was to undermine her professionalism and credibility. The fact that Olivia had scheduled her own performance review for the following week told Sierra all she needed to know: whatever Grissom had planned, it didn't have her boss's stamp.

Even for an old boy like Grissom, who competed with Olivia much like Dennis competed with Sierra, pulling something like this was extreme. Sierra had texted Olivia, tipping her off as professionally as possible to what was going on. So far, Olivia hadn't answered her back.

Neither had Forrest, who had presumably seen Frank Barnett earlier. Olivia would be pissed once she caught on. A brief exchange with Rick had told her only that Grissom had stormed into Frank's office on the day of the fire, but had been suspiciously absent ever since. Later, she would dig deeper on that, and deconstruct it with Forrest. In the meantime, Sierra couldn't blow off the meeting.

"Morning, Superintendent." Sierra was the last person to arrive in the conference room. This time, the long, pine table looked menacing. The superintendent sat at the head, and Grissom to his left. The seat was vacant where Frank Barnett should have been, but it was 9:30 AM on the dot. And the superintendent was a punctual person.

"Morning, Ranger Betts." Ed Ellis rose as she came into the room, something he didn't normally do, but which seemed to bode well. She nodded a neutral hello to Grissom as she passed.

"Sounds like you rescued a camper," Ed continued, extending his hand.

"Yes, sir. I did." Sierra returned a firm handshake and smiled a modest smile.

"Good work." Ed sat down and Sierra followed. "We don't want any fatalities in the park."

Ed turned his attention toward Grissom. "Where the hell is Frank?"

Grissom didn't look so confident when he looked to his left—the hand that held his phone.

"I've got Dennis Peck trying to track him down. He accepted the meeting yesterday, so he must be tied up. But I don't want to take up too much of your time, Ed. Let's just get started."

If Frank had accepted the meeting the day before and Sierra had only gotten the invitation that morning, it confirmed Sierra's ambush suspicions. Frank hadn't wanted Sierra to have time to react. With fewer than three hours' notice and her still recuperating, it's possible he'd been counting on her not to show up to her own disciplinary meeting at all.

Seething silently, she took notice of a brown paper file in front of Clint that was nearly the same hue as the table. It didn't look thick, but it was clear the file was about her.

"As you know, Ed, Olivia is out on maternity leave. I am interim supervisor for Ranger Betts. Pertaining to Friday's fire, there are some reportable issues."

Grissom slid two reports across the table—one to the superintendent, and one to Sierra herself. She began to scan it with her eyes. It was a filled-in printout of the form that was used for official warnings. Astoundingly, the document was three pages long.

Even at first glance, Sierra could see a long, bulleted list of items included in the complaint. When you got the official form instead of just a conversation, it was serious. But her record had been so clean she'd never been on the receiving end of even a conversation. Tears that she would not let show sprang to the back of her eyes.

"I'll start by saying, Ranger Betts, that though I admire your dedication, defying direct orders in a life-and-death matter is a Class 2 conduct violation. For violations of this magnitude, it's customary for the chain of command to be involved."

Grissom gave a nod to Ed.

"I wanted to start out by explaining each of the charges."

Sierra gritted her teeth. Talk about "charges" and "violations" made him sound like an attorney arguing the law in court. They weren't terms that anyone used to describe missteps a parks service employee may have made. She didn't miss how his language attempted to criminalize her.

"The first charge is defying a direct order. That one's straightforward. According to dispatch recordings, you were asked to obey orders to vacate three separate times. There seems to be some evidence that you stopped answering your radio as well."

To her earlier thought, this wasn't a police interrogation room and she hadn't been read her Miranda Rights. Still, she just blinked over at him, a silent prompt for him to continue.

"The second charge is endangering an officer of the law. By defying direct orders, you created an incident within an incident.

Additional first responders were called in to rescue you. You risked the lives of other law enforcement officers, Ranger Betts, a maneuver that could have resulted in loss of life and limb."

A lump rose in Sierra's throat and she swallowed thickly. Of all the accusations Grissom might lob at her today, this was the only one she felt guilty about—the only one she felt she really ought to be punished for.

"I see that now and I've learned my lesson, Superintendent." She turned to the man and spoke earnestly. "Next time I'll listen to incident command. In the moment, I was so focused on the hiker that I didn't think a few steps ahead. When you're on the ground, it's hard to see the whole situation."

The superintendent's facial expression remained neutral, but upon hearing her apology, he nodded in a not-unkind way before looking back at the report.

From there, Grissom launched into the most trumped-up list of bullshit Sierra had ever heard. It was everything from endangering company vehicles to wasting department resources. But her car had been parked up at Greenbrier, exactly where it belonged. And the idea of her act of defiance wasting department resources was debatable. There were already crews dispatched to the fire when she got there. In order for Grissom's claims to be true, there would have had to be additional crews called in to go after her and Eddie individually. She wanted to be sure whether that had actually happened.

At the end of his laundry list, Grissom slid a pen over to her side of the table.

"On the bottom of the third page is where you can sign to acknowledge that you understand."

Sierra was set to open her mouth to request more time to review the "charges" when the door burst open and Olivia stormed in.

"Stormed" might have been too strong a word. Sierra wouldn't make the observation out loud, but Olivia moved slowly. Her baby belly had grown.

For the first time since reading Grissom's email, Sierra's racing heart calmed and her senses were flooded with relief. This was more —much more—than Sierra had expected. Short of Olivia putting in a call to stop the meeting before it started, Sierra had resigned herself to the cleanup that would come in the wake of Grissom's hostile move.

"Olivia. I—" Grissom stammered, then darted his eyes toward the superintendent. "I thought you were on maternity leave."

The superintendent eyed Grissom with suspicion. "Yes, Olivia. I thought you were on maternity leave. That's why Ranger Grissom is presiding over this disciplinary hearing."

Olivia made her way around the table and sat next to Sierra, sinking herself down as slowly and carefully as her body would allow. Sierra promptly slid over a printout of the complaint and threw her boss a grateful look.

"I had some questions about Ranger Grissom's actions, myself," Olivia said. "Good morning, Superintendent Ellis. Ranger Grissom," she added for good measure.

As soon as Olivia began to page through, Grissom started to explain, not sounding nearly as confident as he had a moment before.

"We were just doing a post-mortem of Friday's incidents and discussing feedback that could help Ranger Betts." He extended his arm once again—further, this time—pushing his pen across the table. "She was just about to sign off on the assessment."

"She's not signing anything. Under whose authority did you file a Notice of Warning, Ranger Grissom? Did Barnett put you up to this?"

"He did place me in charge of the fire investigation."

"Yet, Ranger Betts is my direct report. If you felt that Ranger Betts was in need of discipline, can you please explain why you did not report relevant details related to Ranger Betts's role in the fire incident to me?"

Grissom looked to the superintendent, as if to explain.

"I'm sorry. It was my mistake. I thought you were on maternity leave. I mean, given your condition—"

But Olivia cut him off. "Ranger Grissom. Do I look like I've given birth to you?"

Olivia looked utterly exasperated, and she had a right to be. Sierra had heard her explain the difference between being pregnant and working from home versus maternity leave no fewer than half a dozen times.

"Seeing as how we're all here now, why don't we get on with the proceedings?" the superintendent cut in. "Why not give Olivia a minute? Let her weigh in? Olivia, if you're up to doing it now, I'll sign off on whatever we decide here."

Olivia nodded and began her silent perusal of the lengthy document, reaching across the table to grab the pen that had been meant for Sierra, beginning to mark up the page. Her review only took about two minutes.

"Ranger Grissom, as I read these complaints, some of which sound repetitive, and as I look at what lengths you've gone to in order to make sure this disciplinary action happened outside of my view, I have to wonder why. I'll agree that Ranger Betts was wrong to disobey a direct order. And that, in doing so, she placed the park in a position to have to go out to rescue her, but this list of offenses you want her to sign off on is excessive."

"I'd have to agree, Ranger Grissom," the superintendent chided. "And I'd like to hear what Frank has to say about all this."

The door opened again at that very moment and Sierra half-expected to see Frank Barnett. But it wasn't the chief; it was Forrest. And she might have smiled at the mere sight of him if he hadn't looked murderous right then. He had spared Sierra a fleeting glance but had his current sights set on Grissom.

"I heard there was a meeting."

Without waiting for an invitation, Forrest walked to the end of the table and took the open seat at Grissom's side. Next to him, Forrest seemed enormous. Sierra didn't think she was imagining Forrest's silent intimidation, his body and his glare combining to encroach on Grissom in a threatening way.

"Frank's coming, but he's upstairs," Forrest continued. "We just got back from investigating a lead in the arson case."

Grissom's face was reddening. "This is a disciplinary meeting," he bit out.

"Does it have anything to do with the fires?" Forrest didn't wait for an answer. "If so, I think I'll stay. I'm the fire marshal, after all."

"The superintendent's time is valuable. I'd really like us to get back on track so we can focus on outcomes and next steps," Grissom said.

Without invitation, Forrest reached to the space in front of Grissom and swiped the paper with the charges against Sierra.

"You wrote these?" he asked Grissom a few seconds later, who only gritted his teeth in response. "'Cause you got a whole lot wrong."

Forrest was usually subtler about calling people out. Now, he was taking off the gloves.

"In terms of moving forward ..." Olivia cut in before Forrest and Grissom could do any more to antagonize one another. "I can agree to work with Ranger Betts on the first two items—disobeying a direct order and endangering other park officials—from there, I'd like to move on."

"I have a question," Forrest said. "Endangering other park officials. When did Ranger Betts do that?"

Grissom looked and sounded completely put out. "When she put herself in a position where you had to go in and rescue her."

"Only I didn't *have* to rescue her," Forrest pointed out. "I wasn't even on duty."

Sierra's eyes went wide.

"If no one was ordered in to rescue her ..." Forrest said, looking between Grissom and the superintendent, "then I don't think this item sticks. Which leads me to the question, why wasn't anyone officially dispatched to search the area where there were fires? And why wasn't anyone dispatched to go in after Ranger Betts after she disobeyed orders?"

Sierra had never thought of that angle, either. But now that Forrest planted the seed, the fact that no duty crew had been called in was suspicious as hell.

"Sounds like mistakes were made all around," the superintendent commented, referring to both of them but looking at Grissom.

"If it's all right with you, sir, I would like to have the formal disciplinary case dismissed," Olivia said. "As far as I can tell, there is only one legitimate complaint and that warrants only a verbal warning."

"Agreed," the superintendent said.

"Now, onto the matter of Ranger Betts's promotion ..." Olivia continued.

Sierra held her breath. This was what she had been waiting for.

"It is increasingly clear that I'll have to make my wishes known. And just in case I have this baby before her real performance review next week, I'll say it here and now, with witnesses."

Olivia turned toward Sierra then and smiled for the first time since she had arrived, something joyous and genuine taking over her features.

"Sierra Betts is the finest GS-7 ever to have worked in my service. I have never seen such diligent work, strong performance, and a genuine love for the nature in these parks as I've seen from her. I have received more unsolicited commendations about Ranger Betts alone than I have all across others who report to me, combined. And I'll be happy to keep her in my service. Congratulations, Ranger Betts. Effective immediately, I'll have you take on a new role with supervisory responsibilities as part of your new promotion to GS-9."

Sierra grinned back at a beaming Olivia for a long moment, speaking a quiet "thank you" that was about more than Olivia having so much confidence in her. Olivia was thirty-eight weeks pregnant, and yet here she was. When Sierra caught a glance of Forrest smiling at her from where she sat, the moment was almost perfect. Almost. Because Grissom opened his mouth again.

"With respect, Olivia, you've been away from things for weeks. I have the most recent knowledge of Sierra's work here on the ground and the work of the other rangers."

"And if you insinuate one more time that me working from home means that I'm not working or can't or won't perform my role, you'll be the one with a complaint filed against you."

Olivia began to rise, which caused Forrest and the superintendent to do the same, the latter because he was a gentleman and the former because he had probably seen enough. Sierra rose, too, wanting a minute to speak in private with Olivia before she headed out. Grissom looked salty as hell and Sierra imagined he would be even more inhospitable to her now.

As for the issue of his nephew, an investigation would take time. The post-mortem on Friday's fire wasn't scheduled until the following week. But the truth couldn't come out fast enough. Sierra wondered how Grissom had found out that she knew. She would have to talk to Forrest later about that piece. It was clear Grissom's own vulnerabilities had put him on the attack.

Olivia was halfway to the door when it opened once again. Frank had finally arrived, with Sheriff Jeffrey James as his unexpected guest. Despite the fact that the meeting was clearly breaking, both men proceeded into the room and closed the door behind.

"There's been a break in the arson case. I think y'all better sit down."

Chapter Thirty-Seven

FORREST

Though they hadn't yet announced their purpose, Frank's tone told folks everything they needed to know. A tense silence fell over the room. Even for people in law enforcement, who were used to other people in law enforcement buzzing around, the two of them entering the room the way they had held gravitas.

"Ranger Grissom," Frank began, having taken a seat next to Forrest. Jeffrey James had walked around the table and taken the seat across. Except for Buck and Dennis, the entire fire investigation task force was in the room.

"Are you aware that your nephew, Jesse Grissom, and a college friend of his, were both admitted to County General on Friday afternoon, complaining of shortness of breath and chest pain?"

Grissom shook his head. "No. I was not."

"Do you know what circumstances might have led to those symptoms in your nephew?"

"I'm guessing he's a bit young for a heart attack." Grissom said it as if attempting to make light. It fell flat.

"The attending physician determined the cause to be smoke inhalation," Frank went on, without an iota of humor.

Grissom's face reddened.

"Do you know what Jesse's friend told the authorities about the incident when he was questioned?"

"Why don't you tell me?" Grissom asked with a bite.

Forrest didn't know what to make of his reaction. Was he defensive over insinuations about a nephew who could do no wrong in his eyes? Or was he in on it and bitter about what he had to know would come?

"His friend said they were putting out a backyard fire in Jesse's shed. Only, when a fireman was dispatched to the location to make sure the embers were out, they found no evidence of a recent fire. In fact, the only other reported fire that lined up with the timing of their symptoms was the fire in the park."

Grissom said nothing, but all eyes were on him.

"I'm sorry—are you asking me a question?"

That reaction made things clearer. For someone who should have seemed either shocked or worried, Grissom sure didn't look surprised. His demeanor now was odd, his words ranging from flip to outright sarcastic. But, by his body language, he was starting to look sick.

Frank carried on. "When I ran your nephew's plates, I confirmed that his car entered the park on Friday and on the date of one of the other fires."

Grissom laced his fingers together and leaned forward on his forearms a bit. "Jesse grew up here. He's been coming to this park since he was a kid."

"Did he visit you on any of those dates?" Frank probed. It was increasingly clear that this was an official questioning that would go on record.

"I don't know. I would have to look back at my calendar. Sometimes he comes by, unannounced."

Frank looked livid. Ed Ellis did, too. Both of them had a right to be. It was becoming increasingly clear Grissom knew something—something he ought to have disclosed.

"This is serious, Clint," Ed scolded. "If you know something, you'd better say something. And you'd better say it now. It sure is starting to look like Jesse might have something to do with those fires."

"That does seem to be what you're insinuating." Grissom threw as insubordinate a glare as Forrest had ever seen at Frank, who was still Grissom's boss. "But here's my question: if Jesse's starting fires in the park, what's his motive?"

Jeffrey James chimed in for the very first time.

"The sale of psychedelic mushrooms has been linked to his fraternity at NCU. I just got off the phone with the provost. It seems Jesse's been in trouble with campus police. And, I'll be candid, Frank. I've picked him up myself in Green Valley. Underage drinking. Possession. Misdemeanor vandalism. Let him go a couple times because I knew who he was."

Forrest didn't miss the slight roll of Sierra's eyes. He didn't think anyone else noticed. The sheriff's comments quieted the room. Even Grissom shut his mouth and came off of his defense. Forrest recognized the position Grissom was in. Answering questions directly would either incriminate Grissom himself or it would give away his nephew. This was usually the point in an interrogation when the suspect asked to speak to his attorney.

"Look, Clint ..." Forrest started, in his most disarming voice, using Grissom's given name on purpose. "You're an employee of this agency. We don't want you implicated in this. And you're right about Jesse, too. Most of us have known that kid since he was little. But seventy-seven acres burned on Friday. And you know how this works. The truth'll get you leniency. Holding out'll get you a trial and an unsympathetic federal judge. You took an oath. If you know something—and didn't say something—that's obstruction of justice."

Clint's breathing was heavy. His face turned a sunburned shade of red once again, though the anger had drained from his features. More than that, he seemed emotional, nearly verging on tears. Forrest sat close enough to see that Grissom's hands—which he had pulled back from the table at some point and now sat hidden in his lap—trembled. Everyone in the room gave him time.

"I had it under control," Grissom began after a long, silent minute. "At least I thought I did. Jesse came to me—said he was in some trouble with the Wraiths. The two guys he was working with—Buck and Chuck—he'd made a deal with them and he couldn't make good."

"What kind of deal?" the sheriff asked.

"They were supplying his fraternity house, you know, with *party favors*? Not mushrooms, but other kinds. The Wraiths have been tied into that supply chain for years. Hell, when I went to NCU, the club were the ones supplying. And that's been twenty damn years."

"Go on," Ed prodded.

"Somehow, the house ended up owing the Wraiths a lot of money. Jesse said they shook 'em down. Said they owed three times as much for the last delivery than they actually did." Grissom shook his head. "It was all a ploy. Those Wraiths threatened violence if they didn't deliver—they knew the kids couldn't go to the police, and they knew the kids couldn't come up with the money. Then, what do you know? Buck and Chuck straight-up tell them, if they pony up some mushrooms, they'd call it even."

"There's no honor among thieves ..." Forrest murmured.

Grissom let out a bitter, humorless little laugh. "Damned right there ain't. When Jesse came to me about it, my plan was to help get him out of hot water—pay the debt—then help him to cut ties. I thought he got out a year ago."

Now, even Forrest was surprised.

"How'd you find out he was back in?" Frank wanted to know.

"After the third fire this year, I had a report pulled on any license plates that were captured coming into the park on more than one date when there was a fire. I wasn't even thinking about Jesse or mushrooms or any of that business. At the time, I was just doing what anyone would do for diligence."

"Who is we?" Sierra cut in. "You said you had someone else pull a report."

She asked it out of turn, because she wasn't the one in the position to do the interrogating. But Forrest saw it on her face. She wouldn't have asked if the answer wasn't one she already knew.

Grissom gave her a grumpy look, as if she was too smart for her own good. It seemed to Forrest she was too smart for his.

"Dennis Peck," Grissom admitted.

"Wait …" Olivia chimed back in, irritation written all over her face. "Is that why you've been submarining Sierra? Because Dennis knew too much and was blackmailing you? You were about to give *Dennis Peck* Sierra's promotion to cover your own ass?"

Grissom shook his head vehemently. "No—it's not like that. I never asked him to cover anything up. He knew about it. But he said he knew I'd handle things my way."

"So you didn't promise him a promotion …" Olivia probed.

Grissom looked irritated again. "Absolutely not."

"But you did put him in for one," Frank cut back in. "You submitted a request over the weekend."

"Olivia, did you know about this?" Ed asked.

Olivia was still glaring at Grissom. "No, sir. I had his performance review scheduled for tomorrow. Why would you put him in for a promotion without consulting me? And don't you dare tell me again you thought I was on maternity leave, Clint. We were on three calls together last week."

Most other eyes in the room were either on Frank or on Ed. Forrest watched Sierra, who definitely did not look okay. She had on her brave face, but Forrest saw past her veneer. He could finally see how a system built to work against people like her made her devastatingly—tragically—sad.

Out of the corner of his eye, Forrest saw movement. Ed had just written something down. Grissom didn't answer. Because, what did you say to that?

Frank broke the silence by resuming his questioning, his eyes pinned on Grissom once again. He'd come in playing the impassive cop, but now he seemed livid. Not just livid—betrayed. More so than to other people, Grissom had lied to Frank.

"So you figure out Jesse could be implicated and you confront him about what's going on, find out he's back to it with the mushrooms, and decide you can fix it yourself."

Grissom looked ashamed. "I'm not proud of it. But federal arson is a serious crime. First time around—last year—his only charge would have been stealing government property. It could have been third-degree felony mischief, at worst. But this time ..." He shook his head and let out a breath. "Jesse may be greedy, and stupid, and wayward. But he is scared *shitless* of those Wraiths. Now, I don't think he ought to get off scot-free. But he's a kid—not a criminal. And he doesn't belong in jail."

Forrest took stock of the faces around the room as the space descended into silence. Out of everyone, Jeffrey James seemed unfazed. Forrest supposed that was what happened when you'd done the job for so long. Frank, as usual, looked utterly put out. Olivia's eyebrows were raised in surprise. Sierra was stewing about something, and Ed looked grim.

"Is there anybody else who has not been identified, apart from those already implicated in the crime?" Frank demanded.

"No. Not that I can tell."

"What is the status of the other suspects?" Ed asked Jeffrey. "Seems like you have enough evidence to make some arrests."

"Jesse and Sean were taken into custody an hour ago. We did a traffic stop."

"When do you expect to have their statements? I have to report this to Washington."

Jeffrey and Frank looked at one another before Jeffrey said, "It could be a while. An empty bag with mushroom residue pointed to the fact that they recently had narcotics in the car. We believe they ate their inventory in order to avoid being charged with possession."

"Ate their inventory?" Ed looked between Jeffrey and Frank.

"They're tripping their heads off."

Ten minutes later, Grissom walked out of the room with Frank Barnett and Jeffrey James, not in handcuffs, but not a free man. He was headed down to the station in Green Valley and he would get there via the backseat of Jeffrey's car. Letting him walk out with dignity was their final courtesy. Folks would know soon enough. But today, he would be allowed to save face.

Olivia had gone as well, citing a need to get back home before her husband had a fit. Sierra's things were still at her seat at the table, but she had gone to walk Olivia out. Forrest planned to wait for her there. Also on the table were Grissom's phone, his radio, his federal ID, and his badge.

A pensive-looking Ed Ellis didn't move, which meant he was either still processing, or wanted to get something off of his chest.

"How'd this happen on my watch?" he wanted to know.

Right then, he didn't sound like the gruff superintendent who presided seriously but fairly over his domain. He sounded like the Ed Ellis who wore Hawaiian shirts when they went fishing and sat in his boat drinking beer. Maybe it was that energy that made Forrest feel that he could speak freely.

"No one could have guarded against Clint lying to protect his nephew," Forrest began. "But less bureaucracy would have changed how things turned out. I ruled this an arson four weeks ago. If it had been investigated the way it should've been, we'd have gotten our guy sooner. Frank didn't have good incentives to do the right thing. Neither did Jeffrey. Hell, neither did I. Me breaking ranks is the only thing that got this shit figured out."

Ed still looked thoughtful. Forrest didn't want to push the man too far, but there was no better time to say his piece. And he was feeling protective of his woman.

"And how 'bout the part where Sierra didn't even get a shot at the investigation? Frank gave it to Grissom and Grissom gave it to Peck. Olivia's the only one standing in Sierra's corner. If that's not backwards, I don't know what is."

Forrest thought Ed would at least have the decency to look chagrined, but he didn't.

"*Olivia*'s the only one in Sierra's corner?" He half-smiled as he gave Forrest a look. "Olivia wasn't the one who found time on her day off to drive into the smoke and rescue two people from a fire."

Not knowing what to say to that, Forrest opted for nothing. He also opted to get up out of his seat. He wanted a private moment with Sierra. First and foremost to congratulate her on her well-deserved promotion, and then to give her a tiny high five for them solving the case. A glance at his watch told him they could still make her doctor appointment if they left now.

"And, Forrest?" Ed asked, rising from the table himself. "You've got the green light on submitting to the commission. You've earned your shot. And it's obvious I need to spend more time coaching the members of my team who are less self-sufficient and quit standing in your way. My guess is your drone proposal will be met with interest."

Chapter Thirty-Eight

SIERRA

S ierra was the first one up the next morning. She had been up
since dawn, moving around Forrest's kitchen to make a batch of
bacon bites. Jake and Eddie planned on leaving early—or, at least the
teenage version of early. It was seven already. Her best guess was
they'd be on the road by nine.

In the quiet of the morning and the solitude of the kitchen, there
was no point in denying to herself that she would miss Jake. She had
been dropping in on him all summer. He was only ten years younger
than her, but it wasn't lost on her that he'd brought out some sort of
maternal instinct. It got her thinking about how much, one day, she
wanted kids of her own.

Sierra liked Forrest's kitchen. Hers was much better than average
for a ranger cabin, but Forrest's was really nice—spacious and open
and with an island range and counter space that looked out at the lake.
Sierra imagined you could get so carried away with the view while
stirring and blending and rinsing, you'd lose track of timing for
pulling together your food.

Taking the bacon out of the oven had drawn an eager Everest to the kitchen. She drew closer as Sierra began to take it off of its rack. Everest knew she wasn't supposed to beg. She also knew that when Sierra made bites, she could expect exactly one slice for herself.

"All right ..." Sierra picked one up and waved it through the air, helping it to cool faster as Everest stood at attention licking her chops.

Two hours later, Forrest was helping Jake load up the truck. Sierra and Eddie stood on the porch, looking on. Despite the early hour, Jake looked wide awake. He was as hopeful and animated as Sierra had ever seen him and she liked him best like this—not a sad, sulky teenager who was haunted by a dark past, but a survivor looking forward to his future. It made her smile.

"We've been waiting for this day for a long time," Eddie said from where he stood next to her, his eyes fixed on the truck as he watched Jake. "We can't thank you enough for making sure we saw it. Things could've ended differently. In a lot of ways."

It was still hard for Sierra to think too hard about that—about what it had been like when she'd run into a burning forest. Being in the thick of it showed her more than she ever wanted to know about how treacherous a day at work for a fireman could be. She was still coming to terms with being in love with someone with such a dangerous job.

"I'm just glad you're okay. And that you have each other. And I'll admit—I'm a little jealous. Going off on a big adventure ... You have your whole lives ahead of you. It's a beautiful thing." She smiled over at him.

"You and Forrest aren't *that* old. Y'all still have time for a lot of things."

Sierra threw him a look and burst out laughing. "Eddie. I'm twenty-eight."

After the truck was fully loaded, Sierra walked and Eddie hobbled down off of the porch. Jake thanked her for everything, including the bites. Forrest told them not to lose his number and slipped Jake some money. She gave both boys hugs, whether they wanted them or not.

Forrest tucked her under his arm and gave Sierra a little squeeze as they watched the truck drive away, then kept his arm around her shoulder as they turned to make their slow way back toward the house.

"So what'll you do with your week off?" Forrest wanted to know.

"You mean my week of fake suspension?" Sierra had to roll her eyes. Olivia had punished her one legitimate violation with an extra week of rest. Upon her return, she would be moved to her own office at Sugarlands, where she would be reunited with her 49ers mug. It had been found during a search of Dennis's desk.

"I don't know. Eat bonbons. Watch soap operas. Cuddle with Everest. Look for a new place in town."

She had finally achieved her goal of more stable hours and a rank that didn't prefer her to live in the park. Now that Sierra had ranked up to a GS-9, her territory would go to someone new. She would manage a small group of other rangers, including Wendell and Dennis, supposing the latter actually got to keep his job. According to Rick, he was out on a real suspension, pending further investigation of Clint's case. He'd already been tagged out, not for one week, but two.

"About that …" Forrest's arm fell away from her shoulder. He stopped them from walking, right in front of his steps. "I've been thinking."

She squared to face him. "Thinking about what?"

"About you moving in here. With me. To live in my house. Only, it wouldn't be my house anymore—it would be ours and Everest's. It'd be good for her to live by the lake, with her thick coat. The temperature here is cooler than anywhere else in the park. We could redecorate however you want."

Forrest's eyes took on an excitement Sierra didn't think she'd ever seen. Without stopping to give her time to speak, he went on.

"We could put in a Jacuzzi on the deck and sit out here some nights. If you want, I could put up a hammock. We could have friends over and go for boat rides and barbecues and host our families whenever they come. It could be a real good time."

Sierra didn't know what shocked her more—that Forrest had just asked her to move in not three weeks since they'd had their first kiss, or that she was instantly and seriously considering it. Her gut reaction had been a big, fat yes. Her rational brain, which knew it ought to at least question the idea, was waging a weak protest, at best.

And Forrest … this wasn't something he seemed to be mentioning on a whim. It seemed like he'd given the idea thought. More than that, he wasn't casually asking her to consider it—he was selling the idea. He must have taken her silence as a sign of doubt.

"Now, look …" He took her hands. "I know it might seem fast, but I've thought on it for days. You being in this house felt right. And I know it might be too much, too soon. I understand if it is. But you've got a right to know—I don't want to spend a single night away from you."

She wanted to say yes. She wanted to scream it and jump into his arms. Only, she'd been thinking about their future, too—about how right it felt and how easy it would be to fall even deeper in love. But park rangers sometimes rotated parks—especially ones with Sierra's ambitions. Forrest had his own ambitions. He also had deep roots in Tennessee. Did what each of them wanted even intersect? Sierra loved her friends and she loved the park. She loved this house and it was abundantly clear that she loved him. But would he always, only ever want to live here?

"What about a year from now? Or two?" she blurted inelegantly, not yet able to articulate her question.

"I'm fairly sure I'm still gonna love you then."

"Only fairly sure?" she whispered, because making light with him was all she knew how to do.

"Actually ..." He took a shaky breath and gave her a watery smile. "I'm more like one thousand percent sure, but I'm trying to ease you in."

"I love you, Forrest. And you love this place. And I love parts of it, too. But I'm afraid of what'll happen if I fall deeper in love. I want to be with you, but what if I want to live near my family again?"

"Then we pack our bags and go to California. They've got no shortage of national parks. Or fires. I get calls for job offers from California regularly."

Sierra hadn't known that. Half of what scared her was there was a lot she didn't know. She wanted to believe him, and she believed that he believed himself. But what if his own instincts were wrong?

"Forrest. You've got your family ... your nephew ... your house on the lake ... You love it here."

"And God invented plane tickets and FaceTime and all the things you already use. I do love it here, but there are things I'd like about living someplace else. I'd like to live someplace where everyone didn't know all my business. Hell, I'd like to live someplace bigger. If I want axe throwing or even a better selection of restaurants, I've gotta go all the way to Knoxville. And you know I like to eat."

Sierra thought Forrest would be hard-pressed to find an abundance of axe throwing in California. But she did understand his point. And she had heard him talk about the downsides of living away from things. Green Valley was a small town and Bandit Lake was even more remote. Maybe his vision made sense.

Before she could formulate a response, he brought his hand up to cup her face, tucked a stray lock of hair behind her ear and spoke to her in earnest.

"Sierra Betts, I fell in love with you the very first time I saw you ... with the mama bear and her cub. I waited a year for the privilege to hold you, and now that I have, I will never—ever—let you go. I'm in this, Sierra. I'm in it for good. I know you can't believe it just yet. So do what you need to, until you do. Stay in your cabin in the park for a while. Get an apartment in town if I'm moving too fast. But, when you're ready, you come on home."

Chapter Thirty-Nine

"This is beautiful country."

Forrest tucked Sierra under his arm and breathed in a lungful of fresh air as they looked out across the vista onto a valley with a pristine lake encircled by ponderosa pines. The map put them deep in Plumas National Forest, some thirty miles past the state border. They'd crossed into Northern California by way of Nevada an hour before.

"We're gonna love it here." Forrest pulled her closer and gave her shoulder a little squeeze. Arriving in her home state had quieted her, and he wanted to reassure her with his gestures and his words. They'd left Green Valley a month earlier to make their meandering way across the country, visiting parks and seeing sights and stopping along the way.

"The Coast Douglas firs are nice …" Sierra spoke her first words of agreement, though her tone was bittersweet. It had been hard on her to leave Green Valley—even harder on her to leave their house on Bandit Lake—than anyone had foreseen. Four years living in

Tennessee, three of them spent living there with Forrest, and she'd fallen in love with the place.

"Everest knows where she is," Forrest observed.

Off to the side from where they were parked on the turnout was the head of some sort of trail. Everest had run back and forth between the path and Sierra three times already. Her tail wagged and she looked happy and hopeful. It surpassed her standard excitement at the prospect of a hike and the luxury of being out of the car. The farther west they traveled, the more Everest smelled things that she seemed to remember from her puppy days.

They stood there for minutes, watching and breathing. The late morning air was cool and fresh and it held the astringent zest of a plant that Forrest did not yet know. It was more beautiful to him than any of the other dozen places they had been together, which was saying a lot given how much travel they'd fit in during the off-season. But none of those other places were home.

"My brothers wanna take you to some blacksmith they like tomorrow."

The corner of Forrest's mouth quirked up in a smile. Indoctrinating the triplets into the ways of the axe had been one of Forrest's smartest moves. His and Sierra's wedding had been a weeklong affair that culminated with a ceremony and reception on Chase's peach farm. But Forrest had insisted that the backwoods bachelor party that took place the weekend before be attended by Sierra's father and all three of her brothers.

There had been camping and fishing deep in the park at one of Forrest's favorite spots. There had been eating what they caught and campfires and whiskey. There had also been the felling of an old, dead tree for wood—chopping logs, splitting kindling, and shaving tinder. Making all of those possible were an impressive collection of axes and hatchets and mauls. By the end of the weekend, her brothers were in the life.

"See?" He looked down at her with an amused smile. "I knew California was gonna work out."

She turned toward him then and brought her other hand around his waist. When she looked up with her dark eyes in that adoring way she sometimes did, Forrest hoped for the best: a kiss.

"Well, I sure am gonna miss calling you 'marshal.'"

There was something wicked in her smile. There was a certain way she said it when they were in the bedroom that always made sexy times more fun.

"Special Attaché to the Head of the Department of the Interior doesn't quite have the same ring to it, does it?"

Not the sort of ring Sierra was talking about. But Forrest was proud of his new post. They didn't just pass out special appointments like candy.

It had taken six months for Forrest to get his drone proposal approved and another year for drones manufactured to the technical specifications he had ordered to arrive in the park. From there, he had needed an entire fire season to test his prevention theories and measure the results. He'd learned things along the way, tweaked his approaches and made plenty of mistakes. But the program had been a breakout success.

"Neither does Special Consultant to the Superintendent." Sierra pouted a little as she mentioned the title connected to her own new post.

Forrest wasn't the only one whose work at Great Smoky Mountains had garnered national interest. Olivia had supported Sierra in expanding her animal watering system pilot months before Forrest's drone program had even been approved. For a solid year, Sierra had juggled supervisory responsibilities while supporting test programs of her system at other parks. It was because of Sierra that they'd landed their next rotation in the crown jewel of the California parks. They wanted her to implement her irrigation system at Yosemite.

"I could still call you Ranger Winters sometimes …" He trailed off, pulling her in closer. It still wasn't too late for that kiss. He pulled her left hand down until her fingers were interwoven with his own right hand. He never got tired of calling her by her married name and he definitely never got tired of feeling the smooth platinum and raised diamond of the ring on her finger. He nuzzled her jaw for a moment and spoke quietly in her ear. "And you won't hear any complaint from me if you decide you still want to call me marshal. I believe I'm still an officer of the law."

Sierra did let him kiss her then. Her lips felt as soft as ever—and inviting and pliant and sweet. Whenever she kissed him, she moved closer, as if she couldn't stand for there to be a millimeter of space between their bodies. The way she breathed and the little sounds she made always ensorcelled him.

Everest's bark broke the spell, not causing them to break their kiss right away but reminding them of the outside world and the passing of time. They were running rather late. They should have been in California three days earlier. They'd been waylaid by rainstorms near The Badlands for a full two days, then decided to stay an extra day at Grand Teton. They didn't start their new jobs for another three weeks and might have stayed away longer if today wasn't the day when they were slated to arrive at the house.

Her brothers and their families had all taken the week off and they'd rented a luxurious, eight-bedroom house in a place called Sea Ranch.

"I think Everest wants to go for a hike," Forrest said when he finally pulled away.

Sierra gave him a final kiss on his chin before casting a repentant look toward their dog who was trotting back toward them once again, this time with a stick in her mouth.

"We've gotta get all the way to the coast." Sierra glanced at her watch. "It'll still be another five hours even if we drive straight through.

"But we're *not* driving straight through," Forrest baited, more than asked. "Because we gotta make a stop."

"Starbucks?" Sierra smiled and feigned innocence.

"No …" Forrest drew the word out. "We're going to the place you haven't stopped talking about for the past four years and two thousand miles."

* * *

"I'll take a Double-Double, Animal Style with chopped chiles," Forrest ordered proudly. "Two of those, then a cheeseburger, no onion. Two orders of fries, well-done, a chocolate shake and a sweet tea."

The teenager—dressed in a crisp, white uniform, complete with a red apron and a 50s-era soda jerk cap—repeated his order swiftly.

"That's two Double-Doubles, Animal Style, with chopped chiles, one cheeseburger no onions, two orders of well fries, a chocolate shake and a hot tea."

"Not hot tea," Forrest corrected. "*Sweet* tea."

The kid blinked. "Like, tea with sugar in it?"

"Yes—iced tea that is sweetened with sugar." Forrest knew he had an accent but he still spoke slowly, so as to allow the teenager to understand.

"The iced tea is over there, sir. And there are sugar packets by the drink station as well. We've also got Stevia and sugar in the raw."

"What the hell is Stevia?"

"A non-sugar, plant-based sweetener with fewer calories. You can fix your own tea with as much sweetener as you want."

Forrest frowned and threw Sierra an incredulous look. She had raved about this place—made In-N-Out Burger sound like the Mecca of all fast food. She'd even coached him on how to order. Now, her hand was over her mouth and she appeared to be trying not to laugh out loud.

He handed the teenager his credit card, kissed her temple and whispered in her ear, "What kind of fast-food restaurant doesn't serve sweet tea?"

"Literally every fast-food restaurant in California."

After the cashier had given Forrest his receipt and a number to listen for when their order was ready, Sierra led them off to the side. Another half-dozen parties stood waiting. Sensing their burgers wouldn't be ready anytime soon, he tucked her under his arm and smiled through the kiss he pressed to her temple.

"This burger had better be worth it."

Acknowledgments

This book is a dream come true. My biggest thanks goes to Penny for opening up the amazing worlds she's built to let authors who love them play. I imagine it's a tremendous effort on her part to create and manage this space. The Knitting in the City and Green Valley worlds reignited my passion for romance at a moment when I wasn't sure I would ever write again. Writing in the Green Valley world has been a priceless, unforgettable honor.

Writing this book was no solitary endeavor. Sherry Ewing let me grill her about details of the National Parks Service. Eva Moore and Seren Goode were my partners in plot. Jennifer Levine and Rebecca Kimmel were my editors extraordinaire. Nora Everly, Cathy Yardley, L.B. Dunbar and Bhavani Rao lent me their characters for cameo appearances. Daisy Prescott sat down with me to work out ranger world details. And Fiona, Brooke and Penny were always (like, *always*) available.

2020 was a difficult year. It took a village to get me through. My Tuesday night crew—Shannon Monroe, Addie Woolridge, Kara Lockharte, E. Menozzi, Anne Zoelle, Dafina Dailey, and Jackie Yau

—represent the best parts of being in this community. Amy Lane and Anna Stewart kept me on track with many a sprint. Edward Giordano, my assistant, never let me drop the ball. L.G. O'Connor, R.L. Merrill, Daphne Maqsue, Nancy Timpanaro and Joanna Claire are everywhere, always, for anything. And the biggest thanks, of course, goes to my family, who honors my creativity by giving me space to write.

About the Author

Kilby Blades is a *USA Today* Bestselling author of Romance and Women's Fiction. Her debut novel, *Snapdragon,* was a HOLT Medallion finalist, a *Publisher's Weekly* BookLife Prize Semi-Finalist, and an IPPY Award medalist. Kilby was honored with an RSJ Emma Award for Best Debut Author in 2018, and has been lauded by critics for "easing feminism and equality into her novels" (*IndieReader*) and "writing characters who complement each other like a fine wine does a good meal" (*Publisher's Weekly*).

During her career as a digital marketing executive, she moonlighted as a journalist, freelanced as a food, wine and travel writer and lived it up as an entertainment columnist. She has lived in five countries, visited more than twenty-five, and spends part of her year in her happy place in the Andes Mountains. Kilby is a feminist, an oenophile, a cinephile, a social-justice fighter, and above all else, a glutton for a good story. Follow her everywhere @kilbyblades.

Find Kilby Blades online:
http://www.instagram.com/kilbyblades
http://www.facebook.com/kilbybladesauthor
http://www.twitter.com/kilbyblades
https://www.bookbub.com/authors/kilby-blades
https://www.goodreads.com/kilbyblades
https://www.amazon.com/Kilby-Blades/e/B01N4770M0

Find Smartypants Romance online:

Website: www.smartypantsromance.com

Facebook: www.facebook.com/smartypantsromance/

Goodreads: www.goodreads.com/smartypantsromance

Twitter: @smartypantsrom

Instagram: @smartypantsromance

Also by Kilby Blades

Gilded Love Series

Snapdragon

Chrysalis

Vertical

Loaded: A Holiday Romance

Hot in the Kitchen Series

The Secret Ingredient

Spooning Leads to Forking

Modern Love Series

Friended

Ended?

Also by Smartypants Romance

Green Valley Chronicles

The Love at First Sight Series

Baking Me Crazy by Karla Sorensen (#1)

Batter of Wits by Karla Sorensen (#2)

Steal My Magnolia by Karla Sorensen(#3)

Fighting For Love Series

Stud Muffin by Jiffy Kate (#1)

Beef Cake by Jiffy Kate (#2)

Eye Candy by Jiffy Kate (#3)

The Donner Bakery Series

No Whisk, No Reward by Ellie Kay (#1)

The Green Valley Library Series

Love in Due Time by L.B. Dunbar (#1)

Crime and Periodicals by Nora Everly (#2)

Prose Before Bros by Cathy Yardley (#3)

Shelf Awareness by Katie Ashley (#4)

Carpentry and Cocktails by Nora Everly (#5)

Love in Deed by L.B. Dunbar (#6)

Dewey Belong Together by Ann Whynot (#7)

Hotshot and Hospitality by Nora Everly (#8)

Love in a Pickle by L.B. Dunbar (#9)

Scorned Women's Society Series

My Bare Lady by Piper Sheldon (#1)

The Treble with Men by Piper Sheldon (#2)

The One That I Want by Piper Sheldon (#3)

Hopelessly Devoted by Piper Sheldon (#3.5)

Park Ranger Series

Happy Trail by Daisy Prescott (#1)

Stranger Ranger by Daisy Prescott (#2)

The Leffersbee Series

Been There Done That by Hope Ellis (#1)

Before and After You by Hope Ellis (#2)

The Higher Learning Series

Upsy Daisy by Chelsie Edwards (#1)

Green Valley Heroes Series

Forrest for the Trees by Kilby Blades

Seduction in the City
Cipher Security Series

Code of Conduct by April White (#1)

Code of Honor by April White (#2)

Code of Ethics by April White (#3)

Cipher Office Series

Weight Expectations by M.E. Carter (#1)

Sticking to the Script by Stella Weaver (#2)

Cutie and the Beast by M.E. Carter (#3)

Weights of Wrath by M.E. Carter (#4)

Common Threads Series

Mad About Ewe by Susannah Nix (#1)

Give Love a Chai by Nanxi Wen (#2)

Key Change by Heidi Hutchinson (#3)

Educated Romance

Work For It Series

Street Smart by Aly Stiles (#1)

Heart Smart by Emma Lee Jayne (#2)

Lessons Learned Series

Under Pressure by Allie Winters (#1)